# FIRST THE FIRE, THEN THE SWORD

First the great solar flare scorched half the Earth. Then nuclear warheads blindly set in flight devastated the rest.

Earth was a place of horror now, its human survivors murderous savages. Only in a colony on the Moon did civilization survive intact—and even that was threatened. Its last hope was a desperate expedition back to Earth to obtain the fissionable fuel vital to human lunar life—fuel now denied the Moon by a brilliant, ruthless barbarian conqueror.

At the head of the expedition was young Alec Morgan—and the Earthling emperor he came to destroy was his father . . . .

# WHEN THE SKY BURNED

A NOVEL BY BEN BOVA

POPULAR LIBRARY • NEW YORK

All POPULAR LIBRARY books are carefully selected by the POPULAR LIBRARY Editorial Board and represent titles by the word's greatest authors.

POPULAR LIBRARY EDITION



Library of Congress Catalog Card Number: 72-95800

Published by arrangement with Walker and Company

Dedication

To Jay Kay Klein, gentleman songster.

All the characters and events portrayed in this story are fictitious.

PRINTED IN THE UNITED STATES OF AMERICA

# BOOK ONE

# Chapter One

Alec stood at the observation dome's main window and gazed across the tumbled, broken ringwall floor to the bleak horizon.

Hanging above the weary, slumped mountains of the ringwall, floating softly in the blackness, shone the blue gibbous crescent of Earth. It glowed, catching the light of the now-quiet sun on bands of gleaming white, casting vivid shadows across the pitted lunar floor.

From slightly behind him he heard a soft voice:

> "All of beauty's there,
> And all of truth.
> Let me leave this land of mirthless men
> And return to the home of my youth."

Turning, Alec saw Dr. Lord, the astronomer. The old man was smiling faintly; the Earthlight coming through the window caught the wispy remains of his white hair and produced a halo for him against the darkness of the room's dim lighting.

"I didn't realize you were a poet," Alec said.

Dr. Lord's voice was the whisper of a dying man. "Oh yes. Back before the sky burned, when there were still girls to impress, I spent hours memorizing poetry. Between the poetry and the observation work, I made out rather well. You know, working all night at the observatory . . . you ask a girl over to keep you company . . ." He chuckled faintly at his memories.

"Has the Council meeting started?" Alec asked.

"Yes, about ten minutes ago. Your mother said the vote won't come until after considerable debate, and it would be impolite for you to be present while they're trying to decide."

Alec nodded. "I wouldn't want to offend any of the Council members."

"No, that wouldn't do," Dr. Lord agreed.

Turning back to the window, Alec thought, *All of beauty's there, and all of truth . . . and much more, too.*

Dr. Lord moved up to stand beside Alec at the window, and Alec could see their faint reflections despite the purposely low lighting of the observation dome. Lord was ancient, frail, his dead-pale skin stretched over the bones of his face like crumbling antique parchment. He breathed through his mouth, so that his lips were drawn back and revealed big rodent-like teeth, surprisingly strong and healthy in his death-approaching face.

Alec studied his own face and wondered what it would look like if he ever reached Dr. Lord's age. He was taller than the old man, but not by much. Not as big as his father or most of the men he knew. His features were delicate, almost feminine, and his hair curled in golden ringlets no matter how short he cropped it. But he had his mother's dark, brooding eyes. And he noticed that there were tight, angry lines around his mouth. Tension lines. Hate lines.

"I was there when it happened," Dr. Lord muttered, more to himself than Alec.

Alec said nothing, hoping the old man wouldn't go through his entire litany. For a few moments the only sound in the dome was the faint electrical hum of the air-fans.

"We had no idea . . ." Dr. Lord looked as if he was

still dazed by it, even now, fifty-some years later. "Oh, a few theoreticians had proposed that perhaps the sun emits a truly large flare every few tens of millennia . . . but the theoreticians were always coming up with unprovable ideas."

He paused, and Alec tensed himself to beg the old man's permission to leave. But, "When it happened, I was in Maine, at the Moosehead Center, checking out the new array of fifty-meter dishes . . ."

Furious with himself, but not daring to risk impoliteness, Alec stared out at the luminous crescent of Earth. He narrowed his thoughts to the debate going on in the Council. He knew the choice was between Kobol and himself. Kobol had the advantages of age, experience, and no personal involvement. As a Council member, he was physically present at the debate. No risk of impoliteness for him! Alec's only advantages were his mother, and the urgings that were burning inside his guts.

". . . the sky just lit up. For a moment, we thought it was dawn, but it was too early. And too bright. The sky burned. It was so bright you couldn't look at it. The forest around the Center, the grass on the lawns, the buildings themselves—everything burst into flame. The entire world was burning. We were lucky enough to get down into the basement, behind the safety doors, but still most died. Peterson, Harding, Sternbach . . . that lovely Robertson girl. . . . The firestorm killed most of them . . . would have killed more if the rains hadn't flooded the area. Fire and flood—the hands of God scourging us. We thought it was a missile attack, but it was nothing so simple. Everything gone. Everything. The hand of God . . ."

Alec put a hand on the old man's frail, bony shoulder. "It's all right . . . we made it, we survived."

"Yes, here you were all safely underground," Lord said, his soft voice catching, almost sobbing. "But you have no idea . . . no conception . . . the entire dayside of Earth was burned out. Europe, Africa, most of Asia . . . simply destroyed. In a stroke. Whole continents in flames. It was years before we saw the sun again. Years! The clouds covered the whole sky. The cities died. The people starved. A whole civilization destroyed under that burning sky. Just a single flare, a few moments, worth of the sun's energy aimed against us, and ten thousand years of civilization went up in smoke."

"But we survived here. We found you. You're all right now."

"It all burned. The sky burned. There was no place to turn to. Nowhere to go."

Very gently, Alec led the old man away from the window. "Come on, let's get you down to your quarters. You're tired."

Dr. Lord let Alec lead him to the ladderway. Usually it stayed unpowered, and people clambered up and down using their own muscles. But for the old man, Alec touched the power button. A strong whiff of machine oil puffed up from the recess beside the ladder, and a motor whined to life. The steps began moving past them. Alec helped the aged astronomer onto one of the steps and hopped onto it beside him. Wordlessly they descended five levels, to the living quarters.

He left the old man at his door, then followed the rough-hewn corridor toward the settlement's central plaza, and the Council's meeting room. The rock walls of the corridor were lined with pipes carrying water, electricity and heat: the settlement's three necessities. Light tubes shone steadily overhead, not so much for the aid of the pedestrians as for the benefit of the grass that carpeted the floor.

As he padded on slippered feet through the meager, oxygen-producing growth, Alec wondered what it would be like on Earth. To be outside without a suit.

Would he be frightened? There were stories about men going crazy, out in the open with nothing to protect them. And the gravity . . .

With a shake of his head, he dismissed all fears and strode doggedly toward the Council meeting room.

# Chapter Two

There was a crowd in the central plaza. Alec knew there would be, but it still shocked him to see so many people in one place, milling around, not working, almost touching each other at random. The big high-dome cavern was buzzing with a hundred muted conversations.

The double steel doors of the Council chamber were still closed. No one was allowed in or out while the Council was debating. Originally the meeting room had been the only chamber of the first underground base on the moon. The double doors were actually a pressure hatch that had once led into a tube that went up to the surface.

Alec drifted through the crowd aimlessly, careful not to touch or be touched by anyone. He had been too nervous to return to his quarters and wait for word of the Council's debate. But this crowd was making him even jumpier. And he could see that everyone was reacting in the same way: the more people that poured into the plaza, the more excited everyone got. The noise level was building steadily.

He knew most of the people by their first names, of course. But Alec was not in a talking mood.

"You look like a man in need of refreshment."

The voice startled Alec. He turned to see Bill Lawrence, one of the settlement's top engineers and one of his lifelong friends. Thick dark hair cropped short, beard neatly trimmed, Lawrence usually approached the world with a kind of stiff formality that melted into playfulness with his friends.

"Do I look that uptight?" Alec asked him, forcing a grin.

"Everybody's that uptight," Lawrence answered. "Why do you think they're clustering here?"

Lawrence took him by the arm—a privilege allowed only to friends—and guided Alec through the shuffling, chattering crowd back toward the benches that circled the dwarf trees at the far end of the plaza. Several more of Alec's close friends were there, sipping from plastic cups.

Alec sat in their midst, wishing that Lawrence's brittle bones hadn't ruled him out of the Earth mission.

Handing him a cup, Lawrence explained, "Deitz brewed this stuff in his chem lab, in between experiments on rat poison and rocket fuel. It's strictly illegal, but sells for twenty-five units a liter."

Alec took a cautious sip. The liquid burned his tongue and almost gagged him. "Yugh . . . who the hell would buy a liter of *this?*"

"Nobody."

They all laughed.

Zeke, a roundish gold-haired young man who was called "the Bumblebee" because of his coloring and constant air of busy-ness, said, "We're going to turn Deitz in . . . as soon as we finish drinking the evidence."

Alec shook his head. "You'll be dead long before then." He placed his cup down on the bench beside him.

"It's sort of scary seeing everybody hovering around here," Joanna said in her throaty voice. She was tall, dark, leggy, part Russian.

Alec agreed. "Isn't anybody at his job today?"

Lawrence, still standing, eyed the crowd. "Only those with really essential jobs. Everyone else just walked off and came here."

"I don't understand it," Alec said. It *was* frightening.

"Kobol's people had a little parade just before you arrived," said Zeke the Bumblebee. "All the miners and techs . . . they said it was a spontaneous demonstration."

"A parade! Without permission?"

Lawrence nodded grimly.

"First they leave their jobs and then they parade without the Council's permission." Alec's voice sounded shocked, even to himself.

"Kobol wants to head the Earth mission," Joanna said.

"No, it's not just the Earth mission," Lawrence corrected. "It's control of the Council. If Kobol can get his way, he'll head up the mission and then return to take over the Council. Your mother's fighting for her Chairmanship in there."

"Kobol can't defeat her," Alec snapped.

"If he comes back from Earth with the fissionables," Lawrence said, "he'll demand a vote of confidence, and Lisa will be forced to step down."

"Which is why it's important that you head up the mission," Zeke took over. "I sure as hell don't want to see the miners and techs taking over. We'll be overpopulated and run into the ground inside of ten years. Kobol's people never seem to understand that you can grow people faster than you can carve out new farmlands."

"Kobol won't head the mission," Alec said tightly. "And he won't take over the Council."

"Says who?" a new voice shouted at him.

An older man was standing between the bench on which Alec sat and the next one. He was big, shaggy-haired, and wore the fire-red coverall of an ice miner.

"It's impolite to interrupt a private conversation," Alec

replied carefully, noticing that there were several other miners and techs gathered around the bench.

"Oohhh." The miner pursed his lips. "Now we mustn't be impolite, must we? Or perhaps the frail darling boys of the scientists will break into a rash."

Lawrence put a hand on Alec's shoulder. "Pay no attention to them."

Alec forced himself to turn back to his friends.

"Kobol's gonna set things straight around here," the miner continued loudly. "Put you brittle-boned sweethearts in your place. The settlement's gotta be ruled by the strong! You cuties push buttons all day while we break our asses for you. Gonna be a lotta changes."

Struggling to control himself, Alec got to his feet. "Let's get out of here," he said quietly. "There are limits even to politeness."

But the miner stepped lithely around the bench and planted himself squarely in front of Alec. Grinning, he rested his fists on his hips. He was a head taller than Alec, and bulged with strength and self-confidence.

"Hey, don't get upset. I didn't mean to make you cry."

Alec stood glaring at him.

"In fact," the miner continued good-naturedly, "I really should wish you luck on the vote in the Council. You're gonna need it!"

He leaned his head back and laughed; the other miners and techs roared with him.

Alec could feel Lawrence's hand on his arm, pulling at him. "Come on, Alec; you're only embarrassing yourself by listening to him."

"Hey wait," the miner went on. "Listen, kid, I'd vote for you myself if I was on the Council."

Alec blinked at him.

"Sure! I really would. Providing I got the same inducements that the rest of the Council*men* are getting. . . ."

Alec could feel the heat of his anger giving way to something far colder than lunar ice. He pulled his arm free of Lawrence's grasp.

"What inducements?" he asked, in a voice so low that he could barely hear it himself.

"Go ask your Momma, little boy." The miner was grinning hugely now. Most of the crowd in the plaza had swarmed up to surround them.

Alec took a step toward him.

"What's the matter, kid? She's already fucked half the Council for you, why not a couple of real men?"

Alec aimed for the throat. The miner put his hands up to protect himself and Alec slammed into him. They toppled over the back of the stone bench together. Someone screamed, voices shouted, but that was all far away. Alec felt the solid impact of hitting the grassy ground atop the miner's muscular body.

The miner was big and catlike, hard-handed and strong. But he hadn't spent hours each day in the Earth-gee centrifuge, as Alec had for months. Alec scrambled to his feet and turned, saw the miner still in a crouch, knees bent, one hand touching the ground like an ape's.

Looking up at him, the miner grinned. "I heard you got a temper, kid. Now you're gonna see what it costs you."

He got to his feet slowly. Alec stood still, realizing that they were standing between benches now, little room to move. Every nerve in him, every muscle was screaming with rage and anticipation. But he held them in check, waiting, waiting.

The miner towered over Alec, big as his father. He made a feinting move to his right. Alec ignored it. Another left, and again Alec didn't respond. Then he launched a straightarm blow to Alec's head.

Alec slipped under it, kicked the man's knee out, chopped hard at his kidney and brought a cupped hand up into his face. It caught the miner's nose. Blood splattered as he fell heavily against the stone bench.

He looked surprised now, behind the blood smeared across his face. The grin had vanished. He got to all fours, started to get to his feet again, but his damaged knee wouldn't support him. He went down again, on his face.

Alec looked up at the circle of watchers. "Anyone else have something to say?"

Lawrence stepped to him. "Come on, it's over. Let's get out of here."

Alec let his friends lead him through the hushed crowd while the miner's friends bent over him.

They wound up at Alec's quarters, which he and his mother shared. One by one, his friends drifted away until no one remained except Joanna.

They were drinking legitimate liquor now, part of the precious supply that was synthesized each year from the unusable waste products of the farms.

"You know," Joanna was saying, "I think Deitz's rat poison extract tastes better."

Alec grunted. "How can you taste it? Burns the taste buds right off your tongue."

She was sitting on the padded sofa, feet tucked up underneath her. Alec sat beside her. The furniture was all made of lunar stone, the most plentiful material of all, and padded with foam cushions. The room was spacious by lunar standards, big enough for a large viewscreen on one wall, two chairs and a low stone table in front of the sofa. Paintings hung on the other walls, and the ceiling panels glowed with a soft fluorescence.

"It's strong all right," Joanna agreed, smiling at him. "I had no idea you were so strong . . . you handled that miner as if he were a toy."

Alec shrugged. "Spend as many hours in the centrifuge as I do and you'll be strong, too."

"You really are dedicated," she said softly.

He didn't know the answer to that one. Joanna was staring at him, her arctic eyes a stunning contrast to her long dark hair.

"Doesn't anything interest you," she asked, with a smile toying at her lips, "except the mission to Earth?"

"A lot of things interest me," he answered, "but the mission comes first."

"Oh. I see."

*The damned games they play*, Alec thought to himself. *Think of me before anything else.* But he knew that he played the same game himself.

"The life of the whole settlement depends on the mission," he said. "If we don't get those fissionables, and soon, we're going to be in irreversible trouble."

She nodded thoughtfully. "And that's why you've been so . . . inaccessible?"

"I've been in training. Facing full Earth gravity is like carrying six times your normal weight. And then there's been the classes in military tactics, logistics, all the planning . . ."

"You've been involved in those classes since we were all children," Joanna said.

"Ten years," he agreed. "Since my father went Earthside."

She started to respond to that, but he quickly changed tack. "Did you know that the Council's adopted my plan for the mission? I worked it out with old Colonel Dunn, all the details, the men and equipment, the timing—everything. The Council accepted it over Kobol's plan."

"No, I didn't know . . . that's wonderful." But her voice was flat, plainly uninterested.

"I even studied the old tapes on Earth's meteorology . . . rainfall and temperature changes, things like that."

"But what about *you?*" Joanna asked. "What do you want out of all this?"

"Me?" Suddenly he was puzzled. "I want to lead the mission." There was more to it, of course, but he had no intention of telling her.

"But why? What's the reason . . . your own personal reason?"

Alec didn't answer. He couldn't.

Joanna looked impatient. She turned squarely to him, kneeling, sitting on her heels. "Look . . . is it because of your father, or is it to keep your mother secure as Chairwoman of the Council, or what?"

He edged away from her. "It's not for my mother, and certainly not for my father. It's for me. I'm going because I want to go."

"You enjoy risking your life."

"Don't get so personal," he snapped. "It's not polite."

Her mouth was a determined thin line. "Alec, don't hand me any of that politeness crap. We've known each other since we were toddlers, and I want to know why you're so anxious to risk your life. It frightens me!"

"I'm the man best qualified for the job. Nobody in the settlement, from Kobol on down, has scored as high as I have in all the physical and mental tests. I enjoy doing what I'm trained to do."

"And *she* trained you," Joanna said. "She brainwashed you."

Alec jumped to his feet. "I think you'd better leave. You either don't understand or don't want to."

"No! Alec, it's not either of those. I *do* understand . . . more than you do. I want to see you living your own life, not hers. Why should you throw yourself away for her career, her revenge?"

"Get *out!*" Alec shouted.

Defeated, Joanna got to her feet and went to the door. She opened it, turned her head toward Alec briefly and murmured, "You poor fool."

Then she left.

He was almost asleep when his mother finally returned home. After Joanna had left, he paced the room angrily for a while, then went to the kitchen alcove and tried to eat. The cold remains of the food still rested on the cabinet top next to the microwave cooker. He waited for her to call, prowling through the entire three-room apartment endlessly. Then he went to his own cubicle, sat on the bunk and stared at the plastic sheeting that covered the walls of the man-made cave, stared at the hand-woven tapestry that concealed the water tank and fuel cell. He turned off the lights and lay back in the air mattress, sinking slowly into it as it sighed under him, tried to turn off his mind, to become a blank, a zero, a nothing. He shut his eyes. But in his mind he saw that miner's leering face, and then his father's.

"You're sleeping?"

Alec's eyes snapped open. His mother was standing in the doorway, framed by the light from the main room.

"No." He reached up and flicked on the lights. She looked tired.

Watching her as she moved from the door to the chair beside him, Alec could see why every man in the settlement could desire her. Lisa Ducharme Morgan was tall, supple, darkly beautiful. But she was a cool beauty, a distant Diana or Artemis, perfectly attuned to the task of leadership in this tiny hothouse of transplanted humanity set into the cold, sterile lunar rock.

"I heard about your roughnecking," she said quietly. "What were you trying to prove?"

"That you're not a whore," he answered, and immediately regretted it.

But she didn't even blink. "Oh, that again? Another little benefit we have to thank your father for."

"The Council hasn't voted?" Alec asked.

"No." She shook her head wearily. "The debate drags on. Kobol's people are trying every trick they can—even claiming that you're too emotionally unstable to lead the mission. I wouldn't be surprised if that fight wasn't arranged purposely."

Alec thought it over briefly. "It could have been," he admitted.

She leaned toward him, suddenly intent. "Then can't you realize how important it is for you to hold your temper? You broke every social rule we have today; how do you think the Council members will react to that? Save your anger for the real enemy, or you'll ruin everything for both of us!"

With an effort, Alec kept his voice level. "All I want to know is when the Council will vote, and whether or not I will win."

She stared at her son for a long moment. Alec looked back steadily into those endlessly deep, infinitely dark eyes. His own eyes.

"The vote will be tomorrow morning. I think you will win."

"Then I'll go to Earth."

"Yes. Just as your father did," she replied bitterly.

# Chapter Three

The destruction of Earth had not been complete. Even a full-sized nova eruption by the sun could not destroy the solid bulk of the planet.

And the sun had not been so unkind. It had merely released a flare. A very large flare, to be sure. The radiation and energetic plasma particles from that flare heated the dayside of the Earth's atmosphere enough to flash almost all combustibles into instant flame. Over half the planet, forests, grasslands, even cities burned. It was months before the fires died away completely. Years before the smoke finally dissipated. But that was only the first, instantaneous effect.

The storms were the worst. To some extent they mitigated the effects of the fires. But planet-wide hurricanes and tornadoes with scalding rains and winds of nearly sonic velocity tore at every part of the Earth's surface. Storm tides drowned most of the seaside cities of Earth, and most of the people still alive in them. Whole forests were blown down; healthy trees and burnt-out hulks alike. Not only mankind died, but all land life was decimated. And much of the life in the seas.

A few of each species survived. Even a few men. Despite the fact that in the first panicked instants of their planet's agony, they hurled their ballistic missiles at each other. Despite the fact that they seeded the tortured atmosphere with radioactivity and lethal viruses and poisonous gases. Despite all this, a few humans survived.

On the moon, mankind fared much better.

Already dug deeply underground merely to survive the ordinary harshness of the lunar environment, the people of the lunar settlement hardly felt any effects from the flare. Their scientific instruments went manic, of course. Most of their surface equipment simply stopped functioning, and never worked again. The few dozen people who were caught on the surface when the flare made its eight-minute leap from the photosphere to Alphonsus were quickly and almost painlessly killed.

The lunar settlement survived. It was nearly self-sufficient, and for several years had grown enough food to feed its members. Luxury foods were still brought in from Earth occasionally: melons, fish, suchlike. But the lunar colony raised its own staples, and even had a small ranch with goats and pigs.

The settlement imported almost all of its medicines from Earth, and during the first ten years after the disaster epidemics ravaged the lunar population. But the knowledge was there, inside the minds of the survivors, and on the first expedition back to the burned-out Earth, the lunar explorers sought out the plants that formed the basis for much of humankind's medicines. Within a generation, they had learned how to grow or synthesize most of the medicines they required.

The key to the settlement's self-sufficiency was the smelting plant, where lunar rocks were reduced by man-made lightning to gaseous elements: the oxygen, hydrogen, nitrogen, silicon, potassium, carbon and other ingredients that sustained life. The smelting plant needed electrical power, lots of it. The power was supplied by nuclear reactors.

And here is where the lunar settlement was not self-sufficient. Fissionable elements were needed for the reactors: uranium and thorium, from which the breeders could produce high-grade nuclear fuels. Only a tiny bit of uranium and thorium was needed. One expedition to Earth every ten years should fill the bill.

And did. Until ten years ago.

Alec snapped awake the next morning like the sudden step from darkness into full sunlight up on the surface. He dry-bathed quickly and pulled a black jumpsuit over his trim frame.

His mother was already dressed and waiting for him in the apartment's main room. She handed him a cup of soybrew.

"I've decided to bring you with me to the Council meeting."

He took a burning sip of the brew. "Kobol's going to be there?"

"Of course."

Alec watched her primp her thick, wavy dark hair in front of the room's only mirror. The suit she wore was severe, from its high Chinese collar to the loose-fitting slacks that ended in foot-slippers. The color was a demure blue-gray. But still, when she raised her hands over her head that way . . . when she walked and her hips moved rhythmically . . . Alec heard all the whispered gossip again, and all the taunting shouts from childhood.

He could feel his face burning, and his mouth pressed into a grim line.

Lisa turned to him. "You needn't look so uptight. I told you you'll win the vote, and you will. Now come along."

The Council chamber was purposely kept austere. The rock walls were unfinished, bare, rough as the day the chamber had been blasted out of the virgin lunar stone. There were no decorations at all, nothing in the room except the circular table and chairs, and a single portable viewscreen standing in the corner opposite the double doors.

Most of the Council members were already seated around the circular table. Lisa swept in regally, extending her hand to the men nearest her chair, smiling her hello to the rest. She allowed Alec to hold her chair for her, then directed him to a chair almost exactly across the table, which had been set up for him beforehand.

"I hope you don't mind my inviting Alec to join us today," she said sweetly to them. "I thank you for the courtesy shown."

Alec suppressed a smile as he sat down. It was not polite to use your position for a point of personal privilege, but it would be even more impolite for another Council member to object. *But,* he wondered, *how will this affect their voting?*

Several of the Council members nodded to Alec. He knew them all, of course. Nine men, six women. But three of the men were still missing: Kobol and his two closest allies.

"That's the chair that your father used to sit in," said the fat old fool next to Alec. "We saved it for you. Perhaps in a few years you will grace the Council with your membership."

Alec nodded curtly. He didn't trust himself to say anything.

Kobol arrived at last and all the conversations stopped. Flanked by his two henchmen, he stood for a moment at the door and looked straight at Lisa. She returned his glance. Then his eyes flicked away and he moved to his seat.

Alec watched him, and knew that Kobol wanted the Council, wanted to rule all of the lunar settlement, but especially he wanted Lisa. And Alec felt a special brand of hate for Kobol.

The man was Lisa's age. Tall and spare, with a bony, almost cadaverous face marked by deepset eyes that were almost impossible to see beneath dark, shaggy brows. Large, too-prominent teeth. A bushy mustache, partly to show that he wasted no extra water on shaving, but mostly to divert attention from the fact that he was going bald. So Alec was convinced.

As he pulled his chair up to the Council table, Kobol said in his reedy, nasal voice, "Sorry to keep you waiting. Let's get on with it."

Lisa allowed a slight smile to flicker across her lips. "We resume the adjourned session of September fourth," she said for the microphone link to the central computer file. "The question before the Council is: who will command the upcoming expedition to Earth. The nominees are Councilman Martin Kobol, and Citizen Alexander Morgan. Arguments have been heard, and a motion for a voice vote was tabled at the conclusion of yesterday's meeting."

She glanced around the table. "Are there any questions before we vote on the motion?"

"I have a question," called one of Kobol's supporters, a diminutive, bearded old man with the huge eyes of a hyperthyroid and a stentorian voice.

"Councilman Le Strande," Lisa acknowledged calmly.

The little man pushed his chair back and stood up. Pointing to Alec, he said, "Citizen Morgan is a very talented and capable young man. Everyone agrees on that. But he is *young*. Too young, perhaps, to lead an expedition of such critical importance . . ."

"But the Shorter expedition of . . ." someone argued.

Le Strande cut him down with an imperious gesture. "Let's not waste our time by arguing about previous expeditions! Some have been successful, some have been total failures. I might point out that Morgan's own father is responsible for the most disastrous expedition of all, which has been the direct cause for the crisis in which we now find ourselves."

"Surely," Lisa said with razor-edged ice in her voice, "you're not suggesting that my former husband's actions should bar my son from assuming his rightful duties as a citizen?"

"Of course not," Le Strande replied smoothly, "but the Council must consider that every action has a cause. We are critically short of fissionable fuels. Why? Because we have used almost all our reserves. Why? Because our last expedition, ten years ago, did not return any fissionables whatsoever. Why? Because Douglas Morgan refused to return from Earth. *Refused!* And we've spent ten twitching years politely discussing what we should do and watching our fuel reserves dwindle."

The Council members nodded and mumbled agreement.

"Morgan's still down there, turning himself into some sort of barbarian emperor, and thumbing his nose at us!" Le Strande's voice was rising, ringing against the rock walls of the chamber. "He knows how desperately we need those fissionables. He knows we'll die without them. But does he care?"

"No!" several Councilmen shouted.

"And now we're expected to follow the lead of his wife, and send his whelp down there? To help us obtain the lifeblood we need? Or to help further Douglas Morgan's schemes for setting up an empire on Earth that will eventually kill us all?"

Several Council members pounded the table and roared their approval of Le Strande's attack. Kobol sat back, idly tugging at his ear, saying nothing and looking inscrutable behind his mustache and thick eyebrows.

Alec burned with anger. He clenched the arms of his

chair, coiled inwardly and ready to leap to his feet and shout them down. But then he glimpsed his mother's face.

She sat there silent and unmoving, an ice-queen, waiting for the fools to shout themselves out. Only her eyes were live, and they blazed fury.

The Councilors' shouting raggedly tapered off to a few scattered mumbles, then went dead. The chamber became absolutely silent.

Then, in a voice that Alec had to strain to hear, Lisa said, "Councilman Le Strande, your concern for our future has led you beyond the bounds of politeness and common sense. Surely you don't believe that the sins of the father taint the son—and wife, as well."

Le Strande blinked his watery frog's eyes at her. "I, eh . . . I merely want the Council to, um, consider all the facts of this matter."

"Including," she countered, her voice suddenly vibrant, "the fact that I have lost a husband. Renounced him, years ago. Including the fact that my only child has been raised without a father, and feels all the taunts and sick little innuendos that you have so rashly brought out into the open. Including the fact that my son has volunteered to head this dangerous expedition, so that he may prove to the foul-minded and petty-minded fools in this settlement that he is his own man, not a duplicate of his traitorous father! Include these facts in your considerations, Councilors. Include them all!"

They all sank back in their chairs, as if pushed by the force of Lisa's words. Le Strande studied the table top in front of him. Kobol smiled and crossed his legs.

"Madam Chairwoman," called a white-haired Councilor sitting two chairs to Lisa's left.

She nodded to him.

"I regret that the debate is reaching an unfortunate level of incivility," he said. "However, a critical point has been raised by this outburst. Douglas Morgan has committed treason against us. There is no other word for his actions, even though I counted him among my closest friends on the day he left for Earth. The question, then, is: why did he do such a horrible thing? Is there some factor in his psychological make-up too subtle for our tests to discover beforehand? And—forgive me, but I must ask—has this factor been inherited by his son?"

Before anyone could reply, before he himself could think, Alec was on his feet.

Barely controlling his voice, he said, "I will not sit here and listen to my mother and myself being discussed as if we were two specimens from the biology lab."

The Councilor at his right reached for his arm but Alec moved away and started walking around the table toward the white-haired man.

"Since I volunteered for this expedition on the day I reached my majority, I have been subjected to every possible physical and mental test that the medical staff could devise. My record is available to you for the most intense study. And I know you have studied it carefully . . ."

He stopped at the old man's chair. The Councilor had to look up at Alec.

Clenching his hands on the chair's back and looming over the man, Alec demanded, "Have you studied my record?"

"Why . . . er . . . yes . . ."

"And is there any indication of any unbalance whatsoever?" Alec found, deep within him, that his anger was being replaced with another emotion: not joy, exactly, but a thrill, an excitement, the tingle of *power*.

"No . . . the medics gave you excellent ratings . . ."

"So they did." Looking up at the others, sweeping his eyes across the chamber, Alec went on, "I know that I am young. I know that my father failed us all—but he failed no one so badly as my mother and myself. And I also know that I have scored higher in every test, from psychological associations to heavy gunnery, than any citizen of the settlement. If my name were Kobol, or Le Strande, or Nickerson, you wouldn't have made the slightest hesitation in approving me to head the mission. That is the truth and we all know it!"

"You are out of order," Lisa said to him. "Apologize and return to your seat." But her eyes warmed him.

He grinned at his mother. "Sorry. I beg the Council's indulgence."

One of the women Councilors, almost as young as Alec, called for the floor.

"Councilor Dortman," Lisa acknowledged.

Sylvia Dortman had been a strong supporter of Alec's nomination, one of Lisa's most dependable allies.

But now she looked troubled. "There's no sense trying to ignore the problem that's bothering most of the Councilors," she said. "And that problem, quite simply, is trust. We trusted Douglas Morgan to go to Earth and return to us with the fissionables we need for the conversion smelters. He failed us. Deliberately. Can we trust his son?" Before anyone could reply, she raised a hand. "I'm not questioning Alexander Morgan's loyalty or strength of purpose. I'm not questioning his physical or mental abilities to lead this expedition. I'm not even questioning his intentions.

"But the basic fear remains. His father was just as capable and well-liked and respected—more so, actually—than Alec is. And Douglas turned traitor. We don't know why. And, equally, we don't know what Alec will do when he reaches the Earth."

For a long moment, no one said a word. All the Councilors turned to Lisa, waiting for her reaction. Alec sat there like the rest of them, staring at his mother.

At last she said, very quietly, "We are beginning to hear repetitions of previous discussions. A motion has been made to put the question to a vote. Who will second the motion?"

"A question, please." Le Strande again. Lisa nodded to him. "I suggest that we change from voice vote to secret ballot. To assure complete freedom of choice."

Most of the Councilors agreed. The motion was seconded.

"Very well," Lisa said, her eyes closed and her voice sounding infinitely weary. "Let us proceed with the vote."

*Why?* Alec raged silently at her. *Why take the vote now, before these stupid arguments have been put to rest?*

Then he saw the withering look Lisa was firing at Sylvia Dortman, and Alec suddenly understood. *She wants to get the vote in while we still have a majority. She's afraid that our support is crumbling away.*

The Councilors voted by pressing the appropriate button on the tiny panels set into the table at each of their places. Their vote was registered by the computer and displayed on the viewscreen. Fifteen council members, eight votes needed to carry the nomination.

The screen flickered and showed: COUNCIL VOTE. FOR MORGAN, SIX VOTES. FOR KOBOL, FOUR VOTES. ABSTAIN, FIVE VOTES.

Twisted around in his chair to read the screen, Alec felt fear for the first time. *Five abstentions! They could swing the vote to Kobol. Just four of them could!*

"We'll have to take another ballot," Lisa said.

"Madam Chairwoman."

It was Kobol. He had stayed silent through the debate so far, as propriety demanded. Now he rose to his feet, a lanky unfolding of knees and elbows.

"There's been enough debate," he said slowly, nasally, "to convince me that further discussion could split the Council hopelessly and cause divisions that might not be healed for years. I think the time has come for a compromise, in the interests of peace and unity."

"What do you have in mind?" Lisa asked.

Kobol smiled toothily. "If we look only at the various physical and psychological tests that we have all been subjected to, it is clear that Alec is the best qualified man for heading the expedition. But the question of trust—or guilt, really—has been raised."

Alec found that he couldn't take his eyes off Kobol's face. Something was going on behind that mask he wore.

"No one wants to head the expedition more than I do. I think I would do a good job of it. I'm one of the few men who got back from the last expedition. Empty-handed, yes; but at least we got the shuttle rockets back. I know I could fight off any opposition we might meet on Earth—even if it was Douglas Morgan and his barbarian army . . ."

A sigh of understanding went around the table.

"But I also know," Kobol went on, "that for me to insist on heading the expedition could cause irreparable damage here to the settlement. Friend against friend; jealousy and hatred in the place of harmony and cooperation."

*What's he driving at?* Alec ached to know.

"So I would like to withdraw my name from consideration as the expedition's commander . . ."

The Councilors gave a collective gasp.

". . . provided I can be named as deputy commander, serving under Alec."

Alec felt as if he'd been led up a mountaintop and then pushed off.

The whole Council seemed stunned, but soon enough recovered to mumble, nod heads, look back and forth at one another. Kobol sat down while they chattered. Lisa called for order.

Le Strande asked to be recognized. "I've never seen

such a generous, unselfish move in this Council. I suggest that we name Alexander Morgan commander of the Earth expedition, and Martin Kobol deputy commander —by unanimous voice vote!"

Everyone agreed. The actual vote was an empty formality.

Smiling, relieved, happy that the impasse had been broken, the Councilors filed out of the chamber. Each one of them shook Alec's hand—and Kobol's. Alec stood by his chair, still in turmoil inside, until no one was left in the room except himself, his mother, and Kobol.

Lisa was standing behind her chair. It struck Alec that she was using it like a shield, keeping it between herself and Kobol.

"Well," she called to him, "did you get what you wanted?"

Kobol grinned and started toward her. "Not yet. But it's a step in the right direction."

Alec started around the table for his mother.

She said to Kobol, "Martin, I want to . . . thank you. It took a considerable amount of sense and kindness to suggest that compromise."

"I'm always willing to settle for half a loaf, when it looks sure that I won't get the whole thing."

Alec reached her side, but she was still focused on Kobol, who had also closed in on her. Now he was only a few paces away, within arm's reach, actually.

"You're still determined to rule the Council, aren't you, Martin?" she asked.

"The Council—and everyone on it."

Alec said, "And you think you'll be able to use the expedition to enhance your position."

"Of course," he answered guilelessly. "Why do *you* want to head the expedition so badly? You'll be a Council candidate yourself, if you return alive. Someday you'll try to take your mother's place as head of the Council."

Kobol turned back to Lisa and added, "But *I'll* be head of the Council by then, and you'll take your orders from me."

"You're dreaming," she said. But Alec saw that she still hadn't taken her eyes from Kobol's face.

Still grinning, he answered, "Some dreams come true. You've dreamed big dreams, God knows. And now one of them's coming true. Your son is going to avenge your husband's treason. Clear the family name. Preserve your power on the Council."

Finally, Lisa reached out an arm toward Alec. He took her outstretched hand, and she pulled him close to her.

"That's right," she whispered to Kobol, a low, breathless hiss. "Alec is going to achieve greatness. And you can't stop him."

"Stop him?" Kobol chuckled. "I'm going to help him. I've voluntarily placed myself under his command, remember?"

"Yes," she said.

For a nerve-stretching moment the three of them stood there: Alec by his mother's side, Kobol facing them both. Alec saw that the older man and his mother had locked gazes. Kobol's eyes were, as usual, unknowable. But the look in his mother's: her eyes blazed with something Alec had never seen before, something beyond fear, beyond malice, much stronger than hatred.

At last Kobol took a step backward. With a muttered, "If you'll excuse me . . . ," he headed for the door.

After the door clicked shut behind him, Lisa turned to her son.

"He'll try to ruin you, subvert your authority, perhaps even wreck the mission."

"I know," Alec said. "He'll try to kill me."

She shuddered and grasped his arm and pulled him close to her. Alec slid his arms around her waist and let her lean her head against his shoulder.

"No, no, he mustn't . . . he can't." She looked up at Alec, tears in her eyes. "I shouldn't have pushed this so hard. I shouldn't have forced you . . ."

"You didn't force me to do anything . . ."

Her eyes closed wearily for a moment. "Alec, you're still a child. You don't understand any of this. I can manipulate you, the Councilors, everyone . . ." She looked away, toward the door. "Almost everyone."

"I can take care of Kobol," Alec insisted.

"Can you? Will you know what to do, when the time comes?"

"Yes." He was dead calm inside now. "When the time comes, I'll kill him."

"No! It mustn't come to that," she said, suddenly fearful. "You don't understand these things. If it comes to violence, he'll kill you. He'll strike when you least expect it. He could be a million kilometers away and he'll still be able to reach you. It mustn't come to violence, or you'll end up the dead one."

Alec pulled away. "I can take care of myself. And him. And you, too."

"And your father? What of him?"

The old sickening wave of hatred seethed inside him again. "I can take care of him, as well."

"He'll come looking for you, as soon as he learns there's an expedition on Earth."

"Let him. If he doesn't, then I'll go looking for him."

"And when you two find each other . . . ?"

Alec's fists were clenched so tightly that his fingernails were cutting into his palms. "When I find him, I'll kill him."

Lisa Ducharme Morgan smiled. "Tell me again," she said softly.

"I'll kill him," Alec repeated. "For all he's done to you, Mother. I'm going to find him and kill him."

# Chapter Four

The satellite station revolved at a steady one *g*.

Alec had spent at least an hour a day over the past five years in the settlement's big centrifuge, feeling six times his normal weight. His Earth-gened muscles had always responded to the full one-g load without complaint.

But here on the satellite, after nearly a solid month of six lunar gravities, he was worried. He woke in the mornings tired and aching. His back felt sore, the sullen kind of pain that never quite goes away. His pulse thrummed in his ears after the simplest exertions, such as climbing the ladder from the sleeping deck to the observation blister.

At least the blister was in the zero-g hub of the satellite station. Alec warned himself against spending too much time there.

Kobol was already there when Alec poked his head up through the hatch on the blister's floor. The older man was sitting at one of the observation ports, safety belt looped loosely across his lap, peering intently through one of the stubby telescopes before him.

The observation blister had four such ports, equally spaced around its circular perimeter. A fifth station dangled from the center of the domed ceiling. Taking up most of the floor space was a horseshoe set of consoles and viewscreens, where an observer crew of three monitored all the unmanned sensors that watched the Earth.

Alec floated lightly up through the hatch. Touching his slippered feet to the bare metal floor, he bent over slowly and shut the hatch. The action made him drift slightly. He touched the back end of the console horse-shoe, then pushed off and half-glided, half-stepped toward an empty port. The motion reminded him of the ice skaters he had seen at the Imbrium mine.

The sight of Earth so close still made him gasp. A huge curving blue immensity, streaked with dazzling white, changing, showing different colors, different textures even as it slid past his viewport. *It's so huge,* Alec thought. *And so . . . alive.*

"That's the east coast of North America," Kobol's voice drifted to him, like an ancient woodwind playing in its upper register, too refined to be impolite, but condescending, bored by the need to explain everything to inferiors.

"I know," Alec snapped. "And our prime target area. . . ."

"Look through your number three 'scope," Kobol said. "I've got it slaved to mine."

Alec sat lightly on the swivel chair and leaned toward the little telescope on his right.

"Clouds . . ." Kobol muttered.

Through a break in the white, Alec glimpsed brown and green ripples like old lava flows along the edge of a ringwall. But these ripples were razor-back ridges, hundreds of meters high. Or so he had been told.

"There . . . in the clearing . . ."

Alec caught a glimpse of grayness, a slightly lighter form arranged like a lopsided letter X.

"That's the airport," Kobol explained as the clouds covered the scene again. Alec pulled away from the telescope and turned toward Kobol, who was still talking, "The Oak Ridge complex is only a few kilometers from the airport. If it's still intact, that's where we'll find both processed and raw fissionables—enough for half a century, at least."

Nodding, Alec got up from the seat and glided to the monitoring consoles.

"Any activity in that area?" he asked the youth sitting in the center chair.

He turned around to face Alec. "Nothing much . . . at least, nothing that we can detect. No vehicles, of course. No fires or signs of life, the infrareds would pick that up. But the area's heavily forested—the trees have come back pretty well after the firestorms. I don't think we'd be able to detect small numbers of people moving around in there."

Alec glanced at the fifty-odd screens that blinked and glowed across the curving banks of consoles. The other two monitors were steadily watching, touching dials, making notations.

"We've got the strength to handle small numbers of people," Alec said. "You just keep your sensors alert for large bands."

The boy smiled. "Yessir. We'll do that."

*Boy.* Alec turned away. *He's only a year or so younger than I am. But now I'm in command, and therefore officially a man to be respected, by order of the Council.*

Then he saw Kobol watching him, his face impassive behind those brows and mustache. Abruptly, Alec went to the hatch and back down into the living and working quarters.

Speed. Speed and firepower. That would be the key. Alec lay on his bunk and watched the tapes play out on his viewscreen. His compartment was no bigger or better than anyone else's: just a bare little cell with a bunk, desk, chair and viewscreen.

*We've got to get in and out before anyone knows we've landed*, Alec told himself. He knew that his fifty men, armed with automatic guns and lasers, could deal with any ragtag band of barbarians that might stumble across them. But the observers had occasionally seen larger groups, more organized, marching along the crumbling old highways. Some on horses. Even a few mechanical vehicles now and then.

*Suppose they've got Oak Ridge defended?* Douglas knew the value of those fissionables. He might attempt to keep them from the lunar expedition.

*Why?*

Alec stirred uneasily on the bunk. The fabric beneath him was wrinkled and cut into his bare skin annoyingly.

*Why is he doing this? Why didn't he return to us? Why is he trying to kill us all?*

Then a new thought struck him. *What if he doesn't show up?*

That hadn't occurred to him before. *What if I have to choose between returning to the moon and finding him?*

He lay there in the bunk, eyes watching the unfolding scenes of Tennessee's rugged hill country.

"Speed and firepower," he said aloud, trying to force his mind to focus on the mission. "Terrain is the key to speed. Get in and get out before they know you've arrived."

*Do that and you'll never find him.*

Angrily, Alec reached out and punched the viewscreen's OFF button.

Briefings. Exercises. Examinations. Training. The days in the satellite station blurred into a continuous round of automatic routine. Morning briefings on tactics. Physical therapy, mainly running along the central corridor of the satellite for an hour. Then medical exams. After lunch, training: weapons, communications, hand-to-hand combat.

"You're losing weight."

The medic was a woman, a handsome woman. Alec had seen several of the men making fools of themselves, trying to impress her. She was big, with a broad Slavic face and strong, big-boned body that she kept in perfect shape. Her white coverall strained across her bosom and hips.

"It goes with the job," Alec said. "Soon I'll be turning gray."

They were sitting in the tiny alcove off the medical compartment. The main section of the compartment was filled by the automated examination booth and its instruments and computer terminal.

Sitting across the fragile desk from her, Alec realized why men chased her. But she was looking at him with concerned, unblinking honesty.

"What's bothering you?"

*You are*, he wanted to say. But instead, "I'm responsible for the lives of the fifty men who'll be going down there with me. And for the life of the entire settlement, if we don't bring back the fissionables."

"You sought out this responsibility."

"That doesn't make it any lighter."

Finally she broke her gaze away from him, glanced at the data screen on the wall beside the desk.

"I think," she said calmly, "that you are full of shit. Either you're trying to con me, or you're conning yourself."

Alec broke into laughter.

"You find that funny?"

"Sure, why not?"

She pursed her lips in obvious annoyance.

"Look," Alec said, "uhh . . . what is your first name, anyway."

"Lenore."

"Lenore?"

"As in Poe."

"What?"

"Never mind. Am I to assume that I may call you Alexander, instead of Commander Morgan?"

"Alec."

She still hadn't smiled. "Very well, Alec. You're losing weight and you're not turning gray. To what do you attribute this medical phenomenon?"

"Are you a psychiatrist as well as a medic?"

"No. Please answer my question."

Alec leaned back in the flimsy chair. "The answer is—I don't know."

"I think you do."

Without raising his voice, Alec said, "I really don't give a damn what you think."

Now she smiled. But it wasn't sweetness. "You'd better. Because you're not going Earthward until I'm satisfied that your physical condition is up to it."

Alec stared at her, feeling the heat rise inside him. "The tyranny of the medics."

She shrugged. Despite himself, Alec found the movement delicious.

For a long moment they sat there trying to stare each other down. Then she said, "Shall I tell you what my guess is?"

"Why not?" Alec was trying to make it sound casual, but he felt his fists clenching in his lap.

"You're not sleeping well, you're not eating properly. You're edgy, moody, irritable."

"That's guessing?"

"No," she said easily. "That's observation. Now the guess comes. The reason for your condition is—you're scared."

Alec fought down an urge to get out of the chair and

walk out. Still, he could feel the color flaming in his face.

"Not in the sense of physical cowardice," Lenore added quickly. "You've been dragging around here under a steady one-g and feeling lousy. All of us have. But you're worrying about how you'll perform on Earth. You know about the heavy atmosphere, the heat, the terrific humidity. It's got you worried. Too much imagination. Like Lord Jim."

"Who's he?"

"God! Don't you read anything?"

"Sure—military history, tactics, geography . . ."

Shaking her head, Lenore said, "Your problem is that you don't know how to unwind."

"That's your diagnosis?"

"Yes, and I've got a prescription for you." She pushed away from the desk and stood up. Alec realized again how desirable she truly was.

"Prescription?" he asked as he got up.

"Yes," she said, and now she was really smiling. "Tonight I'm going to fix you a special dinner. In my compartment. Twenty-hundred hours. Be there. Doctor's orders."

Alec grinned at her. "The tyranny of the medics."

She *did* fix a special meal. Somehow, out of two standard dinner trays from the galley she managed to add spices, some sort of delicious sauce for the soymeat, and even a golden concoction that tasted almost like lunar brandy.

"I raided the galley and the medical stores," Lenore admitted.

She was sitting on the bunk. Alec had the compartment's only chair. Lenore was wearing shorts and a pullover top, standard off-duty clothes. She filled them magnificently.

"I like your prescription," Alec said. He spoke slowly

and carefully, the brandy was that strong. "I haven't felt this relaxed in months."

"The treatment's just starting," she said, and patted the bunk beside her.

Alec took his glass to the bunk.

"You do feel good?" she asked.

He nodded. "Maybe too good."

"What do you mean?"

"I want to go to bed with you."

"Well," she said, "why not?"

"I don't know. I'm not sure I ought to."

"You're afraid that I deliberately ensnared you . . . manipulated you into this?" She was smiling.

"No, not . . ."

"Well I did," Lenore said. "I've been planning this for several days."

"Really?" Something in the back of Alec's mind told him that he should be upset about that, but it was a distant warning and he ignored it.

Nodding, she said, "Ever since I noticed how uptight you were starting to look."

"Oh. I brought out your motherly instincts."

"Not exa . . . why did you say that?"

He shrugged. "Dunno. What?" Alec finished his glass and reached for the bottle on the desk.

But she asked, "How many women have you made love to?"

He grabbed the bottle. "Thousands. I used to keep a list in my desk back home but it got too long. Had to put it on the computer."

"Come on, really." She held her glass out and he went to refill it. The liquid flowed so fast under one-*g* that the tiny plastic cup overflowed and brandy splashed down onto her bare leg.

"Hey!"

"Hell! I'm sorry . . ." Alec put the bottle down and

grabbed one of the napkins from the desk. He dabbed at the wetness on her leg.

"That's nice," Lenore said softly.

Soon they were kissing each other, but that warning note still sounded off in the back of Alec's mind.

"Why'd you want to know how many girls I've been to bed with?"

"H'mmm?" she murmured. Then, pulling slightly away from him, "Oh . . . just professional curiosity."

"Professional?"

"Medical," she said. "Psychological."

"I thought you said you weren't a psychiatrist."

"I'm not . . . but still, it's interesting how much people are attracted to those who remind them of their parents."

He backed off completely. "You don't look anything like my mother."

Lenore smiled. "And you don't look anything like my father, either. But you have that same sweet, sort of shy wonderment about you. And I tend to be aggressive . . ."

"That's bullshit!"

"Such strong language! Really getting to you?" She seemed amused by it all. "Would you have invited me to your place for dinner? Would it have even crossed your mind?"

"Well . . . maybe not. I thought about you, but . . . you seemed to be busy enough."

"I haven't gone to bed with anyone in the station since we arrived here," Lenore said. "Do you believe that? Six women and eighty men, and I get to fondle each man at least twice a week . . . and I waited for you."

Alec didn't know what to say.

"I even turned Martin down. Twice."

The warning alarm rang in his head. "Kobol?"

She nodded. "Twice."

"Why do you say *even?*" Alec demanded.

She shrugged. "I don't know. I guess because he's sexy. Dark and mysterious. Deadly earnest. He warned me about you . . ." She looked as if she would giggle.

"Me?"

"Yes. He said you wouldn't be interested."

"Did he?" Alec felt the tide of rage building up in him. "What else did he say?"

Lenore looked at him quizzically. "Nothing," she answered quietly. "He didn't say anything else . . ."

"No?" Alec grabbed her arm. "He didn't say that I'm a classic Oedipal? He didn't tell you that I'd like to screw my mother?"

"No . . . Alec . . ." Her eyes were wide and frightened now.

Alec threw his cup down on the floor and stood up. "I don't know what your game is, but you can tell Kobol or anyone else that I'm not afraid of anything. I'm not weak, and I'm not scared! Of anything!"

He turned and reached for the door. She sat huddled in the corner of the bunk. "Alec . . . what did I . . ."

With one hand on the door handle, he said to her, "For all I know, Kobol put you up to this—to see if I have any balls at all!"

"Do you?"

Suddenly he wanted to hit her, smash her face, throttle her. Instead, he grabbed her, pulled her off the bunk, tore the clothes from her body. She gasped and then swung at him. But it was clumsy, hampered by the torn clothing that still hung on her arms. They struggled together. She was a big woman, but he was furious with a murderous rage. He ripped the rest of her clothes off her, pushed her into the bunk. When she tried to get up he cuffed her, hard, with the back of his hand.

She recoiled back onto the bunk, then reached out for the bottle on the desk. By that time Alec had his jumpsuit unzipped. He knocked the bottle away, turned her on her back, and fell on top of her. She snarled at him, teeth bared:

"I'll bite your prick off!"

"Try it."

She struggled briefly, then stopped trying to push him off. "Wait . . . wait . . . at least . . ."

But he exploded inside her, then got out of the bunk.

"Tell Kobol I'm not dead yet," he said.

And he left her there.

# Chapter Five

"And I say we go now!"

They were sitting in the satellite station's tiny mess hall, which also served as a conference room. There were only four tables in the cramped, metal-walled room. At this time of night, the other three were empty.

Sitting around the table with Alec were Kobol, Ron Jameson, and Bernard Harvey. Jameson was one of the few real military men of the settlement, an expert in weapons and tactics. He served the landing force as the commander's chief aide, the man who translated strategy into orders to the men. He had the look of a soldier about him: tall, flat-stomached, the unflinching gray eyes of a hunting hawk. A hard man to panic. Harvey was a Councilor and would return to the settlement as soon as the landing force touched Earth. He was small, round, balding.

"But the schedule," Harvey objected, "calls for your leaving three weeks from now."

Kobol steepled his fingers in front of his face, masking his mouth. "That's when the spring rains will be over and the ground dried out. Travel across country will be much easier then."

Alec said, "If we land at the airport we'll only have to travel a couple of klicks, over paved roadway. We can be in and out overnight."

"But your own battle plan . . ."

"Ron, what do the pilots say?" Alec asked Jameson.

"They'd prefer the airport," he said in his easy drawl. "We've put the high-mag 'scopes on the airfield every pass since you suggested it, and there's plenty of room for both shuttles. The runways are in a sorry state, but they're still better than trying to land in open country."

"The shuttles will be sitting ducks at the airfield," Kobol said. "If the locals counterattack, that's the first place they'll hit."

"Any sign of barbarian bands around the airfield?"

Jameson shook his head.

Tapping the table with a forefinger to make his points, Alec said, "The spring rainstorms keep the natives holed up, prevent them from travelling. In another three weeks, those forests might be teeming with them and we'd have to fight our way into Oak Ridge and back out again. Right now, the only natives who could be there are the locals, who don't seem to be much of a threat. And no matter where we land the shuttles, they're going to be vulnerable."

Kobol looked impassive; Harvey upset.

"If we go now, land at the airfield, we can have the entire mission accomplished in two days, max. Before any barbarian hordes have had time to mass and reach us."

"That's not the way the mission was planned," Harvey insisted. "It's your own plan! The Council . . ."

"The Council gave me command. My decision is that we go now. Tomorrow, if possible. The next day at the latest."

"It's a mistake," Kobol said flatly.

"Maybe," Alec countered. "But it's *my* mistake."

They sat there, under the bluish fluorescent light panels of the ceiling, for a silent few moments.

"All right," Alec said. "That's it. Ron, please get the men ready for boarding as soon as possible. Inform the pilots and maintenance crews."

Jameson nodded.

Turning to Harvey, Alec said, "You can report this back to the Council if you want to."

Visibly sweating, the Councilor replied, "I guess I'd better."

Alec got up from his chair, nodded to them, and walked out of the mess hall. The station's main corridor was dimmed down for night lighting. As he walked through the shadows to his room, Alec told himself, *At least I won't have to see her anymore.*

It took two days.

Two days of checking out the weapons, the communications gear, the food and clothing they would need. Two days of frantic calls back and forth from the station to the settlement. Men who thought they had three weeks suddenly telescoping their homeward conversations into forty-eight hours. Questions from the Council. Technical data from the settlement's main computers to the station's.

Two days of inoculations and medical checks. Alec put off his final medical exam until the last possible moment. Lenore was all business with him, impersonal, clinical. Except as he got up to leave, she said calmly, "Good luck."

He mumbled a thank you and hurried out of the infirmary.

They filed into the two shuttles, fifty men and four pilots glide-walking through the narrow access tunnels that connected the station's hub to the waiting shuttles' hatches. The pilots went first, in their usual blue coveralls. Then came the troops, looking weirdly out of place in olive drab uniforms and metal helmets, with bulky packs on their backs and slung weapons poking awkwardly. They shuffled uncertainly through the tunnels, hands outstretched so that their fingertips could touch the fabric-covered walls for balance.

Alec hovered at the station's hatch and watched his men as they passed him, silent and grim-faced. The only sound were the clinking of metal and plastic, the shuffling of booted feet. When the last of them had disappeared into the tunnel, he pushed himself in, made his way through, and stepped into the shuttle.

Two dozen men were strapping themselves into their seats. Packs and weapons were unslung and stowed in the special overhead compartments. Alec stood at the hatch for a moment. He'd inspected the shuttles a dozen times over the past weeks, but this was the first time he'd seen one occupied since they arrived from the settlement. The usual odors of lubricants and plastic and ozone were overwhelmed now by the smell of human sweat and gun oil. As he made his way up to the empty double seat at the front of the passenger compartment, Alec realized with a start just how old the shuttles were. The plastic flooring was worn thin, the metal walls so scratched that they were starting to look almost polished. The shuttles had been built long before the sun's eruption, and kept in repair by the lunar engineers with a tenderness that approached blind religious faith.

*Our link with Earth,* he knew. *And our only link back home again.*

As he stopped in the aisle beside the seat and slipped off his own bulky pack, Alec wondered if he should say anything to the men. Many of them would have preferred Kobol's leadership to his own, he knew. Kobol had been to Earth on the last raid. Many of the men resented, even questioned, his speed-up of the mission schedule.

"With any luck at all," he said, loudly enough to make them jerk with surprise, halt their private conversations or inner thoughts and look up at him.

"With any luck at all," Alec repeated, "we'll all be back aboard this bucket in thirty-six hours or less. That's why I speeded up the schedule . . . so we could *all* make it back, quick and safe."

They grinned, they nodded, they returned to their buzzing conversations. But it was brighter now, looser. Alec sat down and strapped in.

"Separation in five minutes," said the pilot's voice over the intercom. "Ignition in seven minutes."

Despite himself, Alec tensed. *And if we do get in and out so quickly, what chance will I have of finding my father?* But somewhere deep inside his guts, Alec knew that he and his father were going to meet down there on the surface of Earth. One way or another, they would meet. And one of them would die.

The separation and ignition were so gentle that if the pilot hadn't told them about it on the intercom, Alec would have questioned their occurrence. There were no windows in the passenger compartment, and he felt only the slightest pressure and thump of rocket burst.

"We're on our way, on trajectory, and all systems are in the green," the pilot reported happily.

Alec unstrapped and stood up gingerly. With one hand on the grip set into the bulkhead in front of him, he tapped on the hatch that separated the passenger compartment from the cockpit.

The copilot opened the hatch, and Alec squeezed into the cramped world of green-glowing panel lights and data displays, two bulky control chairs, and dials and switches that literally surrounded the two pilots—spreading in front of them, to their sides, across the console between their chairs, even overhead.

There were windows in front of them, and Alec could see the vast brilliant bulk of Earth sweeping past them.

"Everything on the mark," the copilot said cheerfully. "We'll be buttoning up for re-entry in ten minutes."

Nodding, Alec asked, "How about Kobol's ship?"

"Just got a buzz from them; all okay."

"Can we see them?"

"Not visually." The copilot pointed to a circular screen on the panel in front of him. A luminous yellow arm swept rapidly around it; a single fat dot hovered near the center. Other dots, smaller and fainter, stood out toward the edge of the screen.

"That's them, right behind us," the copilot said. "The other dots are the station and smaller satellites passing this area."

"I see."

"Sorry we don't have room for you up here," the pilot said, without taking his eyes off the instruments.

Alec got the hint. Commander or not, the pilot was in charge here and Alec was in his way. Grinning, "I'll be too busy to say thanks when we land, so I'll say it now. Good flight!"

"Thank *you*," the copilot answered, with a big smile.

Settling back in his seat in the passenger section, Alec repeated to himself, *Speed. Speed and surprise. If there's an enemy out there, don't give him time to think. Don't give yourself time to have second thoughts.*

But he had his doubts, just the same. *What if I freeze up? What if I get to the hatch and I can't step through?*

He glanced at Jameson, sitting across the aisle from him, so relaxed that he seemed almost to be sleeping. Abruptly, Alec pushed himself out of the seat and unlatched the overhead compartment. Guiding his weightless equipment before him, he glided down the aisle to the seat nearest the hatch.

"Would you please take the first seat, up forward?" he asked the startled youngster sitting on the aisle. "Take your gear with you."

Clearly puzzled, the young man did it. Alec stowed his own gear and strapped in next to an equally surprised looking kid of about twenty. He said nothing.

"Re-entry commencing in two minutes. Strap down tight."

It got rough enough to drive other thoughts from his mind. Alec *felt* the shuttle biting into Earth's heavy, turbulent atmosphere; felt the *g* forces that made the straps cut into his suddenly heavy body. His hands were too massive to lift off the armrests. His neck and shoulder muscles cramped under the strain of holding his head up. His palms started to sweat. *Nonsense! It's no hotter in here.*

But every man there knew that the outer skin of the shuttle was bathed in fiery air, hot enough to strip electrons from the atoms.

*Makes a perfect radar target,* Alec knew. *Does he have radars working?*

Then they lurched, staggered. Alec felt himself driven deeply into his seat, then suddenly dropping, his stomach nearly heaving.

"Sorry," the copilot's voice came over the intercom, no longer cheerful. "Bumpy out there. We're through re-entry and flying in the lower portion of the atmosphere. Not too smooth, I'm afraid, but nothing to worry about."

Swaying, bouncing, shuddering, they sat in suffering, frightened silence for an eternity of about twenty minutes.

"There's the airfield. Touchdown in two-three more minutes. Might be rough."

The landing wheel hatches opened beneath them, with a terrific roar. Despite their indoctrination, most of the men were plainly startled.

"Get ready for the landing," Alec shouted over the

wind-rushing noise. "As soon as the pilot gives the word we pop the hatch and start moving."

The impact of hitting the ground was unmistakable. The shuttle bounced once, hit again, then rolled onward with a wild screeching of brakes and roar od retrorockets. Alec leaned against his shoulder straps, felt his head pushing forward.

Then abruptly the noise and motion ceased.

"Okay. We're stopped," the pilot said tersely.

Behind him, Alec heard the main hatch crack open. He took one fast breath, then grabbed at his harness buckle.

Standing up and reaching for his helmet, pack and machine pistol, he yelled to the others, "All right—*move!*"

The man from the other side of the aisle got to the hatch first and swung it open. Alec gestured him back as he slung his light gun over his shoulder.

"Steps are jammed," the man grumbled.

Alec nodded once, then without even thinking about it jumped from the lip of the hatch. He barely had time to realize how fast he was falling when he hit the ground with a solid thump that buckled his knees. He put his hands out to brace himself and managed to keep from toppling over.

Unslinging the gun, he stepped away from the shuttle quickly. The other men were jumping behind him with a steady succession of *thumps* and *oofs*.

"All right, you know your positions," he waved his free arm at them, "spread out and form a perimeter."

They hustled outward, a few limping noticeably. The steps finally creaked out of their slot below the hatch and dropped into place. The final ten men scrambled down them and got to work on the equipment bay hatches. Jameson was the last man out, looking as unruffled as if he'd been at a friend's wedding.

By now Alec was at the nose of the shuttle, watching

the men swing open the cargo hatches. Abstractedly, he saw that the ship's nose was charred and streaked from its burning journey through the atmosphere.

And then it hit him. *I'm on Earth! I'm standing, moving, breathing on Earth!*

He looked around. The sky was gray, not blue, and the sun was hidden behind the clouds. It was nowhere as bright as Alec had expected, and he kept his glare visor up inside his helmet. It wasn't even particularly hot, about the same temperature as the living quarters at the settlement. But there was something else, something strange; air moving across his body, like standing in front of one of the circulation fans. Except that this was gentler, softer, and nowhere near as steady. It stopped and started again, playfully.

The shuttle had landed not on the concrete runway itself, Alec saw, but on the green grass alongside the runway. The concrete was broken and pocked with holes, while the grass was reasonably flat, though bumpy. The shuttle's many-wheeled bogeys looked undamaged; they could get out again.

The entire area around the airport was open and unobstructed. The land seemed to go on forever, with no horizon where it should be. Instead there were dark undulating hills away off in the distance, farther than Alec had ever seen any landscape feature before.

"Alec."

It was Jameson, who had come up beside him.

"Perimeter's established, and the heavy stuff's been rolled out of the cargo bay."

"Good." Alec glanced at his wristwatch; five minutes since touchdown. "Very good. Get the laser trucks up along the perimeter. A couple dozen men can't keep this field secure with nothing but hand weapons."

Jameson grinned tightly. "Sound observation." He turned and started shouting orders.

A shriek split the sky and Alec looked up to see the second shuttle coming in, trailing a plume of vapor behind it. It circled the field once, then came down on the opposite side of the broken runway, screeching and roaring, blowing tongues of incandescent gas out of its retrorockets, tossing clumps of sod and rocks and bits of concrete before it.

Alec hurried to the shuttle as soon as it ground to a halt. Before he could reach it, the ladder was down and men were pouring out to take their assigned positions. Last to emerge was the lanky figure of Martin Kobol.

"Welcome to Earth," Alec called to him.

A burst of machine gun fire punctuated his greeting.

# Chapter Six

Kobol looked as startled as Alec felt. All the men seemed to freeze in place, there by the side of the still-hot shuttle.

"What was that?" Kobol asked.

Alec swung the microphone down from his helmet. "This is Morgan. Who fired and why?"

In his earphones he heard a tinny reply, "Kurowski. I saw someone moving beside the buildings here on the west flank."

"Hit him?"

"Nosir. He dived behind a building when I fired."

Kobol clambered down the ladder. He was listening to the report on his helmet radio, but didn't have his mike down. "It could have been an animal," he said to Alec. "There are all sorts just wandering around loose, you know."

Alec grimaced. "Kurowski, what's your position?"

"As assigned. A hundred meters from the shuttle, on the west flank. Not much cover here . . . I'm on my belly in some sort of cement-lined rille."

"That's a culvert," Kobol murmured. "For carrying rainwater."

"All right," Alec said. "Hold your position. The others will be out there in a few minutes with heavier equipment. If you see anything else, don't fire unless it looks hostile. Conserve ammunition. But call me immediately."

"Yessir."

"I want those buildings searched," Alec said to Kobol.

"It'd take every man we have to search them."

"We can spare half the heavy weapons men, once we've got the trucks spotted around the perimeter."

"That's only six men."

"It's all we can spare. I'll lead the search as soon as the weapons are set up on the perimeter."

Alec headed off toward Kurowski's position, leaving Kobol to supervise the weapons set-up.

He could see the buildings, white and low, with holes in them for windows. A tower surmounted the central building, but its top seemed broken and charred. *Could hide a hundred men in there. And a thousand more in those hills.*

Kurowski was lying in the culvert, white-knuckled hands gripping his gun. Alec crawled down beside him.

"Seen anything else?"

"Nosir. Nothing."

"You're sure it was a man . . . not some sort of animal?"

The kid shook his head. His face was flushed with excitement, or maybe fear. "It stood on two legs, whatever it was. I'm sure of that."

Nodding, Alec said, "All right. We're going to get a search party together. Let's both watch the buildings until then."

It was actually pleasant. Lying there wasn't too uncomfortable, and Alec started to get the feel of this huge world called Earth. The breeze made noises, strange sighings and whisperings. Memories of old poems from his childhood school days started to make sense to him for the first time. And there were other sounds too. Alec had been told what bird songs and insect buzzings sounded like, but he had never heard them before.

"Look at that!"

Kurowski was pointing six centimeters in front of his nose. In the stubby grass an insect was scurrying busily.

"I think that's what you call an ant," Alec said. "Or maybe a bee."

"Bees can fly, can't they?"

"Only the queens."

The heavy weapons carriers finally started trundling into position. There were six balloon-tired armored trucks, driven by smooth-humming electric engines, mounting high-powered lasers. Some of the men hustled up on foot, laden with heavy rocket launchers and machine guns. They began putting the sections of their weapons together, and surrounded themselves with a bristling arsenal of gunbelts and finned rockets.

Alec led six men on a fruitless search through the gutted buildings. They found nothing but burned-out walls, crumbling floors and shattered roofs. And a few startled raccoons and other small animals that had claimed parts of the building for themselves. One of the troopers fired a burst from his automatic rifle at a brown furry something that simply blew apart when the bullets hit it.

"Glad it wasn't a skunk," muttered Beardon, who had made a special study of troublesome Earth animals as part of his preparation for the mission.

By mid-afternoon Alec gave the word to extend their perimeter. Most of the rocket launchers and heavy machine guns were repositioned on the roofs of the buildings, together with the infrared sensors for the night vision. One laser truck was parked in front of the center building. The other trucks prowled the farther limits of the field, about a thousand meters from the shuttles. Troopers patrolled on foot alongside them, cradling their automatic rifles in their arms.

Back inside the first shuttle, Alec reviewed the situation with Kobol. The older man sat heavily in a padded seat. Alec leaned against the armrest of the chair on the opposite side of the aisle.

"We've got to assume we've been spotted," Kobol said.

"Right. I don't think we really have been, but it's the safe assumption to make."

"The shuttles would have been a lot easier to hide if we had landed in one of the valleys nearby."

Alec shook his head. "They're safe enough here. None of the barbarians have weapons that can reach a thousand meters."

"Really?"

"And there's still no report from the satellite of large numbers of barbarians moving our way. So we're safe from a mass attack. For a day or two, at least."

Kobol looked skeptical, but said nothing.

"All right," Alec said. "We move out tonight. I . . ."

"Tonight? In darkness?"

"Right. We have infrared sensors; the barbarians don't. We can move in darkness; they can't and they won't expect us to. I want a dozen men and one of the laser trucks. We have aerial maps of the region, the road between here and the Oak Ridge complex is clearly marked. We can be there by dawn and surprise any possible defenders."

Kobol shook his head. "The men won't want to move at night. And those who're left here will be scared even more, knowing that one-quarter of their strength is off in the dark."

"Martin, I'm not here to engage in debates," Alec said, getting to his feet. "The men will follow orders. By this time tomorrow we can be on our way back home."

With a shrug, Kobol said, "Very well. You're in charge. I assume you'll want to lead the trek to Oak Ridge personally."

"That's right. And I'll want you along to identify the fissionables when we get there."

"Yes, I thought you would. That means we'll leave Jameson in command here while we're both gone."

"Right. He'll keep the men steady."

Getting up slowly from his seat, Kobol said, "You know, if you're not careful out in the dark, you could get shot by one of your own men."

"That's right," Alec replied, keeping his voice even. "I've already thought about that. If it happens to me, though, there's a chance that the same thing could happen to someone else. A better than fair chance, in fact."

Kobol broke into a grin. "That's about what I would expect."

"As long as we understand each other," Alec said, unsmiling.

The night was different.

It wasn't merely a turning down of the lights. It was *dark*. And alive.

Alec rode perched on the front fender of the laser truck, which trundled along quietly carrying the dozen men, including himself and Kobol. The driver, burrowed in the armored cockpit between the fenders, was groping along with the infrared lights and scanners. Up here in the open air, all the ancient tales of ghosts and werewolves seemed only too real.

*It's absolute nonsense*, Alec knew.

But still, there were things out there in the dark. Things that croaked and groaned, things that sighed, sudden cries and strange ghostly hootings.

"Bet that's what they call an owl," said a voice behind Alec.

The clouds had started to lift just before sundown, giving Alec and the men the most heart-catching sight they had ever seen: an earthly sunset, vibrant with reds and flame-oranges that slowly paled to blue, then softest violet, and finally to a star-strewn darkness.

The sky was clear now, and except for a disturbing twinkling, the stars seemed very normal. Where the highway swung close to the trees, however, even the stars were blotted out. All that Alec could see was the twisted black branches of the trees, rustling in the moaning wind, swaying across the faint brightness of the sky.

He shuddered. And not merely from the growing cold.

The truck braked to a stop so suddenly that Alec almost lurched off the fender.

"What is it?" he whispered urgently, leaning over toward the side slit in the driver's cockpit.

From inside the armored compartment, the driver answered, "Something moved out there."

"Something? What?"

"Don't know. It threw off enough heat to register on the scope. Big as a man, maybe more than one."

Alec considered the alternatives for a few seconds. "All right. We're not going to stop. All you troopers get off the truck and walk alongside. If you see movement, tell me on the intercom. Don't fire unless fired upon. Joe, keep the truck apace with us on foot. Let me know what you see on that 'scope."

"Right."

So the ride down the broken, abandoned highway became a walk, a crawl. Alec hefted his machine pistol and snapped its wire stock into place. He walked out in front of the truck, off on the right shoulder of the highway. The road was broad enough for four trucks to pass side by side. But the brush and trees came right up to the edge of the cement. *An army could hide in there.* But Alec saw nothing.

"Something up ahead!" the driver's voice sounded in his earphones.

"I saw something," a trooper agreed excitedly. "It went across the road from left to right. Fast."

Alec said, "Gunner—spray the right shoulder of the highway . . . how far up ahead, Joe?"

"About fifty meters, I'd say."

"Fifty meters, gunner."

The truck stopped. The low hum of its electric motors was replaced by the high-pitched whine of the special generator that drove the laser. In the darkness, Alec could barely make out the ovoid metal mirror of the laser as it moved slightly in his direction, catching the glint of starlight.

Then the whine rose to a shrill crescendo and the woods some fifty meters ahead burst into sudden flame. It sounded almost like an explosion, then a roaring crackle, as the invisible laser beam poured infrared energy into the brush.

In the lurid harsh light of the flames, two large animals leaped onto the highway and bounded across it and into the brush on the other side. They were four-footed, with graceful slim legs.

"Deer," someone said disgustedly.

"Deers have horns on 'em."

"Not all the time!"

"Cease firing," Alec commanded.

The flames disappeared as abruptly as they had sprung up. Alec could smell an oddly pleasing odor: it made him want to cough, yet it touched a cord so deep inside him that he had never known it was there. *Burning wood? Why should it smell so pleasant?*

With a shake of his head, he said, "All right, if there were any people in there, they've taken off by now. Everybody back on the truck."

Kobol hopped up on the left fender and said loudly enough for everyone to hear, "Well, there's your ambush. Two scared deer."

They all laughed. But Alec couldn't help thinking, *He's out there. Somewhere he's out there waiting for us. And he's not alone.*

He checked with Ron Jameson back at the airport twice over the next few hours. No activity there; a quiet night with no movement. The men were sleeping in relays.

Alec found that his own men were dozing off as they rode, clinging to various parts of the truck, sprawling as much as they could on whatever flat surfaces were available. He took over driving himself after the second call to Jameson, and let the driver catch a nap on the fender. Even Kobol seemed to be drowsing, his head bobbing gently as they rode, chin on chest.

In the infrared 'scope before him, the highway showed clearly as a band of orange stretching out ahead, crisscrossed by cracks and breaks. The foliage to either side was pink, except for a small scurrying animal here and there, which showed a brighter red.

"Who's on the gun?" Alec asked softly into his helmet mike.

"Gianelli."

"You wide awake?"

"Depend on it. Got my IR goggles on—they're so damned heavy they're giving me a headache. I couldn't fall asleep if I wanted to."

"Good."

"Glad to hear you're worrying about me."

Alec grinned to himself. "You just keep a sharp eye out . . . especially to our rear. I'm watching up front."

"Yeah . . . I've been doing that. Nothing moving except a few more deer."

"You're sure they're deer?"

Gianelli laughed softly. "Unless men bounce across the road on all fours."

"All right."

Alec was still driving when they topped a rise and the heat-radiating buildings of the Oak Ridge complex came into view on his scope. Almost automatically, he slowed the truck to a gradual, gentle stop. Then he glanced at his wristwatch. *Sun will be up in another hour and a half.*

For a moment he debated waking the sleeping men. Instead, he fished in the pouch at his belt for a stimulant capsule, swallowed it dry, with a hard gulp. Then he swung the cockpit overhead hatch open.

He climbed out into the breeze-murmuring night and stood on the top deck of the truck. Sleeping bodies sprawled everywhere, barely visible in the darkness. Another weird hooting sound floated out from the woods, sending a shiver along Alec's spine.

Stepping over one of the dozing men, he reached the laser gun mount. "Gianelli?" he whispered.

"Yeah."

"Take a nap. I'll stand watch."

Gianelli didn't argue. Alec climbed up into the gunner's jumpseat and silently took the infrared goggles from his hand. The laser was humming softly, set on wide-beam scan, acting as a searchlight instead of a weapon.

The goggles *were* heavy. Alec had to make a conscious effort to keep his head erect as he slowly swung the gun mount around in a complete circle. The faint whine of the drive motors sounded almost comforting, compared to the strange night sounds from beyond the truck.

The trees appeared ghostly white in the goggles, the concrete buildings of the complex down in the valley below them were a hotter shade of orange. The buildings were set out in an open area, with the closest trees hundreds of meters away. The land around the buildings looked dark, lifeless. *Maybe some grass, but not much else.*

As Alec swung the laser around slowly, scanning in a complete circle around the truck, he began to get the uncanny feeling that someone was watching him. At first it was nothing more than a vague uneasiness. But gradually the feeling grew, became a prickling along his spine, a cold fear pressing into the back of his neck.

*Maybe I should wake a few of the men,* he thought. Then he answered himself, *No! You're just nervous. Scared to be out here alone.*

Clenching his teeth, he continued to turn the gun mount slowly, feeling colder every minute. Straight ahead was the road and down on the valley floor, the buildings. Turn and the trees came up, closer, closer, mysterious white branches reaching out toward you, grasping, lifting themselves up into the sky. Keep turning, the road again, the trail back to the airport, the shuttles, safety. Then the trees again, and finally the buildings.

*What if he's out there? Would he have IR detectors? Goggles? If so, then we're sitting here like a beacon, a big, fat, bright target.*

Abruptly, Alec kicked on the foot pedals to reverse the mount's rotation. The electric motors shrilled for a moment, the mount suddenly slowed and stopped, then turned in the opposite direction.

*There! In the trees!*

It was gone before he could be sure what it was. Hot spots, several of them in among the trees. They vanished from his field of view just as the laser beams exposed them.

*Animals,* he told himself. *But are animals sensitive to infrared illumination?*

He glanced at his wristwatch. Still an hour before sunrise, but already the sky beyond the Oak Ridge buildings was beginning to pale. *Could our sunrise times be wrong?* Then, remembering the lingering beauty of the previous night's sunset, and the briefings he had received from Dr. Lord on terrestrial atmospheric effects, Alec realized that the daylight actually started before the sun itself appeared above the horizon.

For a tense fifteen minutes he continued to scan around the truck, moving the beam back and forth randomly, trying to avoid a predictable pattern. He saw nothing. Then it was light enough to snap the laser off and remove the heavy IR goggles.

A couple of the men stirred as the light grew brighter. Alec didn't know which made him feel better: the fact that he was no longer alone, or the end of the dark, threatening night.

They made their way toward the buildings in good order, Alec walking up front on the right point, Kobol taking the three-man rear guard position, the truck in the middle of the spread-out formation of armed, wary men.

The ground around the buildings was barren. Scrub grass straggled here and there in thin patches. Large stretches of ground immediately outside the buildings were bare, broken cement or blacktop. There were some areas of gravel, as well.

As they approached the buildings, Alec began to understand why Kobol had volunteered for the rear guard. He was the only man who'd been here before, ten years ago. Alec wanted to ask him if the buildings looked the same, but to do that, he'd have to ask Kobol up to the point position with him. In front of all the men, he'd have to show that Kobol knew and he—Alec—didn't.

*Screw that.* Alec kept pacing steadily toward the lifeless, gaping buildings, gripping his machine pistol in his right hand, feeling the welcome pressure of its strap riding firmly on his shoulder.

It was a longer walk than he had anticipated. Everything was deathly quiet, except for the vague rustlings and bird twitterings from the woods. No breeze. The sun climbed up into the sky, and it began to get much hotter than he remembered the previous day being. *Does the heat come from the buildings?* Fears about radioactivity sifted through Alec's thoughts. But he kept marching steadily, glancing back at his men and the trundling laser truck only occasionally.

Finally, when they were on the outer edge of the cement pads that surrounded the buildings, he called a halt. Faint dark streaks and stains mottled the broken squares of cement; they'd been made long ages ago, and blurred by years of weathering.

"Stop the truck here, where it can cover the whole area," Alec said into his helmet mike. "Form up in front of the truck."

Kobol walked up to him, thin chest and underarms of his coverall dark with sweat. He looked slightly foolish with the heavy helmet clamped bulbously over his head.

"What do you think?" Alec said, gesturing toward the buildings.

Kobol hiked his shaggy eyebrows enough to make them disappear inside the helmet. "Been a long time since I was here. But it looks about the same."

"That's the main entrance, isn't it?"

Kobol nodded.

"All right. Gianelli, take two men and follow me. The rest of you stay here. Keep a sharp watch all around."

They walked slowly toward the buildings, tension mounting with each step. Alec could see that the windows gaped emptily, there was no glass. The doors were gone too, and the walls were streaked with the sooty reminders of old fires. The interior of the buildings, though, was completely shadowed.

He could feel his heart hammering harder as they climbed the steps to the open, dark doorway. His hand felt slippery on the gun, but Alec was hot, not cold.

They stepped inside.

The floor was littered with broken bits of cement and plaster, dried leaves, other debris that Alec could not identify. The room was large and bare, stripped of everything except the litter on the floor.

"Reception area," Kobol said. "Everything in here was looted long ago."

A sudden fear struck Alec. "The fissionables?"

Kobol grinned at him. "Don't worry. They're too hard to get at, even if the barbarians know what they are and want them. Which they don't. There are all sorts of legends and taboos about radioactive material, you know."

They walked through an empty, desolate building. The rooms were huge, but blackened, charred. Most of the roofs were gone, and the still-climbing sun lit their way through the moldering shambles. Nothing stood except a few sagging partitions. No sign that human beings had ever lived or worked here. Everything caked thick with grime, showing the tracks of small animals. Kobol pointed to some dried grass wedged into a crack high up on a cement wall.

"Bird's nest," he said.

"Creepy," Gianelli said in a low, awed voice.

"The barbarians took everything they could from this building," Kobol explained needlessly. "Burned it, too."

They reached a metal door that opened onto a long metal-ribbed tunnel.

"This is the connector between the main administrative building, here, and one of the processing plants. That's where they produced the fissionables from low-grade natural ores," Kobol's lecturing voice rang irritatingly off the metal wall of the tunnel as they walked through it. "You'll see plenty of heavy equipment in the next building, and beyond that are the storage vaults."

They opened the door at the end of the tunnel.

The room was huge, vaster than any enclosure Alec had ever seen. Sunlight filtered down slantingly through the shattered roof. It was all eerie, and still.

And empty.

The giant processing building had been looted even more thoroughly than the administration area. Nothing remained except the bare walls and a few dust motes drifting through the shafts of sunlight.

Kobol's jaw fell open.

"There's nothing here," Alec said.

"It's been cleaned out." Kobol's voice was strained, shocked.

"The fissionables!"

They ran, the five of them. Kobol in the lead, they raced across the huge empty room, their boots clumping dully on the cement floor. To Alec, it was like a nightmare, running endlessly across the barren, torn-up expanse, this oversized cement box.

He ran as hard as he could, but seemed to be getting no closer to the far end of the one-room building and the metal door that they wanted. Almost unconsciously, Alec noted that the floor was studded with metal fixtures where equipment had once been bolted down to the solid floor. The fixtures looked bright and clean; the equipment had been removed only recently.

They dashed, gasping, up to the heavy metal door. It was slightly ajar.

"The vaults . . ." Kobol muttered, wild-eyed, as he strained to swing the door open.

Alec and Gianelli leaned into it, helping him.

The room on the other side was small, barely big enough to allow all five of them to squeeze in. It was lined with a dull gray metal; three walls were filled with box-sized compartments, like metal bookshelves, but with many separations along each shelf.

"Empty."

Kobol was puffing hard, his face white. "No . . . barbarian . . . did this."

Alec said nothing.

"Only one man . . . knew what . . . the fissionables were worth," Kobol said. "Your father."

# Chapter Seven

Alec forced himself to breathe deeply several times before answering.

"You think he deliberately cleared out this place?"

Kobol nodded, his eyes glaring. "Who else? The barbarians couldn't organize the men and machines you'd need for this. They wouldn't know what all this was for. . . . Most of them have been scared as hell of this place."

Gianelli kicked at the wall. "Chrissake! We came all this way for nothing."

"Your father," Kobol made it sound as if he was accusing Alec, "knew we needed the fissionables. So he's taken them away. He's trying to kill the entire settlement."

Alec returned the older man's stare. "How long can we go on what's left in the settlement?"

"A year, maybe eighteen months. What difference does it make?"

"By that time we'll have the fissionables. If I have to tear this planet apart, we'll find them."

Kobol didn't reply. He merely shook his head.

They trudged slowly back out of the vaults and through the empty processing building, heading for the entryway they had come in through. *The tired march of defeated men,* Alec said to himself. But somehow he didn't feel defeated. He was excited, almost happy. *He's forcing me to seek him out. His first mistake.*

They were halfway through the connector tunnel when Alec's helmet earphones crackled:

"There's somebody . . . toward us . . ." The radio voice was weak and masked by heavy sizzling interference.

"What?"

". . . lone person walk . . . us here on the truck . . ."

Alec hurried through the tunnel and got out of the metal-walled tunnel in time to hear, "Hey! It's a girl!"

They quickened their pace and left the buildings. Outside, Alec could see a lone, slim figure heading for the truck, walking slowly but deliberately from the woods toward them. By the time he and his men reached the truck, she was almost within hailing distance.

"She's unarmed," Kobol observed.

*And very good to look at,* Alec realized. Small and slim, wearing a stained white blouse and long pants that fitted the curve of her hips snugly. Longish, serious, big-eyed face. Long blonde hair wisping in the breeze. She shrugged it back away from her face as she came up to the truck.

Alec said, "Looks like she's got a definite reason for coming here."

"Maybe she's lonesome," Gianelli snickered.

"Not for you, big nose," one of the other men said.

"Can't see anyone else around," Kobol said, scanning the distant woods with binoculars. "But there could be an army in among those trees."

*Like Hannibal's army at Lake Trasimene,* Alec thought.

He watched the girl as she calmly approached them. A stubborn face. Strong jaw, prominent cheekbones, thin patrician nose. Mouth set in a determined line. But the eyes were searching, a little uncertain, perhaps a little frightened.

He could feel the tension among the men as she came closer. *Ridiculous.* A dozen men armed to the teeth, staring nervously at one unarmed girl. The firing bolt of a rifle snicked mechanically. *Scared to death of one girl!* Alec almost smiled.

"Gianelli," he said softly, "keep an eye on the buildings. She might be a decoy."

"Watch the flanks too," Kobol said to no one in particular.

"Rather watch her flanks."

She raised her right hand, palm open, and stopped some twenty paces from the truck. Alec walked out toward her. He knew without looking over his shoulder that Kobol was right behind him.

"My name's Angela," the girl said. No smile. Her voice was flat, unemotional.

"I'm Alec, and this is Mar . . ."

"Alec Morgan and Martin Kobol," the girl said.

"You know my father." Somehow Alec wasn't surprised.

"He sent me here. To warn you."

For an instant, Alec felt as if this entire world hung suspended in time. He could feel the sun on his shoulders and neck, see the bright sky and new green of the woods in the distance, hear the girl's pleasant but wary voice. But it was all as if he were somewhere else, far more distant than the moon, watching the scene remotely.

"We're not frightened by warnings," Kobol said.

"Wait," Alec snapped. To the girl, "Warn us about what?"

She pushed a strand of hair from her face. "There's a raider band heading for the airport. They saw your ships land . . ."

"Why would they head for us? Aren't they frightened . . ."

A smile toyed at Angela's lips. "Scared of a few dozen men? You know how many men the raiders got?"

"We have plenty of firepower."

"I know," she countered. "And so do they. It's your weapons they're after."

Kobol stepped up to her. "You're lying. We would have detected a large group of men moving through this territory. We have sensors . . ."

"No shit?" She turned back to Alec. "Look, your father told me all about the platform you've got in the sky. They can't see the raiders—not well enough. There's at least a couple hundred of them linking up together a few klicks from the airport. We're trying to keep them off balance . . ."

"It's a trick," Kobol said.

She scowled at him.

"Where's my father?" Alec asked.

Angela waved a hand. "Up north . . . seven, eight hundred klicks from here."

"And the fissionables?"

"The what?"

*So he hasn't told her everything.* "The machines and things that were in these buildings. My father has them up north with him?"

She shrugged. "I don't know. The buildings have been empty for years."

*I'll bet.* Turning to Kobol, Alec said, "Come on, we've got to get back to the airport. If there really are several hundred . . ."

"There can't be," Kobol said.

"I don't like being called a liar," Angela snapped. "Especially by a fughead who doesn't know a tree from a turd."

Alec bit his lip to keep from laughing. Kobol staggered a step backward; his lanky helmeted, booted, armed frame retreating from this tiny girl.

"Come on," Alec said, forcing his voice to remain serious. "We can't afford to ignore her warning. Let's move." He reached for the girl's wrist. "You can come with us."

She pulled back slightly. "I can make it faster on my own."

Holding on to her wrist, Alec said, "We've got the truck here; it'll go a lot faster than you can walk."

She stopped arguing.

Once they piled aboard the truck and got rolling, Alec called the ships. "Everything's peaceful here," Jameson's calm voice replied. "No sign of movement except for a few birds."

"Check with the satellite," Alec ordered. "Have them make the most intensive search of this area that they can."

"They're halfway around the world right now. Won't be back over here for another four hours."

"Damn," Alec muttered. "Well, keep a sharp watch. Protect those ships."

"You betcha," Jameson said.

The first sounds of battle came while they were still two ridges away from the airfield.

"What's that?"

It was an odd, muffled sound. Soft thumps, almost like an airlock hatch slamming in a distant corridor.

Alec was sitting up on the laser mount, his legs dangling over the edge of the turntable platform. Angela was sitting beside him.

She tensed at the sound. "Mortars. Will must've made contact . . ."

Alec yelled down to the driver, "Top speed! Get this thing back to the ships!"

The electric motors whined and strained, but the overloaded truck didn't seem to move any faster.

Angela said over the rushing wind and another trio of explosions in the distance, "Will Russo . . . he's one of your father's friends . . . he's got a small group of us here, trying to tie up the raiders long enough to give you time to take off."

"William Russo," Kobol snapped. He'd been standing behind them. "He didn't die after all; he turned traitor along with Douglas Morgan."

Alec had to twist around and squint up, into the noon sun, to see Kobol.

"We ought to put out some flankers," Kobol said. "These woods could be swarming with barbarians."

"No, they're not on this side of the airfield," Angela said.

Alec scrambled to his feet, beside Kobol. "If we send out men on foot, we'll have to slow down the truck. Let's keep making as much speed as we can."

"Thirty klicks per hour?" Kobol looked disgusted.

Alec snapped, "It's better than walking."

"And if we're ambushed?"

"We'll fight from here."

It was a tense ride. The truck was agonizingly slow, and seemed to take forever getting through the spots where the trees and brush crowded up to the very edge of the highway. The men kept their weapons in their grips, straining their eyes on the foliage. Alec saw that they were sweating, despite the cool shadows of the trees and the wind blowing against them.

He kept watching Angela. She seemed concerned, but not frightened. *She's not expecting trouble*, he reasoned, *so neither should I.* But his palms were still slippery.

Kobol was in constant touch with the ships by radio. Alec had taken off his helmet and hung it by its chin strap on the platform railing.

He sat down beside Angela. "Do you know my father well?"

She nodded. "He's my father too."

"Wh . . ."

"Stepfather," she added. "He and my mother, before she died . . ." Her voice trailed off and she looked away from him.

Alec's teeth were clenched so tightly that his jaw throbbed.

Angela turned back to face him. "He loved her very much," she said. "It wasn't just a man taking a woman. He's taken real good care of me since I was a little girl."

Alec said nothing. There was a knot inside him that tightened with every heartbeat.

"You really live on the moon?" she asked.

"Yes." His voice sounded like a dying croak, even to himself.

"I said something wrong?"

"Nothing that I didn't already know, I suppose. But . . ." He shook his head. "I didn't expect to meet a stepsister. My mother will be very interested."

"Oh . . . yeah, I see."

"Do you?"

"I think so." Her chin went up a notch.

Alec shook his head. "I think not."

"There's the airfield!" Gianelli's voice rang out. "Hot damn! Those ships look *beautiful!*"

Alec got to his feet just as an explosion erupted in the trees on the far side of the airfield, billowing black, flame-streaked smoke into the sky. The thundering roar reached his ears a split-second later. It felt almost like a physical blow.

"They're getting closer," Angela said. For the first time her voice sounded tinged with fear. "Will can't hold them back much longer."

The truck was plummeting down the highway now, descending from the last ridge and racing full tilt for the ships. They were still parked together, gleaming silvery in the glaring sunlight, looking strangely out of place in this land of soft greens and gray-brown concrete.

The other laser trucks were gathered in a semi-circle on the far side of the shuttles. But as far as Alec could see, no weapons were being fired.

"Look, over there!"

Alec turned to follow a trooper's outstretched arm, and saw three men who had just emerged from the woods off to the right of the ships. Even without binoculars, he could make out the lean shapes of guns slung over their shoulders.

They stopped and waved their arms over their heads.

"Wait!" Angela yelled, as the men on the truck swung their weapons toward the trio. "That's Will! Don't shoot."

Before anyone could stop her, she jumped off the truck and ran toward the three men.

"Hold your fire," Alec snapped. He pushed up to the driver's cab and rapped on its roof. "Get over there, where those men are." Turning to the troopers, he commanded, "All of you except Kobol, off the truck and get to the ships. Now."

Their faces showed they didn't like what was going on, especially trotting a kilometer or two in the open, with those dark woods nearby. But they obeyed Alec's orders.

The truck pulled up alongside Angela. She stopped running, and the three men walked easily toward her. They were dressed in nondescript, rag-tag clothes: cut-off shorts, ancient gray shirts, one wore a vest, only one had boots. But they each had clean weapons and bulging cases of ammunition slung on straps.

Alec clambered down from the truck to meet them. Kobol stayed up on the laser mount, with the heavy copper mirror of the weapon pointing its blunt face at Alec's back. *In half a second he could fry us all,* Alec knew.

Angela was smiling like a child. She reached out for Alec's arm, as if to drag him an extra step or two toward the advancing men.

One of them had moved out ahead of the other two. Angela said, "Alec, this is Will Russo. . . . Will, Alec Morgan."

"Oh-ho! So you're Doug's boy!"

There had never been a dog or puppy in the lunar settlement. Alec had seen videotape children's shows, though, years before. Suddenly the image of a huge, friendly, St. Bernard puppy flashed into his mind: he remembered it overpowered everyone else in the story with well-meaning enthusiasm that knocked down grown men and destroyed furniture. Will Russo was a big, shambling, grinning, happy St. Bernard pup. Like many truly big men, he was slightly round at the shoulders, from leaning over to deal with people smaller than himself. His face was round, with slightly protruding eyes, ruddy cheeks, reddish curly hair that was matted down with perspiration, an easy soft grin.

"It's a pleasure to meet you," he said. His voice was the velvet tenor of a balladeer. But he grabbed Alec's hand in a massive paw and pumped it heartily. "Sorry we've got to be so brief, but there's a lot more of *them* than there are of *us*. We can hold them off you for maybe another half-hour . . ."

Another explosion punctuated his words.

"The woods are just swarming with them. Those shuttles of yours are a prize they really want."

"Casualties?" Angela asked.

Russo frowned. "Some . . . it's been mostly hit and run until now. Just starting to get serious."

Another explosion. Closer. Alec's ears rang.

"Wait a minute," Alec said to Russo. "I've got to know a lot more about what's going on here . . ."

"Good Lord, this is no time for explanations. You've only got . . ."

Alec planted his fists on his hips. "I'm not leaving until I find out certain . . ."

A high, sighing noise like the rushing of air through a punctured bulkhead broke into their conversation.

"Incoming!" one of the men yelled.

Russo dove into Alec, knocking him down. Before Alec could say or do anything, a series of explosions blasted the universe into flame and unbearable noise and shock. Clods of earth pattered down. Alec could *taste* the acrid smoke.

He was on his belly, face down in the grass. Head buzzing, he slowly looked up. Angela was on her knees, a trickle of blood wending a thin red line down her arm. Russo was lying on his stomach alongside her.

"Looks like you're right," he said, without the slightest show of fear or anger. "You're not leaving."

He pointed, and Alec saw that one of the shuttles was burning.

# Chapter Eight

Alec stared at the burning shuttle. A huge gash was torn in its side and flames flickered in the dark smoke that was pouring out of it.

"We've got to silence that mortar," Will Russo said, "or the other shuttle will get it, too."

Alec leaped to his feet and sprinted for the truck. Kobol was already screaming into the radio, "Get the other shuttle the hell out of there! When the fire gets to the propellant tanks . . ."

Scrambling up onto the laser mount, Alec motioned Kobol to silence. He grabbed his helmet and jammed it on, saying into the mike, "This is Alec Morgan. Get every possible man into the undamaged shuttle and take off at once. Do you understand? At once."

Kobol argued. "They can only hold twenty-eight . . ."

Again, Alec gestured for silence. "Acknowledge that order! Who's in charge down there?"

His earphones hummed meaninglessly for a moment. Then, "This is Jameson. The shuttle can't take more than thirty-some men, even if they're lovers."

"Pack them in," Alec snapped. "No time for arguing. Leave the trucks and equipment."

Staring down at the airfield, Alec saw the intact shuttle start to taxi away from the burning one.

Jameson's voice came on again. "We've got three wounded men here, maybe more."

"Get them aboard the shuttle. I want a dozen volunteers to stay here with me. The rest can squeeze into the shuttle. Use the cargo space; the trucks can stay here."

Russo and his people, including Angela, had come up to the truck. The big redheaded man was looking up at Alec, squinting into the brightness of the sky, and grinning at him.

"Say, could you use some of these weapons to drive off the raiders?"

"Come on aboard," Alec said. He ducked under the laser mount's guard rail and kicked on the driver's roof. "Get us moving. Fast!"

Hanging onto the rail as the truck lurched into motion, Kobol leaned his worried-looking face to within a few centimeters of Alec's. "I'm going to go out with them, on the shuttle. I'm not staying."

"Fine," Alec snapped. "Just make sure you stay in touch. I'll tell you when to come back and pick up the rest of us."

"Right," Kobol said.

They stared at each other for a long moment. *He has no intention of coming back for me*, Alec thought. *And he knows that I know it.*

The truck bounced crazily across the grassy field. Two more shells landed near the runways, but too far from either shuttle to do anything more than churn more craters in the ground. The smoke from the damaged shuttle seemed to have died away, or at least thinned out considerably.

"Maybe the fire's gone out," Angela said over the noise of the rushing wind and occasional explosions and gunfire from the woods.

Russo shook his head. "I doubt it."

Alec stood behind the driver's cab and watched his men streaming toward the good shuttle, now parked at the farthest corner of the field, away from the fighting. The laser trucks ringed the rocket, like a defensive wall. But they weren't firing. A few men were standing beside them, looking out toward the forest where the fighting was going on, gawking like spectators trying to decipher a strange ritual.

The rest of the men were scrambling into the shuttle's main hatch. And not looking back.

Alec's truck pulled up alongside the rocketplane. Its silvery finish was now pitted and scratched; it looked dirty now, sullied by the base elements of earth.

Jameson was standing at the hatch when Alec got there. "We're just about loaded. Fifteen men volunteered to stay with you. The pilot's checking the ship to see if there's any damage that will prevent takeoff."

Russo came up beside Alec, pawed once at his nose, and said, "Lookit, I don't want to butt into your affairs, but if you don't start using these laser weapons to clear out the woods at the far end of the field, you're not going to be able to get the shuttle out of here."

"All right," Alec agreed. "Where are the men who're staying with me? I want a driver and two gunners on each truck."

Jameson said, "I'll get them moving."

"You're staying?"

"Yep."

Alec grinned at him. "Good. Thanks."

Kobol grabbed Alec by the arm and pulled him off a few steps. He whispered, "You trust these people?"

"Russo? Yes, why not? He's helping to keep the raiders off your backs long enough for you to get out of here."

Kobol's dark expression sank even more. "That's what

*he* says. I haven't seen any raiders, or any of his men. Only the mortar fire. It could be *his* mortar."

Alec shook his head. "Listen . . ."

"No, you listen. There's enough room in the cargo bay for the rest of the men. Including you."

"I'm staying."

"To find your father."

"To keep those raiders off your back. . . . And to get my hands on the fissionables that we came for."

It was Kobol's turn to shake his head. "We both know why you're staying. I hate to see you killing good men for your own personal reasons."

Alec wanted to take him by the throat. "Then why don't you volunteer to stay with me, and let one of those good men get away safely?"

Kobol grunted. "If you want to be a fool, don't expect me to join you." He turned and went to the shuttle's ladder. He climbed up to the hatch, then turned and looked down on Alec.

"I'm taking these men back to the satellite station. From there I'll make a full report to the Council. I'm sure they'll be interested in your activities. So will your mother." He grinned his toothy mirthless grin. The smile of a man who had just outmaneuvered his enemy.

Alec started for the ladder, but it began to pull up and slide into its recessed slot. The hatch swung shut. Alec's last view of Kobol was of the older man standing at the hatchway, grinning in triumph.

"Alec," Ron Jameson called to him.

He turned and saw Jameson standing a respectful few meters away.

"We're ready to roll," Jameson said.

It took Alec a moment to re-focus his thoughts. He strode down the line of trucks and swung up onto the one he had been riding earlier. Will Russo was already sitting in the gunner's jumpseat.

"I've spotted my other men in two of your trucks," Russo said. "They know the territory pretty well."

Alec tightened the chin strap on his helmet. "All right. Let's get moving. You can call the shots." Then a thought struck him. "What happened to the girl?"

"Angela?" Russo blinked his big watery eyes. "I sent her on ahead. She'll tell our people to fall back, so they won't get caught by our own fire."

The truck was moving now, heading toward the other end of the field. As they jounced across the broken runways and uneven ground, Alec noticed that the fighting seemed to have died down. No more explosions or gunfire coming from the shadowy woods.

"Steer wide of the damaged shuttle," Alec said into his helmet mike. "No telling . . . ."

The shuttle exploded with a violence that nearly tore him off the truck. The truck itself bounced and shuddered as a huge ball of white-hot flame burst out and reached for them. Alec could feel its heat searing his face.

The driver swung the truck around viciously, pulling away from the fireball. Hanging onto the laser itself for support, Alec saw the fireball transform itself into a dark tower of uprushing smoke that ballooned out into a mushroom shape, far overhead.

"By golly, she really blew," Russo said, in an awed voice.

Within a few moments they were back on course, racing as fast as the truck's electric motors would push them toward the woods. For the first time, Alec could see figures moving in the distant foliage, through his binoculars.

They looked ragged, bare arms and legs, no two of

them wearing the same kind of color of clothes. But they all had weapons, and they were forming a skirmish line at the edge of the woods.

Alec passed the binoculars to Russo. "Are those your people?"

He glanced quickly. "Nope. They're the raiders. And they've got grenade launchers, looks like, so I'd start squirting them with the lasers at the longest range possible."

As Alec started giving the necessary orders over his radio, three quick, dull popping sounds came from the woods.

"Mortar fire," Russo said calmly.

He wore no helmet, he had no body armor. He simply sat there on the jumpseat, impossibly big for it, hanging over the edge of the laser mount with the ground rushing past a meter or so below his dangling feet. He looked completely at ease. Even happy.

Three mortar shells burst up ahead of them. Alec winced at the noise.

"Aren't you scared?" he yelled to Russo.

Will grinned. "I guess so. But I learned a long time ago that it doesn't help. So I ignore it."

Alec stared at him.

"Say," Russo's expression changed to purposefulness. "If we swing this one truck out of line and head up into the woods down there," he pointed to the far left, "we could probably sneak up on those mortars and get 'em."

Alec heard Kobol's voice in his head, *You trust these people?*

"All right," he said slowly. He reached for his helmet mike.

Russo waggled a finger at him. "Better not use the radio. They might be listening to us now . . ."

Another set of mortar shells exploded, one of them

close enough to make the truck bounce. Alec crouched involuntarily and heard shrapnel *ping* against the side of the truck. A roar of flame sprang up ahead of them. The other trucks were starting to use their lasers. He heard distant shouts as the woods burst into fire.

Leaning down toward the driver's cab, Alec gave instructions to swing off to the left.

Ten minutes later they were edging slowly through a narrow lane in the foliage, climbing a steep grade toward the top of a ridge.

"How do you . . ."

"Shh!" Russo put a finger in front of his lips.

Alec moved over next to him. "How do you know," he whispered, "where the mortars are?"

"I'm guessing," Russo whispered back. "But they don't have too much range, so they've got to be up along this ridge someplace."

The truck's motors were almost completely silent at this crawling speed. The foliage was thick enough to brush against Alec's legs as he squatted on the laser mount platform. The back of his neck burned, and it hurt when he tried to move his head. A tree branch dipped close, caught momentarily in the laser's cooling fins, then sprung loose as they inched past.

It was impossible to see farther than a few meters ahead in this brush, and not even that far along the flanks. *We could get ambushed anywhere along the line here, and there are only the three of us.* Far behind them, Alec could hear the crackling of flames and the sharper barks of staccato gunfire. The trees over their heads blotted out most of the sky, but to Alec it seemed to have turned gray. Smoke?

Then there was a roar like far-off thunder. But it didn't grumble into silence. It grew, it increased, louder and louder until the truck itself began to vibrate.

"The shuttle's taking off!"

Alec stood up full height and strained for a glimpse of it through the heavy foliage. A flash of silver roared by overhead, and then the thunder diminished, dimmed, grew fainter and fainter until . . .

The monstrous crack of a sonic boom split the air. Alec had never heard it before, but he smiled despite the shock and pain. "They've made it. They're on their way."

"Good." Russo bobbed his head happily.

*Kobol's going back to the satellite. He could return to the settlement and be with my mother in another few days. Even sooner, if he pushed it.*

Russo put his big paw on Alec's shoulder. "Listen!" he whispered urgently.

The soft popping sound of a mortar firing.

"Stop the truck."

It stopped. The mortar sounds came again, off to their right. Somewhere in the thick foliage. The trail they were following curved in the opposite direction.

"We have to leave the truck," Russo said. He checked the sliding bolt of his automatic rifle. It moved smoothly, with an efficient-sounding *click-click.*

Alec bent down over the driver's rearview slit. "Stay here and stay buttoned up. If anybody bothers you, fire the laser by remote control."

"Right," came the muffled reply from inside the armored cab.

Alec swung his machine pistol off his shoulder. It was an ugly, short-muzzled weapon with a long magazine built into the handgrip and a wire brace that could be rested against shoulder or hip.

Russo was already on the ground, poking at the bushes alongside the truck. Alec jumped down beside him.

"Got your safety off?"

Looking down at his gun, Alec saw that it wasn't. Red-faced, he flicked the catch with his thumb.

Russo grinned at him. "Don't want to run into some strangers without being able to say hello right away."

They started into the brush, walking crouched over, Russo in the lead. The foliage was thick and scratched at Alec's face, arms, legs. The mottled sunlight made his neck burn even more, now that he was bent over. Insects were droning everywhere, and within a minute Alec felt itches and stings he'd never known before. It didn't seem to bother Russo at all, so Alec fought down the urge to swat and scratch.

The popping sounds were getting louder, and more frequent.

"They've got a lot of ammo," Russo whispered back, over his shoulder. "Using up their whole winter's production in hopes of getting your stuff."

"Hope they haven't hit any of the trucks," Alec answered.

"The trucks must be doing pretty well, judging from the number of rounds those guys are firing."

They flattened out on their bellies and crawled under some tangled, low-lying vines. Then Russo hissed:

"Freeze!"

Alec stayed absolutely still. He could feel his heart pounding, feel the ground slightly moist and yielding underneath him, feel the damp heat soaking into his body. He was sweating, beads of stinging salt dripping into his eyes.

Russo slid back alongside him. "Up in that big tree, at the top of the ridge . . ."

Alec looked at the tallest tree, standing out against the sky, enormous arms spread widely, newly leafed in bright green—and a man was crouching on one of the lower branches. He had a pair of binoculars up to his eyes.

"Spotter. The mortars must be within shouting distance of him."

"Let's get him!"

Russo shook his head, "If we pot him before we know exactly where the mortars are, all we're doing is warning the mortar crew. Come on, follow me."

Slowly, quietly, slithering like snakes, Russo led Alec down away from that spot. They started to make a wide circle of the area. After several minutes, Alec realized what was heppening.

*He's swinging around behind the spotter. Behind the mortars.*

It took at least a quarter-hour, Alec judged. He didn't get a chance to look at his wristwatch, they were too busy moving. Finally Russo got cautiously to his knees, looked around, then rose to his feet.

"Come on, get up, stretch your legs. Gonna need all the speed we can get."

They were on the reverse slope of the ridge now. The big tree that the spotter was using was now barely visible, only its crown poked above the ridge line.

"Are you sure that's the same tree?" Alec asked. "They all look alike."

Russo said, "Not after you've been here a while."

"All right. Now what?"

"Now we take a couple of deep breaths, then run like hell for that tree. Shoot the spotter as soon as he turns around, and spray the mortar crew as soon as they come into sight."

"You're sure they're there?"

Nodding, Russo said, "Yep. Although I haven't heard any firing for the last few minutes. They might be packing up to move out."

"All right," Alec said. "Lead the way."

"Okay . . ." Russo sucked in a deep breath. "*Now!*"

They dashed up the remaining fifty meters of waist-high brush to the top of the ridge, Russo in the lead. Alec saw him bring his gun up to about armpit level and fire off a three-round burst. The sudden noise of the gun made him jump, despite himself.

Something fell from the tree, a blur that Alec noticed out of the corner of his eye because now he was at the top of the ridge and there were eight men frozen in mid-motion. They'd been dismantling the mortars. The tubes and bipod supports and a half-dozen remaining shells lay scattered around them as they looked up, some crouched, some standing, one of them ridiculously mopping under his chin with a florid red cloth.

For a split instant Alec saw it all frozen in front of him. Then the men dived for their weapons. Alec heard and felt himself firing his gun, it kicked and chattered in his hands. Sprays of dirt sprouted in the midst of the startled men. Four of them jerked backward immediately, arms flung out and mouths open. Two others seemed to stagger, reach for the guns that were resting on the ground, then fall over them. Two more dived for the brush and started scrambling downslope, away from Alec and Russo.

Alec realized he'd been firing from the hip, simply spraying the area with bullets. He straightened and brought the gun to his shoulder, sighting carefully . . .

Russo tapped his shoulder. "That's enough, let them go."

"But they'll . . ."

"Good God, man, what do you want? We've killed seven men and got their mortars and personal weapons. What else?"

For the first time, Russo seemed annoyed. Not angry, really, but annoyed in the way a parent gets upset with a foolish child.

Alec put his gun down. "How do you know they're dead?"

Looking at the bodies sprawled below them, Russo answered, "If they're not now, they will be soon."

Slowly they walked down to the scene. Under the big tree, the spotter lay unmoving, blotches of red welling over his body, his legs crumpled beneath him, his face contorted. Alec turned and looked at the six men near the disassembled mortars. His stomach heaved.

They were broken apart. Huge gaping wounds ripped through their bodies. One of them had no face, only an oozing mass of red and gray.

Someone was groaning. Alec turned his back and tottered away from the sight and smell. Everything was going blurry. But he could still hear.

"Please . . . please . . ."

"I'm sorry, son. There's nothing I can do for you."

A single shot.

Alec leaned against a tree and threw up.

After what seemed like hours, Russo came up beside him. "First time you've seen men killed." It wasn't a question.

Alec mumbled, "First time . . . I've been responsible."

Russo said, "Okay . . . you take their weapons back to the truck. Take it slow and easy. You'll need to make a half-dozen trips. I'll bury them."

"You'll . . . what?"

With an almost bashful shrug, Russo said, "Someday somebody's going to kill me, and I wouldn't want to be left aboveground to feed the maggotts."

"But you killed them."

"Yep. And now they need burying." Russo paused a moment, then added, "You kill enemies when they're in a position to kill you. If they're running and weaponless, you let them run. If they're dead, you bury them. And you don't take prisoners unless you've got a good reason to."

"Those are the rules of war here?"

"The rules of survival."

By the time they had finished their work and navigated the truck back down to the airfield, the battle there had been long finished. Russo left Alec with his own men and trucks at the edge of the charred, smoking woods, and went off into the late afternoon shadows of the forest, saying he would be back before sundown.

Jameson gave an accounting of the battle. "They kept melting back into the trees. We couldn't follow them in there with the trucks, so we just kept patrolling around the edge of the woods, squirting at them whenever they fired at us. They lobbed a lot of mortar rounds at us, but we caught most of the shells up at the top of their trajectories, with the lasers."

Two of the trucks were damaged, but still running. Several of the men were hurt, none killed.

Jameson peered off into the woods, where Will Russo had gone. "Are those people on our side, or what?"

Alec shrugged. "They were on our side today. I'm not sure of what happens next. Keep everyone alert."

"When does the shuttle come back for us?"

"When I call it."

Alec could see what Jameson's next question would be, but he didn't ask it. After a moment's hesitation, he simply said, "I'd better set out some guards." He walked away, leaving Alec standing alone.

The helmet radio had only a limited range, but each truck had a radio powerful enough to reach out to the satellite station when it was overhead. Alec climbed into the nearest truck's empty cab and turned on the radio that was set into the panel alongside the driver's seat.

No answer from the satellite. After several minutes, he realized, *It's below our horizon again. Damn! And all the timetables were in the shuttles.*

He climbed out of the cab and stepped back down onto the grass. Far out in the middle of the airfield the blackened skeleton of the destroyed shuttle lay broken and still smoldering.

Alec looked around at the now-silent forest, the darkening sky, the lengthening shadows of approaching dusk.

Suddenly he realized that they were completely alone on an alien, inhospitable world.

# Chapter Nine

The sun was already hidden behind the trees when Will Russo appeared again. He walked alone out of the forest and toward the semicircle of trucks parked at the edge of the airfield.

Despite himself, Alec was glad to see the man. When Jameson told him that Russo was coming, Alec went out to the guard perimeter to meet him.

"You're not bedded down for the night yet, are you?" Will asked, right off.

"No, not yet."

"Good, good." He looked genuinely pleased. "We've made camp up on top of the first ridge," he waved vaguely in the general direction, "and I think it might be a good idea for you to camp with us."

Alec said nothing.

"What's left of those raiders are still skulking around here somewhere," Will explained, "and, well, our two forces camping together'll be strong enough to discourage them from trying anything during the night. We'll both be able to sleep easier."

*My trucks and weapons and your experienced woods fighters,* Alec thought. Nodding, he asked, "Can the trucks get up there?"

"Oh sure . . . I'll show you the trail."

"All right." Alec turned and called for Jameson.

Will grinned boyishly. "Fine. Wonderful. In union there is strength."

The trail up to the top of the ridge was narrow and tricky. One of the trucks slipped in a rain-sliced gully alongside the barely visible trail and it took nearly an hour to pull it out again. The men had to use primitive muscle power to lift the truck's rear wheels out of the foliage-choked gully; the other trucks' electric motors began to overheat when they tried to tow the truck free.

It was full night when they finally got to the top of the ridge. Alec, perched on the cab of the lead truck, saw a handful of people sitting quietly around a meager open fire. One of them was Angela.

"Is this your whole force?" he wondered aloud to Will, who was sitting on the fender alongside the cab.

"Oh no . . . we've got twice again as many people set out as guards. Didn't you see them as we came up the trail?"

Alec shook his head, a gesture that was lost in the darkness.

The trees thinned out along the top of the ridge, so there was ample room to park the trucks. Alec told Jameson to have the men sleep on the trucks, and have at least four men awake and using the infrared scanners at all times.

"I'm not so sure that four men is enough," Jameson said quietly.

They were standing beside one of the trucks. The camp fire was far enough from them so that no one else was in earshot.

"What do you mean?"

"I don't want to be an impolite guest," he answered softly, hitching his thumbs on his gunbelt as he spoke, "but—well, why should they be so helpful to us? Especially if they're the people who stole the fissionables.

Why did they stick their necks out to help us drive the barbarians away, and why are they offering to share their camp and their food with us? It doesn't make sense to me."

Alec was forced to agree. "At least it's better than sitting out there in the open, alone. And we don't have enough rations to last more than another day or two."

"I just don't know," Jameson said skeptically. "Suppose what they're really interested in is getting these nice shiny new trucks for themselves? It wouldn't be too difficult for them to slit our throats while we're sleeping."

Somehow the picture of Will Russo murdering men in their sleep didn't match in Alec's mind with what he had already seen of the man. Still:

"All right. Tell the men to sleep in the cabs of the trucks. Button them up and don't open for anyone except a recognized member of our group."

Jameson was silent for a moment. In the distant light of the campfire, it was impossible to read the expression on his hawkish face. At last he said, "Okay . . . but I still don't like this."

"Things could be better," Alec admitted. "But they could be a lot worse, too."

"I suppose."

"Keep somebody on the radio. The satellite ought to be in range sometime tonight."

"Right."

Jameson turned back toward the truck, and Alec walked slowly toward the campfire. Angela was sitting there. He could see her long hair gleaming like hammered gold in the firelight.

The fire itself was fascinating. Strangely twisting, dancing, flickering, the flames formed shapes and memories before his eyes. He stared at it, then found that he was staring *into* the fire, deep inside the dancing flames, watching the logs glowing bright red and the flames licking up from them, orange and yellow and blue and . . .

"Hello. Had dinner yet?"

Alec pulled himself away from the hypnotic flames. "What? . . . Oh, no, not yet."

"What's the matter? Feel okay?"

"I'm all right . . . It's just . . . I've never seen an open fire before. It's fascinating."

"Oh. Yeah, I guess so."

They sat together beside the fire, and for the first time Alec noticed that there was a blackened metal container rigged on a set of poles, hanging over the flames. Angela called it a "pot." It looked to Alec as if it had started life as a gasoline tank, but now it was cut down, its corners battered and dented.

"Grab some stew from the pot and make yourself to home," she invited.

Alec stood up and bent over the pot. Inside was a shimmering mess of bubbling liquid, with lumpy dark shapes poking out of the seething surface.

Thinking of all the injections and pills he had taken before leaving the satellite, Alec stirred the concoction with his knife, then jabbed at one of the shapes. He held it at arm's length, dripping and smoking, as he returned to Angela and awkwardly squatted on the ground beside her.

"It won't hurt you," she laughed at him. "It was only a rabbit, even when it was alive."

"A rabbit?"

It was the first time he had seen her laughing. "Don't you have anything you can use for a plate? The stew's got plenty of good things in it—carrots and leeks and all sorts of herbs."

"Uh . . . this is fine. I've got a messkit back at the truck, but just let me taste . . ." He bit into the rabbit.

*Pain!* Alec had never felt anything so hot inside his mouth. Coughing, gagging, burning, he finally swallowed the chunk whole.

Angela was pounding him on the back, looking worried, and shouting in his ear, "You want water? Are you okay?"

"I'm fine," he croaked, eyes tearing. "My mouth is a mass of second-degree burns and there's a lump of dead rabbit stuck sideways in my guts, but otherwise I'm fine."

The eight or nine people—mostly men—around the fire were staring at him. But they quickly looked away and went back to their own conversation. Alec managed to down a few bites of the meat without further trouble, and found that it was good. Good enough to make him realize that he wanted more.

"I'll go find my messkit," he said, starting to get to his feet.

"No, don't bother," Angela said. "Here, use my plate. I'll wash it off, okay? Then you don't have to go all the way back to the trucks."

She leaned forward to reach a small tin of water that was resting on the ground near the fire. While she washed off the metal plate and spoon, Alec wondered, *Why does she want to keep me away from the trucks?*

He ate in wary silence, wondering vaguely how long the immunization shots they had given him on the satellite would protect him from the local germs. The stew was hot and strong, unlike anything he'd ever tasted before. Angela offered him water in a metal cup.

When he had finished the meal, he washed off the utensils himself and handed them back to Angela.

"Is your mouth okay?" she asked, suppressing a grin.

"I'll survive." In fact, with the hot meal inside him, Alec felt fine and strong. Except for the sunburn glowering on the back of his neck.

"I'm sorry about that. Guess I should have warned you. I didn't realize . . ."

"It's all right," he said. "And the food was great. Many thanks. . . . Now, I think I'd better be getting back to my men."

She got up with him and started walking alongside. Alec realized that the only weapon he was carrying was his knife. She was completely unarmed.

"Look." She pointed. The moon was rising above the tree-fringed horizon. It was nearly full, bright and serene and glorious.

Alec stared at it. The lights of the settlement's surface domes couldn't be seen.

"What's it like?" Angela asked.

"What?"

"Living there . . . on the moon."

"We don't live on it," he said. "We live in it, underground. You can't walk around in the open like this; you need a suit and helmet."

"Why?"

"There's no air . . ."

Her eyes widened for a split-second, then went crafty. "Wait . . . if there's no air, how come you can live there?"

So they sat on a convenient rock, watching the moon rise higher into the night sky, playing tag with the occasional silvered clouds, while Alec explained about lunar life to her. *She doesn't really know*, he realized as he told her what a dazzling sight the Earth is. Before long he found himself watching her, instead of the moon. In the soft light from his home, she seemed to float pale and golden against the darkness. *Lord, she's beautiful!*

She turned to face him, "This is the first time anyone's told me about these things. Dad—I mean, your father . . ."

Alec felt his heart turn to ice.

"Funny," she said, still smiling but with puzzlement in her voice. "It's kind of hard for me to call him Dad now . . . knowing he's your father."

"He never told you about the settlement?" Alec asked, his voice sounding flat and distant, even to himself.

Angela shook her head. "He'd always change the subject when I asked him about it. After a while, I guess I just stopped asking."

Alec stood up. "I've got to check on my men. Good night."

"Oh." She sat there for a moment, then got to her feet. "Good night, Alec." She turned and headed back toward the campfire.

He didn't trust himself to say anything more, to call after her. So he tramped in the opposite direction, to the trucks.

Disregarding his own orders, Alec slept out in the open, on a stretch of mossy ground near the trucks. He wrapped himself in a plastic tarpaulin and kept his machine pistol beside him. Still, he hardly slept at all.

The sun awoke him after what seemed like fifteen minutes of dozing. After checking with Jameson to see that everything was all right with the men, Alec walked stiff-jointed and aching to the campfire. It was smoldering low, but one of the women was putting fresh logs into it.

"Well, you're up bright and early," Will Russo called to him jovially. He was standing a short distance from the fire, holding a steaming cup in his hand.

Walking around the fire to confront Alec, he said, "Here, have some herb tea. It's not terribly good, but it'll help you wake up. If you'd like to shave . . ."

Alec shook his head blearily. He got the cup almost to his lips, then remembered the searing pain of the previous night's stew. His mouth still felt raw.

"Uh . . . thanks." He handed the cup back to Will. "I'll just take some water."

Will shrugged. "Have you made contact with your satellite yet? Are they coming to pick you up?"

"Not yet," Alec said, going for the water can by the fire. "We've got someone on the radio right now, but no luck so far."

He drank from the can, and again worried about catching some local disease.

"Well," Russo was saying, "I'd hate to leave you out here in the woods all by yourselves, but we can't hang around here much longer."

"I understand," Alec said.

He left Will by the campfire and walked quickly back to the trucks. Going to the cab of the first one he came to, Alec pulled the medical kit from its niche behind the driver's seat. The pills were all in neatly labelled vials, but the labels weren't all that specific in their instructions. More than half the pills were already missing, besides. Trying to remember what he'd been told, Alec took three different pills, swallowed them dry.

"Oh, there you are." It was Ron Jameson.

Alec swung down from the cab. "What is it?"

"Radio contact."

Alec followed Jameson to the third truck. Gianelli was in the cab, a huge pair of earphones clamped around his face, squinting with concentration.

"Yeah . . . yeah . . . still coming through clear. Okay, here he is now. Hold on . . ."

He took off the earphones and held them out for Alec. "The satellite's relaying a call from home. Kobol's back at the settlement already."

Fitting the earphones over his head and adjusting the lip mike that swung out from the right earphone, Alec thought: *Kobol! He pushed on to the settlement on a high-gee boost. Must have burned every gram of propellant between the satellite and the Imbrium mines.*

The big, cumbersome earphones blotted out all sounds except for the hissing, crackling static of the radio. Alec could see that Gianelli was saying something to Jameson, but he couldn't hear their voices.

"Hello . . . hello . . . Alec Morgan?" The communications tech was a girl, that much Alec could tell. But her voice was faint and streaked with static interference.

"Yes. Go ahead."

A pause. Then, "Alec, this is Martin Kobol. Can you hear me?"

"Yes."

It took about two and a half seconds for Alec's word to get to the moon and Kobol's response to reach back to Earth. A discernible pause.

"Good. Now listen. I've just arrived back at the settlement. The Council will be meeting in an hour. Everything's completely upset here—all our plans, everything. There's a threat of real panic through the entire settlement if we don't act carefully and reassure the people. They were all depending on getting those fissionables."

"I know." *Spare the political speeches!*

Pause. Then, "We've got to work out another plan. Can you hold out down there on the surface for a few days?"

*Or a few weeks? Or months?* "Yes, I think so."

"Good. Now listen. Stay where you are, hold tight, while we figure out the next move."

"No."

A long pause. Not merely because of the distance this time.

"What was that?"

"I said no," Alec repeated. "We know where the fissionables are. We're going to get them."

"You can't . . . I mean . . ."

"I can and I'm going to. We'll keep in touch with the satellite," Alec said.

"This is psychotic! You're going to force us to pull one of the old shuttles out of mothballs, track your movements . . ."

"Stow it, Martin. We came here for the fissionables and we're going to get them. Everything else is a detail."

Kobol's voice, when it came, was almost a woman's screech. "You can't travel across the continent and find him, you fool! You'll kill yourself and your men with you."

"You'd hate that, wouldn't you?" Alec shot back. "Listen to me, Martin. We can travel across country. And we can live off the country, too. There's plenty of food here."

But Kobol was saying, "I don't care what you do to yourself, your own personal grudges are your business, not mine. But to risk the rest of those men without even giving them a chance . . ."

"Good-bye Martin. Tell the Council that I'm following their prime directive: I'm going to get the fissionables."

The time lag between their statements was turning the conversation into two separate monologues. "And there's medicine," Kobol was saying, but more calmly now. He was more in charge of himself, obviously thinking fast while he spoke. "You'll be exposing those men to all the diseases of Earth . . ."

"I want to talk to my mother now," Alec said, "Please put her on."

"Your inoculations can't keep you protected . . ." Kobol stopped, then answered, "Your mother's busy preparing for the Council meeting. By the time we could get her here to the communications center, the satellite would be below your horizon and out of range."

"All right. I'll want to talk to her tomorrow."

The pause again. Alec could sense Kobol's mind working during the hiatus. "Very well. I'll tell her. In the meantime, I want to warn you again that you should not endanger your men. The Council won't look favorably on any foolhardy action. You should stay where you are until we've decided on the next step."

"Too dangerous," Alec countered. "We've already been trapped here once. I don't want to let it happen again."

Kobol's voice was starting to fade. "Your orders are to stay where you are."

Smiling tightly, Alec answered, "No good, Martin. We're in much more danger here than we will be on the move. I'll expect a call tomorrow. And I want to talk to my mother then. Now I'm going to put Gianelli back on. Give him the ephemerides for the satellite, so we'll know when you're in contact range."

Alec pulled the earphones off his head and handed them to Gianelli. "Quick, before the satellite gets out of range."

Still sitting in the driver's cab, Gianelli took the earphones with a slight, quizzical grin. "Gonna make heroes out of us," he muttered.

Jameson said nothing. Alec left the truck and went searching for Will Russo. Halfway back to the campfire, which a pair of men were now burying under loose dirt, he spotted the big redhead striding toward him.

"Looking for you," Will said.

There was something about the man, his big gangling stride, the way his arms hung loosely at his sides, the innocent-looking grin on his face—Alec found it impossible to distrust him.

"I've been looking for you, too," he said.

"Have you been in touch with your people?" Russo hiked a thumb skyward.

"Yes. If you don't mind, we're going to travel northward with you . . . I want to find my father."

Will's grin broadened. "Good. Good. I've just got a message from him. He's only a few klicks off, in a town named Coalfield."

"Here?" Alec suddenly felt weightless, all the breath knocked out of him.

"Yep." Will nodded. "Just a few klicks west of here. We can be there in a couple of hours."

# Chapter Ten

Alec scarcely noticed the countryside rolling past as he sat on a fender of the lead truck, heading for the town where his father was waiting.

They came down out of the ridges and woods, all of his own men and Russo's people riding on the trucks. They bumped up onto a road, but it was not a wide concrete highway like the one between Oak Ridge and the airport. This was a narrow, twisting blacktop road, cracked beyond description. Weeds and grass grew in the cracks.

Behind him, he could hear Gianelli talking with Angela.

"You mean you walk all the time?" he was asking, incredulous. "Carrying all your food and guns?"

She sounded almost amused. "Sure. We ride when we can find something to ride on. There aren't many cars or trucks left in running condition—mostly the electric ones that need sunlight for their solar batteries. Not much fuel for the gas-burners."

"So you walk?" Gianelli asked again. "And carry everything on your backs."

"Unless we can find horses or other pack animals. I covered five hundred klicks on a cow last year, when I hurt my leg."

"Which one?"

"The right."

"Looks pretty good now." Gianelli's voice had a leer in it.

"It's fine. And you can keep your hands off!"

Alec turned and said evenly, "There could be five hundred raiders in those trees. Play some other time."

Gianelli's face reddened and his mouth squeezed down into a thin, hard line. But he moved away from the girl.

Angela looked at Alec for a wordless moment. Then he turned away.

Up ahead he could see the first buildings of the town. His hands felt suddenly wet, shaky. He tightened his grip on the edge of the fender with one hand, shifted the machine pistol's belt across his shoulder with the other. *He's here. Somewhere among these buildings . . .* Every sense in him peaked, brightened. Alec could hear his pulse throbbing in his ears, feel his breathing quicken. *He's here!* But deep within him, something was telling him to run, to get away, anywhere but this one place. Journey across the whole face of the planet, travel back to the moon, get away anywhere, anyhow, anyplace.

Yet he was impatient to meet the man he had come to find.

Alec knew from his study tapes that this was a small town. But it still dwarfed the lunar settlement. *All these buildings, aboveground, out in the open!* And their variety: one floor, three floors, brick fronts, wooden slats, something that looked like stone blocks. Windows staring down at him, empty, gaping, dark. Street after street after street, branching every hundred meters or so.

But empty. Dead. No one lived here. No one was on the streets. No vehicles. Nothing in sight except the silent buildings and windblown dust billowing through the empty streets.

He looked across to Will, perched on the other fender.

"Town's been deserted since the sky burned," Will said. "People come by once in a while, but nobody lives here permanently. Too tough to grow food, and too hard to defend the town against raiders."

"How do you know which building my father's in?"

Will grinned hugely. "Oh, Douglas'll be in his usual place."

It turned out to be a one-floor brick building marked, U.S. POST OFFICE—COALFIELD, TENN.—37719.

Will suggested that the trucks be spread around the building in a defensive perimeter. Alec passed the order on to Jameson, while the truck he and Will were on trundled into the parking area behind the building. Nestled under a protective overhang sat a single squarish, open-topped vehicle. Alec recognized it from history tapes as a jeep.

As he got down from the truck, Alec wondered where his father found the fuel to propel the jeep. *If he can cover long distances in it, then he must have fuel depots spotted along the way.* Then Will Russo was beside him, clasping one of his arms and ushering him through a doorway that had long ago lost its door.

It was dark inside. They walked down a narrow corridor, turned a corner.

And there he was.

He was standing in the center of a big room, surrounded by empty shelves and broken, shattered wooden desks and tables. The roof was partially gone, so the sunlight streamed in, and dust motes danced lazily in the still air.

The room was large and open, but Douglas Morgan seemed to fill it. He was big, hulking broad-shouldered and thick-bodied. Will Russo was as big, Alec instinctively realized. But where Will was a grinning, happy oversized puppy, Douglas Morgan was a towering gray bear.

His face was square and strong, with iron-gray hair rising in a bristling shock from his forehead and framing his powerful jaw with an iron-gray spade-shaped beard. Even his eyes were gray. They stared straight at Alec now, unblinking, pinning him where he stood.

*I don't look anything like him,* Alec heard his own inner voice saying. *No wonder he hates me.*

"You're Alec, eh?" His voice was loud, demanding, even in normal conversational tone. "You have your mother's genes, all right."

*And not yours? Or are you angry because yours might be recessive instead of dominant?*

"I'm Alec."

"Well, come over here and let me see you. I'm not going to bite you."

Alec walked slowly toward his father. The man was just as big as all the childhood memories that were flooding through Alec's mind; a mountainous man, with a strong commanding voice to match.

They stood confronting one another. Neither offered a hand. Neither smiled. Despite the sun beaming down through the broken roof, Alec felt cold, numbed at his core.

"He's a good fighter," Will's voice broke the staring match between them. "He helped me take a nasty mortar nest. Handled himself very well."

Douglas nodded. "That's something."

"I vomited afterward," Alec snapped.

Douglas' heavy eyebrows went up. "Did you? A sensitive soul, hah? Well . . . killing a man's no joke. But be glad you were the one who could get sick, not the one you got sick over."

Will said, "Why don't we sit down and have something to drink? It's been a dusty ride up here, and I sort of feel like celebrating."

"Celebrating what?" Douglas asked.

"Your reunion!"

"Oh. That." He smiled sardonically. "Sure. Obviously

you've found some liquid lightning along the way. So uncork it and we'll have a little party. Just the three of us."

"It's in my pack." Will bounded back toward the door.

"Sorry we haven't had the place dusted and decorated for the big occasion," Douglas said to Alec. "Eh . . . the furniture's a bit nonexistent. Care to sit over here?"

He gestured elaborately toward the floor next to a scarred, battered wooden counter that ran across the front of the room.

Alec shrugged and dropped down onto his heels. He watched as Douglas stiffly, slowly sank down into a sitting position. He leaned his back against the partitions under the countertop with an audible sigh.

"Caught a cold in my back during the spring rains," he said, without turning to look at his son. "Makes it merry hell to bend."

Will came back, holding a metal flask in his big freckled hand. He sat down on the floor facing Alec and Douglas. Grinning, he unscrewed the cap of the flask and sniffed at its contents.

"Wow! Shouldn't keep this in the hot sun."

Douglas reached for it and took a cautious sniff. "I'll bet I could get fifty klicks to the gallon on my jeep with this stuff." He passed the flask to Alec. "Here, you're the guest of honor. You get the first shot. If you survive, maybe we'll try it."

"It's not that bad," Will said, trying to look aggrieved. "The farmers that sold it to me swore that they brewed it last summer."

Alec took the flask and brought it to his lips. The fumes coming from it seemed to crawl right up inside his eyeballs, making them want to water. He took a sip. It stung and tasted sour. *Don't cough!* he commanded himself.

"Not bad," he said calmly, his voice only partly strangled.

Douglas took the flask from him. "Well if you can stand it, I suppose I can too."

Alec watched his father take a long swallow of the liquor, as his own sip burned its way down to his stomach. They passed the flask around for another round before Douglas said:

"We have a lot to talk about."

"Yes, we do," Alec agreed.

Will said, "Maybe I ought to do . . ."

"No, stay right there," Douglas commanded.

*That eliminates talking about mother*, Alec thought. Aloud, he said, "The fissionables are gone."

"Right. We took them north . . . er, for safekeeping."

"We need them."

"I know you do."

"Then why did you take them away? Why didn't you bring them back yourself? Why did you turn your back on us and stay here in this mudhole?" All in a rush.

Douglas had the flask in his hand. He looked at it, then shook his head once, abruptly, as if he'd made a firm decision. "*That* is a long story. But it all boils down to one unavoidable fact. The lunar settlement can't survive by itself. It needs Earth. Otherwise, it's going to die."

"Of course!" Alec snapped. "We need those fissionables . . ."

"It's not the fissionables," Douglas turned toward Alec and leaned one elbow heavily on the sagging wooden shelf behind him. The wood creaked. "There's more than the fissionables involved . . . far more. The life of the settlement itself."

"I don't follow."

"Look—the settlement was never intended to be entirely self-sufficient. Right? When the sun flared up they were suddenly thrust on their own. No more support from Earth."

Alec said, "And we've been on our own for fifty years now. Doing fine."

"You *think* you're doing fine!" Douglas' voice was rising. "But take a good, unbiased look at the settlement. You're still operating on the machinery that was there before the flare, right? No one's built new reactors, new processing plants, new rocket shuttles, eh? No one's even expanded the solar battery fields, or tried to set up the processing plants to run on the voltages that the solar batteries produce. No, instead you keep sneaking back to Earth to grab fissionables for your reactors."

"So?"

"So what happens when you've used up all the fissionables you can find? What then?" Douglas demanded.

"That won't happen for centuries!"

"Centuries, millennia . . . what difference? The point is," Douglas insisted, "that it will happen one day, and unless you people have the knowledge and the guts to work out new devices—like fusion generators, for instance—then you're going to die. All of you."

Alec said, "But that's so far in the future . . ."

"Then what about medicines?"

"We synthesize all the medicines we need."

"Oh sure you do, certainly," Douglas sneered. "But how many people in the settlement are too brittle-boned to make the trip to Earth? How many of your own men are going to suffer sunstroke because they don't have enough melanin in their systems? And that's a beautiful burn you've got on the back of your neck, by the way."

Alec was starting to feel confused. "But those are hereditary things . . . medicine can't . . ."

"Exactly!" Douglas pounced. "What about the four or five people each year who die of cancer in the settlement? Huh?"

Bewildered, Alec replied, "Cancer's unavoidable . . . everybody knows that . . ."

"Oh it is, is it?" Douglas glanced over at Will, then turned back to Alec. "It happens that cancer-arresting drugs were being manufactured on Earth before the sky burned."

"They were?"

Douglas nodded. "And the incidence of cancer is rising in your settlement, at a rate of five percent per year. In another generation . . . pffft!" He snapped his fingers.

"No . . ."

"I calculated it out myself, and that was more than ten years ago. Cancer, birth defects, other genetic diseases—all on the rise in the settlement. Because of inbreeding. The genetic pool of the settlement isn't big enough to be viable!"

"No wait . . ."

"No! You listen. The settlement is dying. It's too small and inbred to survive. Oh sure, maybe you'll get along fine for another fifty years or so . . . but I doubt it. There were already a lot of strains visible when I left. I'll bet there's a lot more tension in the air now. Nobody knows how to build new equipment; you've got some smart engineers and technicians, but no scientists to speak of. A few astronomers. And the genetic diseases are being quietly brushed under the rug because nobody knows how to treat them, or what to do to get rid of them."

"He's right," Will said. "I was a medic, you know. What Douglas is saying is absolutely right."

Alec glared at the two of them. "So you decided to let the settlement die. You left with no intention of coming back."

"That's just about a hundred percent wrong," Douglas said. "The settlement will die—*if it stays alone.* I'm trying to save it by forcing you people to reconnect with

Earth. And to do that, I've got to build a viable civilization here on Earth. Right?"

The molten lava of rage was burning through Alec's guts. "That's a fancy way of saying that you're conquering a little empire for yourself down here, and you're going to force the settlement to become part of it."

Smiling, Douglas replied, "I can see that your mother's been educating you." He shrugged elaborately. "Call it an empire, a renaissance, an attempt to hold back the complete annihilation of mankind as a species . . . call it any goddamned thing you want to! But I'm going to bring the shreds of civilization back together, one way or the other. And I want you to work with me. You're my son, and . . ."

"And someday I'll inherit all this?" Alec shouted at him. "The heir-apparent? The crown prince?"

"Something like that," Douglas muttered.

"Then you're a fool! Don't you know that crown princes spend their lives planning the emperor's murder?"

Douglas said nothing. He simply sat there on the dusty floor and stared at his son. Then, slowly, he struggled to his feet and walked out of the room.

Alec didn't move.

Will Russo shook his head sadly. "I shouldn't stick my nose into the damned thing . . . father and son, after all. But, dammit, that was a lousy thing to do to him. He's been waiting ten years to see you."

"So he saw me," Alec said, suddenly weary of the whole thing. "What was he expecting? Congratulations on leaving us? A hero's medal for turning his back on five hundred human beings so that he could play emperor down here?"

"There's a helluva lot to this that you don't understand."

"No." Alec got to his feet. "I understand him perfectly. He can rationalize all he wants to, but the simple fact is that he'd rather be a king down here than a responsible citizen of the settlement. And he's going to try to make us submit to him by holding the fissionables. He knows we can't survive without them."

"You won't survive even with them," Will said gently. "That's the point he's trying to make."

The afternoon seemed infinitely long. Alec paced alone through the dead streets of the town, kicking up dust, watching the weeds and a few scraggly flowers tossing in the warm wind. Trees grew tall and dark in all directions around the town, but somehow the trees planted along the streets were nothing but dead bare skeletons.

It took Alec several hours to calm down, to regain enough self-control so that he could face his own men without being afraid of trembling hands or cracking voice. *He's convinced himself that he's right,* Alec thought. *And he's convinced Will and the others, too. Everything mother told me about him is true. He's able to rationalize it all: leaving us, not caring if we live or die. And he claims it's for our own good! The bastard!*

The flaming beauty of the sunset went unnoticed. Only when it was getting dark enough to worry him did Alec return to the trucks. He lost his way several times among the many diverging streets, but finally he found the post office and his men. They were eating with Will's people, gathered around an open fire in front of the post office building.

"There you are," Jameson said as Alec stepped out of the shadows cast by the trucks. "I was starting to think I should send a couple of scouts out to find you."

"No need," Alec said.

His own men and Will's were intermingling freely.

The girls among Russo's people were there, laughing and charming the men. Angela wasn't in sight, though. Alec sat on the ground by the fire and shared in their communal dinner. He didn't bother asking what was in the pot. It was tasteless—at least, he tasted nothing.

Angela showed up as he finished eating.

"Dad wants to see you," she said tightly.

He rose and started walking off with her, quickly. Despite her small size, she kept pace with him. *Small,* he couldn't help thinking, *but tough. Battle-hardened.*

"Hey Alec, where you going?" Gianelli's voice called through the flickering shadows cast by the campfire. "Don't do anything we wouldn't do!" The laughter of several men followed them.

They walked into the darkness, around toward the back of the post office.

"He's not your father," Alec said grimly.

Her chin went up a notch and she snapped, "More than . . ." Then she seemed to catch herself, think better of it. "That's right. He's not really my father."

"And you're not my sister."

"So?"

"So just remember that."

Her voice went brittle. "I'll keep it in mind."

Douglas was sitting in his jeep; it was still parked behind the post office building. The only light was from the stars, the moon hadn't risen yet.

"Thank you, Angela," Douglas said quietly. "If you don't mind, I'd like to talk to Alec alone."

"I don't mind . . . Dad." She put special emphasis on the last word, Alec thought.

"Well?" Alec asked, standing beside the jeep. He could barely make out the expression on his father's face, in the darkness.

"What are your plans?"

Alec hesitated, then lied, "I'm not sure yet. I'll have to talk to Mother and the Council . . ."

"She's on the Council?"

"She chairs it."

Douglas grunted. "I might have guessed. Matriarchal societies always wind up with a queen bee."

Alec clenched his fists but said nothing.

"Listen to me," Douglas ordered. "In the next few days you and your men are going to come down with dysentery. It's not fatal . . ."

"No. We have pills and . . ."

"Bullshit! The pills won't do a damned thing for you, take my word for it. Once you start eating the local flora and fauna, your gut bugs change and you get dysentery. It's inevitable. And although it won't kill you, it'll make you wish you were dead. You'll be in no condition to travel or to defend yourselves. Unless you're safely off in the shuttles, you'll be helpless here. And I can't afford to have my people sit around here for days on end, protecting you."

"So take off," Alec snapped. "We don't need your protection."

"You could come with us."

"And help you build your empire?"

"Help save your mother and everyone else in the settlement!"

"I'll save them—by getting those fissionables."

Douglas shook his head, a ponderous negative motion. "No. That's something you can't do. They're too far from here, and too well protected. You'd be dead long before you got within a hundred klicks."

"I came here for the fissionables."

"You'll get yourself killed."

"You're going to kill me?"

"I don't have to lift a finger!" Douglas was starting to

sound exasperated. "There are a thousand ways of getting yourself killed here: raider bands, diseases, injuries . . . hell, you could even starve to death, if you know as little about survival as I think you do."

"I'm going to get those fissionables, one way or the other."

Douglas suddenly turned sarcastic. "Oh are you? Well . . . you're going to find that that's just a leetle hard to do. In the first place, when you talk to your mother, she's going to order you back home. I know her, and she won't have her precious son running around here in the open, where he might stub his toe."

"You might have known her," Alec flashed, whitehot, "but you don't know me."

"That's true. And it's a shame I never will. Because you're either returning to the settlement or you're going to be killed inside of a week."

"We'll see."

"Indeed we will. It's a shame your education is going to prove fatal. You might have eventually turned into somebody worth knowing. You're stubborn enough to be my son, I'll give you that much."

With that, Douglas reached toward the jeep's dashboard and gunned the engine to life. The sudden roar made Alec hop back. Without another word, Douglas put the ancient machine in gear, making a horrible metallic grinding noise, then zoomed off in a cloud of dust and acrid gasoline fumes.

Alec stood there for some moments before he realized that he might have killed the man then and there.

# Chapter Eleven

Alec expected an argument from his mother the next morning, but he got none.

He sat buttoned into the armored cab of his truck, alone and isolated from the others. He reported everything that had happened so far, and ended with his decision to head north and find the fissionables.

His mother's voice sounded strangely faraway, much colder and more distant than the four hundred thousand kilometers between them.

"You must do what needs to be done," she said, metallically, icily, amid the cracklings and hisses of sunstatic.

"When I locate the fissionables you can send reinforcements for us."

He could sense other forces, other emotions working in her mind. "Very well, Alec. The Council will accept your plan. I'll see to that."

"And Kobol?"

The hesitation in her voice was more than the lag of lightspeed. "There are ways of handling Kobol. He won't stop you."

"You'll need to bring out the other shuttles and make supply drops for us. We're going to need medicine and ammunition, fuel for the truck generators."

She said, "That will take time . . . several days, at least. Probably longer."

"All right. I'll keep in touch through the satellite. It

might be a good idea to put an automatic relay satellite in synchronous orbit, so we can keep the communications lines open all the time."

Her voice was fading; the satellite station was passing out of range. "I'll try, Alec. I'll try."

"Take care, Mother. Be careful."

"And you, Alec. Do what needs to be done. Find him and do what needs . . ." her voice dimmed to an inaudible whisper.

Alec sat alone in the truck's cab for several minutes, feeling flushed and weak. *Got to control myself*, he thought. *I'm responsible for fifteen lives.* He reached for the door handle and a sudden stab of pain seared through his middle. His head swam.

Dizzily, he stumbled out of the truck. It was cooler in the morning air. He took several deep racking breaths and forced the pain down.

"You," he called to the nearest man, who was poking into the truck's fuel cell, behind the cab and under the laser mounting.

He looked up. Alec recognized him but couldn't recall his name. "Find the medical tapes and read out the information on dysentery. Remind Gianelli to get all the available data on the subject when the satellite's in range again."

The man looked blankly at him. "The satellite won't be in range again for twelve hours, will it?"

Alec nodded, bringing up the dizziness again. "Right. Do it."

"Yeah, okay. Dysentery?" He started to look scared, instead of puzzled.

Slowly, fighting against the nausea that was gripping him, Alec made his way along the line of trucks, looking for Ron Jameson.

He found Jameson at last, calmly sitting on the ground with his back against a truck's tire, cleaning an automatic rifle. The weapon was spread on a plastic sheet before him, broken down into its many glittering metallic parts. Jameson was deftly applying oil to the firing mechanism as Alec tottered up to him.

Looking up, Jameson said, "You've got it too."

"And you?" Alec sagged to a sitting position beside him.

Jameson nodded. "Had one siege last night. Not much fun."

"We're all going to come down with it. And Douglas is pulling his people out."

"I know. Will Russo was around looking for you. He was pretty shame-faced about it, but he's leaving before noon."

Leaning his head against the truck's cool metal fender, Alec closed his eyes. "That means we'll be on our own . . ."

"With diarrhea and vomiting as our constant companions." Jameson said it flatly, without humor or malice.

"What can we do?"

"They're not sending the shuttle for us?"

"No. . . ." Another cramp made Alec gasp and fight for self-control. "We're going north to find the fissionables."

Jameson was silent for a long while. Through pain-blurred eyes, Alec watched him. He was looking around the street they were in, his hawk's eyes registering every detail of the buildings and intersections, his mind obviously working at top speed.

"Well then," he said at last. "I guess we'd better get these trucks inside some of the buildings, where they won't be spotted so easily. And we'd better pick buildings that are arranged so that the trucks can support each other with crossfire, in case we *are* attacked. We've got to defend ourselves with a troop of sick pups."

"We've got the advantage of firepower," Alec said.

Jameson gave him a withering look. "Won't do much good if the gunners are crapping their guts out when it's time to pull the triggers."

Alec couldn't stand anymore. He lurched to his feet and staggered off to find some privacy where he could be thoroughly sick.

The sun was almost straight overhead when he forced himself back to the street where the post office stood. He was drenched with sweat, yet shivering. He stank. His knees were trembling with the mere effort of keeping himself on his feet.

A pair of strong arms grabbed him from behind.

"My God, you really do have it, don't you?" Will Russo said. His usually carefree face was dead serious now.

"I'll be . . . all right . . ." Alec managed.

Will led him to the post office and sat him down on the floor. Squatting on his heels next to Alec, he said:

"Look, we've got to go. There's a lot going on further north that needs our attention . . ."

"Then go." Alec fluttered a hand at him.

"Let me finish, dammit! I know you feel like you're going to die, but you won't. You'll be okay in a few days. But the thing to avoid is fever . . . it weakens you to other infectious diseases. Now, do you have any anti-fever medicines—aspirin, anything like that?"

"Yes . . . but nothing much more."

"You don't need it. Gobble aspirin and use water baths to keep your temperature down. Same for everybody."

"All right." Far back in his mind, Alec withdrew from the idea of using water for bathing. *Water's too precious.*

"Okay," Russo went on. "Now, I see that some of your men are still strong enough to start moving the trucks inside garages and store fronts and such. That's good. Keep out of sight and maybe nobody will bother you."

Alec said nothing.

"Now, the raider pack we tangled with has apparently left this territory. But there'll be others prowling around, you can be pretty sure. I've asked some of the local farmers to sort of watch out for you, warn you if any packs come into the area. The locals don't like the raiders and they've always worked with us pretty fairly. So they'll at least try to warn you."

"Good."

"But don't depend on them too much," Will warned. "They're not going to risk their own necks to help you. Stay alert. Especially at night."

*Sure*, Alec thought. *Stay alert. We'll be lucky if we can stay conscious.*

"Well . . ." Russo got to his feet. Towering over Alec he said, "Good luck. I hope you get through this okay and we can meet again."

*When we do, we'll be pointing guns at each other*, Alec realized.

The first night wasn't so bad. Before the moon rose one of the men thought he saw someone prowling along the street and fired a burst of automatic rifle fire at him. Everyone roused, the sick and the well, but the alarm was over just that quickly. Once the moon came up it was fairly bright, and the town became absolutely still.

At least, as far as Alec's men could tell.

The next day it clouded over by mid-morning and began to rain early in the afternoon. Alec lay in absolute misery on the floor of the post office, next to the two trucks that had been trundled inside there. The rain poured through the broken roof, adding rivulets of soaking water and a chilling, soggy air to the agonies that they all felt.

Ron Jameson was the strong one among them. He was

on his feet, moving from building to building, truck to truck, man to man, carrying medicine and discipline and —most of all—morale.

But with Alec he was grimly straightforward.

"I palled around with some of Russo's people while they were here," he said, as Alec lay painfully shivering across the double seat of a truck cab. Rain drummed on the roof.

Hunched over the makeshift pallet, Jameson went on, "From what they told me, the farmers in the valleys don't like the raiders, but won't help us as long as the raiders leave them alone."

"Will said they'd warn us." It took all of Alec's strength to gasp it out.

Jameson's fierce eyes bored into Alec. "Better not depend on it. And the way it's raining, the raiders could march into town with a full brass band and we wouldn't see or hear a thing."

"How many . . ." Alec had to take a breath ". . . men are on their feet?"

"They're starting to recover. We've got seven or eight who're good as new, almost."

"Out of fifteen."

"The worst is over. I think you got the biggest dose of all."

Alec smiled weakly. "Good. Wouldn't want anybody else . . . to go through this . . ." He had been vomiting the aspirin and antibiotics. The cramps and diarrhea weren't so bad now, but he was cold and utterly weak. Nothing stayed inside him.

"We'll make it," Jameson said, forcing a smile. "Once the sun comes out again we'll be okay."

Alec translated, *If we get through tonight we'll have a chance.*

Alec drifted to sleep. When he awoke, it was dark. The rain still pattered on the cab roof, but it seemed lighter now, softer. Cramps again. He pushed himself up to a sitting position and the pain washed over him in waves. Dizzy, he grabbed at the truck door and half-fell, half-slid down to the floor.

It was wet. The drizzling rain felt almost good on his head and shoulders. Clutching at his midsection, Alec staggered out toward the back door. If any of the men noticed him, they gave no indication. He saw no one.

He was fumbling with his belt when the first explosion came.

It lifted him off his feet and slammed him into the muddy ground ten meters from where he'd been standing. The back wall of the post office was a sheet of flame and it collapsed in surrealistic slow motion, crumbling in on itself. Sparks and flaming debris soared upward. Men screamed.

Alec rolled over on his back in the ice-cold mud. Gunfire. Men yelling. The high-pitched whine of an electric generator running up to top speed.

He rolled over onto his stomach again and saw four men running toward him. In the flickering light of the flames he could see that they were armed. Then a truck smashed its front end through a store front across the parking lot. The running men turned to flame as the laser hit them. Their clothing burst into fire and they danced, screaming, their hair and flesh ablaze. They fell and the ground bubbled where the invisible laser beam struck. The pencil line of boiling earth marched across the parking lot toward Alec, close enough for him to hear the hiss of atoms wrenched into plasma phase.

Then the beam swung away. More explosions. Another truck pulled free of a building that was collapsing. But the truck itself blew up, hurling pieces of men and machinery so high into the air that they were lost in the shadows.

Alec couldn't move. He lay there soaked in mud and

his own excrement and watched the raiders methodically seize the buildings around the blazing post office. Running, cursing men backed away across the parking lot, firing as they headed for the one truck that was still fighting.

Then another truck appeared, trundling slowly around the post office building. A dozen black-dressed men raced for it, trying to capture it intact. The laser caught them in the open and they instantly became gibbering torches. Men appeared on the rooftop of the building where the first truck still stood, but they must have been Alec's men, for they sprayed automatic rifle fire down across the parking lot wherever they saw men moving.

Then a third truck came up on the other end of the parking lot. Its laser was silent, but Alec could see a squad of men crouched on the mounting platform, behind the cab, and more men walking stealthily behind it. *They've taken that one*, he realized, *but they don't know how to work the laser.*

Jameson must have realized the same thing. Alec assumed it was he directing the fight from the first truck.

The captured truck edged halfway across the parking lot before it was caught in a cross-fire from the other two lasers. The men screamed and burned, the tires exploded and the truck slumped to a halt. Then a beam must have found the hydrogen and oxygen lines of the fuel cell. The truck fireballed, searing Alec with its glaring heat.

Then it all stopped. The truck burned sullenly, the post office was a twisted mass of smoking ruins. The firing stopped. No more shouting, no more movement. In the distance, Alec could hear a truck moving. It seemed to be going away.

*Christ! They wiped us out and I lay here like a turd.*

Alec forced himself to his hands and knees. A burst of gunfire splattered bullets into the mud not more than five meters in front of him. He flopped on his face again.

A couple of rounds of gunfire went off from somewhere behind him. But nothing more from his own men.

*They think I'm one of the raiders! If they turn the laser on me . . .* Alec started to shake again, and not from the cold or sickness this time.

*I could call to them. But then the raiders would shoot me.*

So he lay there in the chilling mud while the rain slackened off and died, while the fires around him burned down to embers, and the sky gradually brightened into dawn.

He didn't realize he had dozed off until someone yelled close by, "Hey, it's Alec!"

Before he could do or say anything, two men had grabbed him and started dragging him toward the trucks, which were now in the open, parked side by side.

One of them was Gianelli. "Where are you hurt?" he kept asking. "Where'd you get hit?"

It took considerable effort to tell them that he wasn't hurt at all. The men still alive and able to move gathered around him as he was carried-dragged to the trucks. But when they saw that his deepest injury was nothing more than soiled pants, they slowly drifted away from him.

After an hour of cleaning and changing clothes, Alec felt strong enough to take some food. Jameson had a small cook fire going between the trucks.

"You're okay," Jameson said.

Alec nodded.

"Clothes fit okay?"

"Not bad. Where'd you get them? We didn't . . ."

Jameson said flatly, "From the dead. Ours and theirs."

Alec's mouth popped open but no words came out. Finally he recovered enough to ask, "How many . . . did we lose?"

"Three killed, five wounded. Two pretty seriously, the other three are cut and scratched."

*We're down to a dozen men.* "They got away with one of the trucks."

"It cost them twenty-two dead."

"And wounded?"

"They dragged most of their wounded away." Jameson looked away from Alec. "The others died this morning."

A single pistol shot cracked through the crisp morning air. Alec jerked in surprise.

"There's the last one," Jameson said.

"I got caught between you and them," Alec mumbled. "Went out to . . . never even got my pants down."

Jameson nodded. "I figured something like that."

He excused himself and left Alec alone. While Alec was trying to get some hot broth down, he heard one of the men muttering:

"I don't care if he does hear me! He sat it out while Ollie and the rest of 'em were getting killed. Some leader!"

And then Jameson's voice, quiet, calm. "Maybe you don't care if *he* hears you, but if *I* hear you make another crack like that I'll break your jaw. Understand? He was sick . . . he still is."

The reply was mumbled too low for Alec to hear.

He leaned his back against the metal of the truck and held the warm cup of broth in both hands. *A dozen men. Twelve of us and two trucks to cross the country and find Douglas and the fissionables. And most of the men think I'm either a coward or a madman. Or both.*

He squinted upward toward the newly risen sun. It felt warm and good, strengthening.

"All right," he whispered to it. "Two trucks and twelve men. We start north. Now!"

# BOOK TWO

# Chapter Twelve

It was pleasantly cool among the trees. The sun still felt hot, falling in mottled patches through the swaying branches, or lighting up a larger clear area of grass. The breeze had a tang to it. It was gusting in from the northwest. The leaves were already falling, and their colors were fantastic. Alec had never seen such reds and golds before.

But he wasn't paying attention to them now. He lay on his belly atop a carpeting of soft leaves at the edge of the forest. Out in the open valley below stood a walled village. A cluster of little huts with thin plumes of smoke curling from a few chimneys.

Ron Jameson lay beside Alec, "They picked a good spot. Couple of klicks out in the open. Nobody can get to them without them seeing him first."

Nodding, Alec raised his binoculars to inspect the wall around the village. Cinderblock, mostly. Some newly made brick. Wooden gates. The materials must have been scavanged from some of the abandoned cities nearby.

He noticed a few men working the cornfield between the woods and the village. No women were in sight, although they might have been in among the rows of two-meter-tall stalks.

"They're greedy," Alec said quietly. "Cornfields planted all the way down from the wall to the edge of the woods. And more on the other side of the village."

Jameson grinned. "Perfect cover."

"More than that," Alec pointed out. "There's a well-used road leading past the farther fields and out of the valley. They must be carrying on trade with other villages."

"Maybe they supply Douglas' people? If he's got a sizable army he'd need food from villages like this."

Nodding, Alec scanned the area again. A cloud of dust caught his attention, off along the road toward the farthest end of the valley. "Truck . . . no," he saw, "it's a wagon, pulled by horses."

He handed the binoculars to Jameson. "Empty, heading in toward the village. Driver and two gunners."

"Wasn't there another one yesterday?" Alec asked.

"That's right. Gianelli spotted it."

"Then there'll be more. Good. We can make a Trojan Horse."

"A what?"

Alec smiled. "You'll see."

All through the summer Alec drove his tiny band northward, toward the area of Douglas' headquarters. Not that he knew where it was. Only that it was north, near the lakes.

The laser trucks ran down and stopped after the first days. Alec had to burn them, rather than let them fall into barbarian hands.

With the loss of the trucks, they also lost their only link with home, the radios capable of reaching the satellite and, through relay, the moon. Alec had the radio transceivers themselves taken from the trucks and carried along.

"Whenever we find a power source, we can make contact again," he said.

Gianelli grumbled at the extra weight: eight kilos per transceiver. Jameson distributed the components among four men. Gianelli still grumbled until the other men made it clear that they wanted a link home, a channel to safety, no mattter how tenuous. So Gianelli got them to take turns.

They talked with Kobol and Lisa and the other Council members sporadically, whenever they could surprise a village or an armed outpost that had a suitable electric power supply. Lisa had supplies dropped for them, but with zero success. The supply vehicles were unmanned and virtually unguided, catapulted from the moon to the satellite station, and then nudged into a re-entry trajectory by the satellite crew. They flamed to Earth like great meteors, either missing the area Alec's men occupied by enormous margins, or being reached first by barbarians who plundered the food, ammunition and supplies inside, long before Alec's men could find them.

So they lived off the land. They raided villages and took what they needed. Alec tried to do it peacefully whenever he could, but it wasn't really possible to take the food people had grown for their own stomachs, and leave them nothing but good wishes, and do it peacefully.

They lost three men in such raids. In one of them the seemingly indestructible Jameson took an arrow in his thigh that left an infected wound. He still limped.

Twice they tangled with other raider bands, and fled for their lives. The other raiders were bigger and knew the countryside much better. They had apparently staked out loose territories for themselves, and drove away any trespassers.

*Feudalism*, Alec thought. *They protect the villages, and in return the villagers supply them with food.* He shrugged to himself. *Well, it's a step up from barbarism.*

The fourth man they lost was on their first entry into a city.

Their sporadic contacts with the satellite had at least

provided them with information about the radioactivity levels of the cities. Most of the cities were untouched by bombs or fallout, although there were areas such as Washington and New York where the bombing had been so heavy that the entire seaboard was still dangerous for at least fifty kilometers inland.

But the satellite couldn't warn them about the diseases that still lingered in the rat-infested cities. Nor about the crazed, ghoulish people who haunted the dead and empty buildings.

They had reached the Ohio River, travelling mostly on foot since the trucks had failed. The summer heat was like a weight pressing on them, although thankfully they had adapted to the sunshine and developed protective tanning of their skins. They travelled in trucks or cars wherever they could find them, but had to abandon them when they ran out of fuel. Once in a while they would find horses, but these were usually guarded more passionately than food or women by the farmers of the villages. And Alec found it very strange and difficult, the first few times they had managed to filch some horses, to be riding on a vehicle that had a mind of its own. It wasn't merely a matter of steering it; you had to fight a battle of wills to make the beast do what you wanted it to.

Cincinnati was to their west and still dangerously radioactive, the satellite sensors showed, from the bombing of the big U.S. Air Force base in nearby Dayton. The cities along the Ohio River itself were mostly abandoned, emptied because the surviving people couldn't feed themselves inside their cities. And the diseases that had broken out had been worst in the cities.

But the cities, empty or not, were treasure houses of canned food, ammunition, clothing, maps, compasses, vehicles, and even vast fuel dumps that still held some gasoline. Even after fifty years, the surviving people shunned the cities with superstitious dread.

Pittsburgh was different.

Alec's band numbered twenty-three when they reached Pittsburgh. The newcomers were mostly young, several still in their teens, with only the faintest fuzz on their chins. They had joined Alec's band from the villages, for adventure, for safety, for loot or women or any of the ancient reasons that turns a boy into a would-be warrior.

When they staggered away from Pittsburgh, only nine of them were left. The city was teeming with rats and other rodents that carried diseases—and with wild-eyed, half-starved ragged screaming things that could barely be recognized as human. They fought as madmen fight, swarming into Alec's men by the hundreds, oblivious to the murderous fire they faced, piling up their dead in the broken filthy streets and still coming, clawing over the corpses to get at the living.

It took two days to get clear of the city, and they had never penetrated close to the heart of it. Constant fighting, day and night, until the men and their ammunition were both exhausted. Jameson hit on the idea of torching the buildings all around them with the precious fuel they had been carrying in a cargo truck they had picked up earlier.

With that, and the paper and trash and scant fuels they were able to find in the buildings themselves, Alec's men built a wall of fire between themselves and the city barbarians—retreating slowly back toward the countryside behind a curtain of flame and smoke.

They left Pittsburgh on foot, nearly unarmed, totally exhausted.

Of the fifteen men who had stayed with Alec at Oak Ridge, only six were still alive. The three other members of the gaunt-faced band that staggered away from Pittsburgh were newcomers, farm boys.

They moved off northward again. They stole or

bluffed or bartered their meager possessions for food and ammunition. When they felt stronger, and had added a few new recruits to their number, they raided villages, mostly at night.

Alec learned from a woman in one village that the local raider band was planning to follow and destroy them. So he retreated hurriedly, leaving a plain trail for the raiders to follow. They walked into his forest ambush. Alec's fourteen men, using a mixture of weapons from the automatic rifles to longbows, killed thirty and took the weapons that the fleeing survivors left behind.

Alec travelled now with an automatic rifle cradled in his arms. Its weight was his comfort. He nurtured it, kept it carefully oiled and working smoothly. It protected his life. He slept with it by his side, as if it were a woman.

Now it was autumn. They were in the lake country, in the area where Douglas made his headquarters.

Alec lay on the leaves with his rifle comfortably tucked alongside him. The village before them, he was now convinced, must be supplying Douglas with grain.

"We'll strike tomorrow," Alec told Jameson. "We'll take the village and hold it long enough to replenish our supplies, get fresh horses, and question them about Douglas' headquarters."

"Maybe they've got trucks or cars," Jameson said, almost wistfully. It was such a difference from his usual, flat tone of voice that it startled Alec into realizing, *He doesn't like riding horses any more than I do.*

"Maybe," he said, keeping his smile inward.

"Be easier to take 'em at night," Jameson said. "Why wait till tomorrow?"

Shifting slightly in his prone position, enough to make the leaves crinkle under him, Alec disagreed. "No. Tonight they'll bottle themselves up inside that wall. Probably there'll be dogs out among the huts that would set up a yowl as soon as we approached. Do you feel like trying to get over that wall while the villagers are shooting?"

"Not unless we had some explosives," Jameson admitted.

"Which we don't."

"We could get some . . . there are cities less than two days from here. Probably still some goodies in them."

"Explosives would've been taken long ago," Alec countered. "No, we hit them tomorrow when the gates are open and the men are working in the fields. Maybe we can take the village without firing a shot."

Jameson said, "Maybe." But he didn't look convinced.

They camped in the forest that night without a fire. Fifteen men, ranging in age from Jameson's thirty-some to the newest recruits' pink smooth cheeks. They gathered around Alec, standing, sitting on the leaf-softened ground. The only light was a shielded flashlight that had been taken from a city. Its batteries were low and the glow from it was feeble.

Alec looked around at his "army." They carried all their possissions on their backs: guns, bows, blankets, sacks of food. They were tough, feral, the survivors of disease and hunger and fighting. Even his eight remaining lunar friends were no longer distinguishable from the Earthmen. They weren't sophisticated citizens of the moon anymore; they were battle veterans, wary-eyed, grimy, dressed in tatters. But their weapons were clean, oiled and ready.

Alec cleared leaves away to make a bare spot on the forest floor. He used a stick to draw a crude map of the village.

"Ron, you and our two best bowmen have to circle around and be in position here," he pointed, "along the road. When the afternoon wagon comes, you take it. Quietly."

Jameson grunted acknowledgment.

"Gianelli." Alec looked up and saw him lazily paring his fingernails with a nasty-looking knife he had acquired. "You take six men and wait here farther down the road . . ."

"Christ, I gotta go all the way around the village?"

Alec said, "Yes, but you'll get to ride into the village in style. Ron will bring up the wagon and you and your men will get aboard. If Ron isn't driving the wagon when it reaches your spot, you'll have to take it yourself."

He nodded sourly.

"I'll have a longer walk than you will," Jameson said. He was deadpanned, but Alec knew he was joking.

"Yeah . . . and you'll have a longer ride, too," Gianelli returned.

"Just make sure you take a good look at who's driving that rig when it gets to you," Jameson went on, seriously. "Getting shot by your own men can spoil your entire day."

"Ahh . . . don't go chicken-shit on us," Gianelli growled back at him. "Your hands'll start shaking again and you'll burst into tears."

They all laughed, a guarded deep-throated chuckle. Jameson's rock-steady imperturbability was so unshakable that it could be joked about safely.

Alec cleared his throat and got their attention back. "All right. The rest of us," *five men, will it be enough?* "will work out way through the cornfield and enter the village by the gate on this side of the wall."

They spent another hour talking it over, checking wristwatches to make certain that the attack would be properly timed and coordinated, picking out the special assignments for each man once they were inside the village wall.

"All right," Alec said at last. "If everything goes right,

we can take the village with hardly a shot. We'll be inside while most of their fighting-age men will be outside. Do your jobs right and we'll be drinking their wine tomorrow night."

But when the morning came it was raining. A cold, chilling rain, driven by a harsh wind.

"They won't be coming out to work the fields in this downpour," Jameson said.

Alec sat under a plastic tarpaulin, his boots pasted with sticky wet leaves. They didn't look pretty in the gloom and rain. The other men were skulking here and there, trying to keep dry as best they could. It was impossible.

"Come on," Alec said abruptly. "Let's take a look." He couldn't sit in the wet misery any longer. Wrapping the green tarp around his shoulders, he pulled his helmet on and waited for Jameson to pull the cowl on the raincoat he had acquired on one of their raids.

They squished through the soaked forest until they reached the edge and could see the village.

Jameson looked up at the sky. "Clouds're pushing along pretty fast west to east. Bet this breaks up before long."

Alec said nothing. The village was buttoned up tightly. Smoke came from most of the huts, swirled along by the wind. The gates in the wall were firmly shut.

"Look out toward the west," Jameson said. "It's brightening."

It was lighter out toward the low hills that marked the western end of the valley. *Maybe . . .*

They tramped back to their soggy camp and arranged a signal to show that the incoming wagon had been taken: an arrow, fired straight up, exactly on the hour or half hour. Alec could spot it with binoculars from the cornfield, and even if a villager noticed it, it probably wouldn't set up an alarm.

By midmorning the rain was beginning to slacken, and the western sky was definitely clearing. Alec dispatched Jameson and his two bowmen. An hour later, Gianelli left with his men, grumbling as usual. "Fuckin' rain . . . we're not gonna be able to do a damned thing. This is all a fuckin' waste of time."

But he went.

Shortly after noon the rain stopped and the sun broke through. The four men left with Alec—youngsters, all of them—smiled and joked together like a quartet of cubs. They knew they'd soon be in action, and they roughhoused to hide the tension.

Alec himself smiled up at the sun and let its warmth bake into his upturned face. He stood on the edge of the woods and felt the sunshine driving away the cold and damp and fear inside him. The sky cleared bright and blue, and Alec risked a glance straight at the sun, squinting at its mighty radiance, squeezing his eyes shut and seeing its after-image burning against his closed eyelids.

*How could you?* he asked the sun. *How could you destroy us, turn us back a thousand years, make us live in fear and hatred?* The sun did not answer. It beamed down on the children of Earth as if nothing evil had ever happened anywhere in its domain.

An insect buzzed by his ear, startling Alec back to reality.

*What if they don't come out to work the fields?* he suddenly asked himself. *Maybe it's too late in the day for them to start . . .*

But even as he was thinking it, the gate swung slowly open and a handful of men walked out, carrying implements over their shoulders. *Weapons?* Alec focused the binoculars on them: hoes, rakes, shovels. Only two rifles, and they looked ancient. No ammunition bandoliers.

He swung the glasses toward the western hills. *No*

*sense starting into the cornfield until the wagon's in sight.* Then he realized, *There'll be no dust cloud. The rain's probably turned the road into mud. And slowed down the wagon, as well.*

For nearly an hour he searched what little he could see of the road. Most of it was hidden by the grain fields, but up by the edge of the hills it stood out fairly clearly against the grass.

Finally the wagon appeared. Alec could feel the breath whoosh out of him in an exhalation of relief. It was moving slowly, still nothing more than a smudge crawling along the road, even in the binoculars. But it was there. Judging its speed carefully, Alec went back to the camp and ate a little cold canned meat with the four youths.

"All right," he told them afterward. "Let's move."

They checked their weapons and ammunition, then wrapped the guns in plastic or cloth to make sure there'd be no tell-tale clinking as they wormed their way through the cornfield. Slinging ammo bandoliers over their shoulders, they headed for the edge of the woods. Alec hefted his automatic rifle, then cradled it in the crook of his arm.

Helmets daubed with mud to keep them from glinting, they walked slowly to the edge of the woods, then ducked down and crawled down the slope that bottomed out at the beginning of the cornfield.

Slowly. Slowly. The five of them were spaced out far enough so that they could slip past the villagers working between them, but still they stayed close enough to cover each other with gunfire, should a fight erupt.

It was 1400 hours. The sun burned down on the ripe corn. Insects droned lazily. Wishing for the thousandth time that the helmet radios' batteries hadn't worn out, Alec half-crouched among the tall corn stalks and put the binoculars to his eyes. He scanned the sky for the sight of an arrow. Nothing. They took a cautious half-hour to penetrate deeper into the cornfield. Twice they came close enough to villagers to hear them talking to each other. At 1430 Alec searched for the signal again. Again nothing.

The field was wet and muddy, but the sun was baking sweat from Alec's armpits and neck. He could feel it trickling hotly along his flanks, while his boots squished in the mud. The plants still had droplets clinging to their leaves and gold-shimmering tassels.

At 1500 he saw a flicker of color zip past the binoculars' field of vision. *A bird?* It seemed to be going up. As if to confuse him, a pair of black birds flapped squawking out of the field.

"What's got them shook up?" a voice called.

"Prob'ly a mole or somethin'," came the answer from several rows across the field.

*It must have been Jameson's signal,* Alec decided. *It had to be.*

He peered through the corn plants and could barely make out the figure of the kid on his left. He rustled a stalk to get his attention. The kid looked white-faced, frozen with surprise. Then he realized it was Alec and grinned sheepishly. All the while he held his carbine pointed straight out, ready to fire. Alec motioned him toward the village wall. The kid nodded his understanding.

Same thing for the kid on the right. Pass it on.

They got to the edge of the cornfield. No more than fifty meters separated them from the gate. An old man was sitting on the ground, his back against the wall, snoozing gently in the hot sun. An ancient shotgun lay across his lap.

Alec waited long enough to give his four youngsters plenty of time to reach the edge of the planted field. Then he stepped out and paced quickly, head ducked low, and snatched the shotgun from the old man's hands.

"Huh . . . wha . . ."

Alec handed the gun to the kid on his left as he hissed, "Not a sound, grandfather. We don't want to hurt anyone."

They stood him up and marched him inside the gate. "Close it," Alec ordered. The old man did it, while Alec left one youngster to watch him and marched past the quiet huts toward the center of the village.

He could hear the horse-drawn wagon clattering and creaking up ahead, but couldn't see very far along the narrow lane that twisted between the rows of huts. Then a man's deep voice rumbled, "Hey, what the hell's going on?"

Quickening the pace, Alec made his way to the cleared area at the center of the huts. Jameson was standing atop the wagon, an automatic rifle resting on his hip. Gianelli and his men were already fanning out around the edges of the clearing. The two young bowmen were swinging the big gate shut.

About three dozen villagers were in the clearing, most of them women. A few small children clung to their mothers, already frightened.

A couple of older men were easing back away from the wagon. Alec and his men came up behind them.

"You'd better stand still, all of you," Alec ordered.

They froze in their tracks.

"We don't want anyone hurt," Alec said, loudly enough for everyone to hear. "We don't intend to hurt any of you."

He stepped to the center of the clearing, under Jameson's protective gun. "Gianelli, take your men on a hut-to-hut search. I want everyone out here. If there's any trouble," he pointed to the three men who now stood glaring before his trio of youngsters, "these three will be shot immediately. Then the others." Alec glanced at the women.

"There won't be any trouble unless you make it," one of the women spat. She was lean and as hard and splintery-looking as the logs from which the huts were made.

"Good."

They secured the village quickly, Gianelli's men routing out another half-dozen aged men and women and a few more children. Plus a fair-sized pile of guns, including a few carbines and a submachine gun. With many boxes of ammunition, all new-looking. *Manufactured within the past year, I'd bet.*

Then Alec had the men reopen the gates and stay out of sight behind the wall, awaiting the return of the men from the fields.

The villagers were returned to their huts and told to stay inside and stay quiet.

Jameson, satisfied that everything was under control, jumped down from the wagon. "Not bad," he said. "Forty minutes to seize, search, and settle the prisoners."

Alec relaxed enough to grin at him.

"Got a surprise for you," Jameson told him. He started for the back of the wagon. Alec followed him.

"Did you have any trouble taking the wagon?" Alec asked.

"No. Driver and two gunners, same as the past few days. Coming in for corn and hay. They didn't put up a fight as soon as they saw we had them covered. Left the driver and one gunner by the road . . ."

He pulled back a ragged covering from the floor of the wagon.

"Angela!"

"She was the other gunner. Tried to shoot me, too, before the driver convinced her she'd only get all of them killed."

She was lying on the wagon's grimy floor, her wrists

bound behind her, her ankles tied together. A gag was stuffed in her mouth. Still, she looked furious.

"Thought you'd want to talk to her," Jameson said.

Alec jumped up on the wagon and pulled the gag from her mouth.

"I should've shot you," she snarled at Jameson. "If I'd known you'd do this to me . . ."

"Quiet," Alec snapped. "Quiet. Ron just didn't want you to give off an alarm." He started to untie her wrists.

"I would have, too!" She yanked her hands free of the loosened cords and sat up, reaching for her ankles.

"What are you doing on a job like this?" Alec wondered.

"What's wrong with a girl on guard detail?" she raged. "I was the only one with guts enough to fight."

"That could have caused a lot of shooting," Alec told her. "A lot of people might have gotten hurt. We're not trying to hurt these people."

"Not much!" She pushed him away and scrambled to her feet. "You just want their food and weapons. Leave them hungry and defenseless."

"No," Alec said firmly. "What I want is what I came to Earth for: the fissionables. We've fought our way acrooss the country all summer to get here. I know he's not far from here, and the fissionables are here too." He took her by the arm. "Where is he?"

She looked at him. There was a silly scrap of straw clinging to her cheek. She brushed it away.

"He's not far. And when he finds out what you've done, *he'll* find *you.*"

"That's fine," Alec said. "One way or the other, it doesn't matter. But I still want to know where he is now and where the fissionables are stored."

Angela shook her head. "It wouldn't do any good, even if I told you. You'd just get yourself killed. You can't storm the base with a dozen men."

"I can get more."

She turned away.

"All right," Alec said. He hoped off the wagon, then turned to help her down. She jumped down on her own. Frowning, he turned to Jameson, "Find an empty hut and lock her in it."

# Chapter Thirteen

The sun swung down and touched the western hills. In small groups the village men came back from the fields, to be taken and disarmed—their faces slack with shock—by Alec's men. By nightfall the entire village was safely under guard.

"Hey!" Gianelli shouted in the flickering light of the fire they built in the center of the village square. "We found the wine!" He waved a wicker-covered jug over his head, then put it to his lips.

Alec was sitting by the fire, eating with Jameson. "Better make certain that no more than a couple of those jugs are opened," he said. "Put the rest under guard or break them. And keep the villagers inside their huts; I don't want any of our men grabbing their women. I want to stay as friendly with these people as we can."

Jameson nodded, put down his scraped-clean plate, and moved off into the shadows.

Alec spent a fruitless couple of hours questioning the village men. None of them admitted to knowing where Douglas' headquarters was, except that it was west of their valley. For years they had been sending grain over the western road, in exchange for protection.

They spoke seriously and politely. They shared the wine from several jugs together. They would reveal nothing.

But they spoke of his father as "the Douglas." Like "the Lord."

"You can see," Alec said, being careful to allow a long time between his sips of wine, "that he isn't keeping his end of the bargain. Where is your protection?"

"It will come," said one of the men, sullenly.

"Protection should protect," Alec countered, "not revenge. My men could have burned your village, raped your women, murdered all of you."

"Ahhh . . ." said the old man who'd been napping by the gate. "The Douglas knew that you weren't any ordinary raider band."

"What?"

"He told us weeks ago that his son might pass this way . . ."

"Shut up, you old fool!" a younger man snapped.

But Alec waved him down. "Douglas came here and warned you that his son might raid your village?"

The old man looked troubled now, uncertain. "Eh . . . it was something like that . . . perhaps I've got it wrong . . . I forget a lot nowadays . . ."

*So he's expecting us,* Alec thought.

They changed the subject, or tried to. Alec steered it back to the location of Douglas' headquarters. Jameson joined the circle around the fire, but still the villagers would admit nothing. Finally Alec bade them goodnight; they got up and returned to their huts.

Jameson watched them drift off into the darkness. "Be easier to watch them if we packed them all in one or two huts."

"Let them sleep in their own beds," Alec said. "We've got all their weapons, and they don't want any trouble."

Shrugging, Jameson said, "They didn't tell you much, did they?"

"Enough. Did that wagon crew have any food with them?"

"No. Didn't see any."

"Then Douglas can't be more than a day's ride from here. Over the western road."

Jameson nodded. Then he asked, "So what do we do now? The girl's right, we can't just walk up to Douglas and expect him to hand us the fissionables."

"No—but we can call down as many men as the settlement can provide. And I think we can recruit some of the people around here. They can't all be totally loyal to Douglas. They'll join our side for a share of the loot . . . especially when they see the army we can put together."

"You really think Kobol's going to mount an army for you?"

"Not for me," Alec said. "But for the fissionables, they'll have to." *Even if Kobol's gained complete control of the Council, he'll have to come after the fissionables.*

In the dwindling firelight, Jameson still looked doubtful.

"What's going on in your head?"

The hawk-faced man pursed his lips. "Well . . . some of the men don't think we'll ever get back to the settlement. They think we've been written off."

"That's not true."

"It's what they think," Jameson said. "And maybe . . . well, they're not all that unhappy about it. This is a big world here. We could carve ourselves a nice chunk of it, if we wanted to. Some of the men have even been wondering why we don't join Douglas . . ."

Alec almost swung at him. At the last instant he checked himself, already leaning toward Jameson with his fist clenched and ready.

"Join the traitor? Let the settlement die?"

"They're letting us die."

"They'll send the help we need, when we're ready for it."

"It better be soon, if you expect to have any of these men following you."

Alec stormed to his feet. "It will be." He was blazing hotter than the fire now, not trusting himself to say any more. He started walking off.

"Wait," Jameson called. He was unbuckling his gun-belt as he walked up to Alec. "If you're going to go strolling in the dark, you'd better have at least a pistol. Don't trust anybody."

Alec's anger softened, backed off slightly. "All right," he said. "Thanks." He strapped the gun to his hip.

He walked off down a crooked lane between two rows of huts. The stars were out, and Alec could recognize Orion rising sideways above the southern horizon. *It'll be winter soon. We've got to get it done before the snow starts.*

He paced along the bare dirt path slowly, thinking, planning. *Got to find a power source for the radios. Douglas must have a few tucked away here and there, this close to headquarters. Find one, make a raid, stay long enough to get the message off to the satellite.* A new thought struck him. *The satellite sensors ought to be able to pick out his headquarters, now that we know it's in this region. He couldn't hide anything that big.*

A sound pulled him up short. A gasp, heavy breathing. He flattened himself against the cool wall of the nearest hut and slid the gun from its holster.

Again. A muffled sound, almost a groan, but stifled.

Carefully, Alec edged along the wall. A dim light was glowing faintly from a doorway further down the row. He headed for it on tiptoe. More gasps, the sounds of feet scuffling, then whispering:

"C'mon cutey . . . come across . . . you won't look too good if you don't . . ."

Alec stepped into the hut, gun level at his waist.

In the wavering light of a single candle, he saw one of

the kids who'd gone through the cornfield with him, pinning Angela's arms behind her back with one brawny arm and holding his meaty hand over her mouth. Gianelli stood before her with his long, slim knife. Her shirt had been torn off and three welling red slashes were already streaking down one breast to the nipple. Her eyes were white with pain and terror.

"Gianelli!"

He wheeled around. The knife blade was red.

"You wanna find out where your father is, I'll find out," Gianelli said, his voice low and shaking with excitement. "I'll get a lot more out of her, too."

"Get away from her," Alec said.

The kid let his hand drop from Angela's mouth, but still held her arms.

"Listen," Gianelli said, "I've had a bellyfull of your orders. I'll get what you want from her and then I get what I want."

The gun's blast was deafening in the tiny hut. Gianelli slammed back against the wall, his mouth open in a soundless "Ooohhh . . ." Alec fired again and he dropped the knife and slid to the floor.

The kid stepped away from Angela, toward Gianelli's slumped body. "I . . . he told me . . ."

Alec fired once more and the kid's face dissolved in an explosion of blood.

Angela screamed and Alec grabbed her, pulled her out of the hut into the clean night air, leaving the stench of gunsmoke and blood behind them.

"They . . . they . . ." she gulped.

"They're dead," Alec said. He still held the gun. His hand was trembling so badly that it took three tries to slide it back into its holster.

Jameson was the first to reach them, a carbine in one hand. Half a dozen other men pounded up right behind him.

"What happened?"

"I just killed two men who couldn't follow orders. Drag them out into the village square and leave them there."

They were a quiet and subdued group of men when they left the village the next morning. The villagers stood mutely around the two corpses in the square as Alec lined his troops together and marched them out of the gate, down the westward road. Angela walked beside Alec.

She seemed still dazed. "You're just going to . . . leave them there?"

Alec hadn't slept all night. His head throbbed. "Let the villagers bury them . . . in the fields. Make good use of them."

"Why . . . ? You didn't have to kill them."

He turned to stare at her. She looked as bleak as he felt. "You wanted me to leave them with you?"

"I . . ." Angela ran a hand through her blonde hair. "In some crazy way I feel like it's my fault . . . partially, anyway."

"I shot them. They deserved it. If I had to do it all over again, I'd do it exactly the same way."

She shuddered visibly. "Because it was me."

"Because they were acting like scum!"

"With me. If it had been one of the village women . . ."

"I'd have done the same thing," Alec said coldly. "Don't flatter yourself."

They walked in silence for most of the morning, heading for the hills that bordered the western edge of the valley, under a sky of rolling fat cumulus clouds that checkered the landscape with warm sunlight and suddenly cool darkness. Angela kept pace with the men.

"Jameson found out last night that there's a relay station for horses over the first row of hills," Alec said to her. "Is that true?"

She hesitated, then nodded. "Yes. And it's built like a little fortress."

"I'd like to get some horses for us. Can you talk the people there into giving us some peacefully, or will we have to fight?"

"They'll be on the alert for you. The wagon driver and other gunner from yesterday . . ."

"I know. But can you talk them into giving us the horses without fighting? Maybe we could trade some of our ammunition or blankets."

She turned defiant. "They won't trade. And why should I help you?"

"You've got a damned short memory."

"No. A long one."

"All right, be tough. We'll get the horses anyway."

Which they did, by the simple expedient of threatening to shoot Angela if the men holding the station didn't give them all the horses in their guarded corral. Alec held Angela up on a hill, far enough from the station so that the men there couldn't hear her, but could see her plainly enough. Jameson did the negotiating.

Angela was smoldering. "You're using me!"

"That's right," Alec said. "But it's a lot better than killing people, isn't it?"

She was too angry to answer.

Toward sunset, they were riding side by side, at the end of the ragged line of his band. Their two horses were plodding in step.

"Still angry with me?"

"Yes." But she looked more sullen than angry.

"Are you in pain?"

"No, I've been riding since before I could walk."

"I didn't mean that. . . . I meant your, eh, chest."

"It hasn't bled anymore. The bandage is still in place. Want to inspect it for yourself?"

"Dammit!" he shouted. "I didn't do it to you!"

"You killed them. You shot that boy."

"You ought to be glad that I did."

"You're a murderer and you expect me to love you for it?"

"You wanted me to leave you alone so they could carve you into little pieces?"

"So it's my fault!"

He knew he was red-faced, he could feel his cheeks burning. The other men kept their eyes strictly forward; no one turned to look at them.

Lowering his voice, Aleec said, "Yes, it was your fault. You were right this morning. If it hadn't been for you I wouldn't have killed them. I lost control, I couldn't stand to see them alive, I . . ."

"All right," Angela said soothingly. "It's all right. I've been a terrible bitch. I'm sorry."

They rode together in silence until it grew too dark to ride further.

# Chapter Fourteen

Alec slept with her that night. Without a word of prearrangement they walked off together from the campfire and took their blankets from their packs on the horses. Side by side, still unspeaking, they moved off into the darkness.

He made love to Angela gently, tenderly, trying to avoid hurting her. She held him, touched him, kissed him, moved with him until the both forgot about her injury.

In the morning they bathed together in an achingly cold lake that stretched several kilometers wide. Alec still couldn't feel at ease using water so lavishly. *This world is so rich!*

By the time they were dressed and heading back for the campfire, Angela said, "You'll have to go back to the moon, won't you?"

He couldn't take his eyes from her gold-framed face: lovely, troubled, serious.

"Not without you," he said.

Nodding, she answered, "I know. I'll have to leave him . . ."

"Who?"

"Father."

"You mean *my* father."

She almost smiled. "Is there such a thing as foster-incest?"

"You will come with me?" Alec asked.

She didn't hesitate at all. "Yes." But her voice was so low he could barely hear her.

They had reached the camp, by the side of the road. The men were milling around, cooking eggs from the village over the fire, grooming the horses, cleaning guns.

"All right," Alec said to her. "I'll need a radio—or rather, the electric power source for the radios we're carrying. Not for very long, maybe an hour or two."

Angela thought for a moment. "You won't be able to get one without a fight. The closest power source I know of is at a perimenter fire base, about twenty klicks from here . . . up in the hills, off the road."

Alec shrugged. "If I can't radio to the satellite for a shuttle, we can't return to the settlement."

A horse neighed somewhere off behind them. The sun was up over the distant hills now, flooding the valley with warmth and brightness. The valley floor was lushly green, except for the squared-off patches of harvested grain. The wooded shoulders of the hills were an unbelievable pallette of reds, golds, oranges, browns, set off here and there by the somber deep greens of pines and hemlocks.

Angela said, "If I help you get a radio for a few hours, you'll go back to the moon?"

"With you."

"You'll give up this idea of trying to get the fissionables and go back?"

"Yes," Alec lied. *She's only trying to protect him,* he told himself, despite a deeper voice that said, *She's trying to protect you!*

Reluctantly, as if she knew she was doing the wrong thing no matter what she did, Angela said, "All right, I'll show you where the fire base is. They have a radio there that can reach the headquarters transceiver, and that's about fifty klicks away."

"That should be plenty of power for our radios," Alec said, forcing himself to keep his voice even.

"I don't like it," Jameson said, staring off into the distant valley, as if he was looking for signs of danger.

He and Alec were standing at the edge of a gently rising meadow that ended in a thickly wooded hillside. The road they had travelled along was farther down the slope. The sun was high overhead, but the wind was cold enough to make Jameson push his hands deep into the pockets of his worn, tattered pants.

"We're deep inside their territory. They know we're here, from the wagon driver and gunner. Anybody with enough brains to feed himself can figure that we would hit that particular village. Now we're going in deeper."

Alec said, "You're missing the point. This is their territory, all right. But look at how big it is. They don't have enough men to patrol every hectare. We can stay in the woods, keep on the move, until we rendezvous with the reinforcements."

Still scanning the distances, Jameson countered, "And you think he's just going to let a few shuttles land within fifty klicks of their home base? Without opposition?"

"By the time they can get some opposition mounted we'll have seized enough territory so that the shuttles can land and take off safely. Before they can organize a big-enough counterattack, we'll have reached their headquarters and found the fissionables."

"Maybe," Jameson said. "With luck."

"No luck! We don't need luck. Just enough men, and good timing."

"Well . . ." Jameson looked at Alec at last, and stuck out his hand. "Good luck anyway. You're marching yourself right into the bear's cave."

Alec let his hand be engulfed by Jameson's. "I'll be

back tomorrow. And inside of a week or two we'll all be home."

"Yeah." Jameson's voice went dead flat. As if the word *home* was starting to take on a different meaning.

Alec thought about it as he and Anngela rode out of the woods that afternoon and headed up the rolling slopes of the hills toward the fire base.

*Home is the settlement. The moon. Where it's safe and clean. Where Mother is.* And where it's cramped and small. Where life is rigidly determined by the amount of air and water available. Where the colors are whites and grays and pastels. Where you speak in polite restraint and wait your turn in the hierarchy that governs all.

Twisting around in the saddle, looking over the glorious autumn plumage of Mother Earth and the even wilder grandeur of the flaming sunset, Alec could see why some of the men might be tempted to stay here.

A flight of birds sped far overhead in a ragged vee formation. Alec's heart leaped at the sight of them. Their queer honking sounds drifted across the landscape.

"Winter's coming," Angela said.

Alec nodded. The birds were heading roughly southward. He took another look at them, fading into the distant purple-reds of the dying day.

He forced his thoughts back to the settlement. *No winter there. No seasons at all. How is Mother holding out? Can she still handle Kobol? Is the Council still loyal to her?*

But as he asked himself these questions, Alec found that he was watching Angela riding beside him, swaying softly and crooning to her horse as it plodded up the grassy hillside.

They reached the top of the highest hill, and the firebase.

Alec saw that the base was small; it couldn't hold more than twenty men. It was ringed by a wooden fence topped with metal spikes. The gate was open, but guarded by two alert youngsters.

Even in the twilight, they recognized Angela at once.

"Angie! We thought you'd been taken prisoner down at the village. There's some raider scum in the area . . ."

"I'm all right," she smiled at them as she got down from her horse. "The raiders have left the village. This is Alec . . . he's from the village. He came along with me, for protection."

The two boys shook Alec's hand. And they *were* boys, no more than fifteen. But they carried their guns well and eyed Alec carefully, despite Angela's lie.

Inside the wall, two ancient artillery pieces stood on makeshift wooden wheels, poking their heavy snouts skyward. Alec had seen such weapons on history tapes. They fired lumbering inert projectiles that contained explosives. Sure enough, there was a pile of such shells next to each piece. *Must take two men just to lift one*, he thought. He also noted there were only six shells per gun. *Of course, they must be either as ancient as the guns themselves, or damned difficult to make properly.* There were plenty of smaller weapons in sight: machine guns mounted on the wall, small rocket launchers, canisters crudely marked FLAMMABLE with hoses that ended in pistol-grip nozzles attached to them.

They unsaddled their horses and slung their bags over their shoulders. Alec's bag was heavy with the radio transceiver. One of the boys led the horses over to a roofed shelter that was already stocked with hay.

The other boy led them down the narrow earthen steps that went into the complex of bunkers that honeycombed the ground underneath the firebase.

The firebase commander was an older man, graying at the temples. "Your father's putting together dozens of search patrols to find you," he said sternly, as if she was a little girl who'd wandered off into the woods.

"I know," Angela replied calmly. "That's why I want to radio him and tell him I'm all right."

The commander nodded curtly and took them to the radio room. The equipment looked old and impossibly bulky to Alec. He stood at the doorway with the commander glowering beside him and looked over the power generator and its connections while Angela got the radio operator to put her in touch with headquarters.

At last she pulled off the headphones and looked up to Alec and the commander. "He's already out in the field with Will Russo. They'll send a rider out to tell him that I'm okay."

"Good," the commander said. "I suppose you'll be spending the night here?" He made it sound like a cross between a challenge and a complaint.

"Yes, I'd rather not travel in the dark."

The commander gave Angela his own bunk, set into a curtained niche cut in one end of the bunker's main room. He showed Alec a cot among a dozen others, in a separate room, connected to the main room by a low narrow tunnel some two dozen steps long.

They ate in the main room with the commander and six other men. Then they went their separate ways. Alec stretched out on his bunk and actually fell asleep, almost at once.

He awoke to the sound of snoring. The room was dark. Slowly his eyes adjusted to the faint glow coming from the tunnel entrance. Most of the cots were occupied now by sleeping men, and in the darkness Alec thought the form next to him was the commander himself.

Carefully, noiselessly, Alec got up and reached into the bag he had slipped under the cot. The radio felt solid and reassuring in his hands. He ducked into the tunnel and went slowly to the main room. It was empty, and lit only by a small electric light. The power generator hummed softly, bringing a smile to Alec's lips. He pulled a wrinkled, weathered hand-written time-table from his shirt pocket and checked it carefully. *Another half-hour before the satellite could possibly be over the horizon.*

After a moment's hesitation, Alec quickly climbed the earthen steps and poked his head out of the bunker's only entrance. Four men were standing by the walls, slumped with boredom or hunched against the cold, looking outward. Two more were sitting by the fire, talking to each other in low, serious tones.

Alec ducked back inside. Angela was sleeping behind the curtain that partitioned off the commander's cubicle. He nodded. *Everything's as good as it's going to be.*

He went swiftly to the radio room and closed its makeshift wooden door, jamming it as tightly as he could against its frame by pressing his entire body weight against it. There was no way to lock it.

He put the transceiver down on the operator's desk and spent the next twenty minutes connecting it properly to the power supply. Then he sat at the desk, slipped the earphones over his head and swung the tiny mike next to his lips. Then he spent an eternity waiting to hear the satellite's automatic beacon ring out against the steady hiss and sputtering of cosmic static.

The eternity ended after eleven minutes.

"Hello, hello," he called, as loudly as he dared. "Come in satellite station. Answer."

Another eternity, seconds long, and, "Alec . . . Alec! Is that you?"

"Yes. Can you hear me all right?"

"Faint but clear. Go ahead."

Alec gave his approximate position, then said, "Get the Council to send the strongest force they can put together down here as soon as possible. Within the week, at most. We can locate the fissionables and take them, if we move quickly. Tell my mother that one quick, decisive stroke can win everything for us. Airdrop me an electric power supply, weapons and ammunition. I'll find it if you can drop it within a ten-kilometer radius of the location I just gave you."

"All right, but . . ."

"No buts! I want a strong force down here, as fast as the Council can put it together. Men, weapons, trucks . . ."

"That's what I've been trying to tell you!" the voice from the satellite said. "Kobol's already landed a force of a hundred men—almost two weeks ago. Trucks, lasers, rockets . . . everything. Took five shuttle flights to get them all on the ground."

"Kobol! Two weeks ago? Where . . . where did he land?"

"Far south of you . . ."

"Oak Ridge?"

"No, further south. Someplace called Florida. I think."

Alec sat in the harsh light of the naked overhead bulb, stunned.

"Hey Alec . . . you still there?"

He nodded, then realized that it was a meaningless gesture. "Yes. . . . Listen. Get this message through to my mother. Tell her we're within a few hours' striking distance of Douglas' headquarters and the fissionables. Tell her to shuttle Kobol's force here. Order him here! Remind him that I'm still the commander of this mission, by order of the Council."

"Yes sir." The voice went formal.

"All right. And get that power supply to me right away. Tear away one of the bulkheads up there, if you have to, but I've got to re-establish communications within twenty-four hours and I can't do it without the power supply."

"Will do!"

Alec signed off. For many long minutes he sat there,

wondering what Kobol was doing and why. But his mind was too tired to think straight. Slowly, he disconnected his transceiver, then stealthily edged the door back to its open position and stepped into the bunker's main room.

Douglas was sitting at the table in the center of the room, making the place look crowded with his bulk. Angela stood beside him, staring at him with cold fury.

"You made it through the summer, I see," Douglas said. He was smiling, but there was no humor in his voice.

# Chapter Fifteen

For a stunned moment, Alec didn't know what to say or do.

Douglas seemed to enjoy his surprise. "Do you really think you've been out of my sight for a minute since you landed on Earth?" He spread his big hands in an all-inclusive gesture. "From the minute you touched down at Oak Ridge you've been under surveillance. I've been impressed, you learn very quickly. There were only three or four times when I was tempted to help you."

"You haven't lifted a finger," Alec snapped. "We fought our way here on our own."

"That's right," Douglas agreed. "You spent the summer working out an experiment—in survival. The experiment was a success. You survived. You even helped us to handle some of those raider bands." He laughed, loudly enough to make the underground bunker shake, it seemed. "Lord, they'd get their attention all focused on your pitiful little gang and start licking their chops. Then Will would come in after them and clobber them. It was sweet."

"Glad to have been of help."

Douglas' laugh faded to a cocky grin. "I've never turned down help from any quarter. I'm not too proud to accept your help."

"As long as you can get your way."

"Of course."

Still standing at the doorway to the radio room, Alec asked, "And what about my pitiful little gang, what are you planning to do to them?"

"Will's going to speak to them in the morning. Offer them a chance to join us. Most of them will, I expect. The rest will be escorted out of my territory, politely but firmly. Maybe they can work their way south again and link up with Kobol."

Shrugging, "We heard your radio conversation on the monitor in my jeep."

"We . . ." Alec looked at Angela. She refused to meet his gaze. For the first time, anger began to seep in and replace the surprise that had numbed him.

"Well," Douglas said, hauling himself to his feet, "get yourself some sleep. We travel at sunup."

He went to the stairs and started up. Angela followed him. She glanced over her shoulder at Alec for a brief instant, but said nothing.

*Bitch!*

Strangely enough, Alec slept deeply through the rest of the night. Dreamlessly. He awoke with a slight sense of guilt at feeling so rested.

Douglas' jeep was parked halfway down the hill. Alec was marched to it by an armed man as soon as he got up. No breakfast, no formalities; none of the firebase crew said a word to him.

The morning was raw and chilly. Thick gray clouds covered the sky from horizon to horizon, making the rolling hills seem somber and grim, muting even the wild colors of the autumn trees.

Douglas was already at the jeep, wearing a dark blue coat over his nondescript clothes. Angela was talking with him, very seriously. She had a blanket wrapped over her shoulders.

The guard sat Alec in the back seat. Angela started to go around the jeep to sit beside him, but the guard looked questioningly at Douglas.

"It's all right," Douglas said as he slid in behind the driver's wheel. "Let her sit back there with him. You ride shotgun up front. He won't try to run away. He's been waiting to see our base all summer, eh, son?"

Alec said nothing.

With a shrug, Douglas added, "If you're lucky, maybe I'll even let you see where the fissionables are stored."

Angela climbed in beside him, the guard swung into the right front seat and laid his heavy black pistol on his lap. Douglas glanced at the threatening sky, then started the engine.

It wasn't the same jeep that Alec had seen before. This one had an electric engine; it purred instead of roared. Starting slowly, it gathered speed as it jounced down the hillside and found a narrow trail that wound among the hills.

The wind was raw and sliced right through Alec's thin shortsleeved shirt.

"Here," Angela said over the wind's rush, "have some." She pulled a metal cylinder from under the front seat and took the top off. Steam wafted from its innards.

Alec accepted it wordlessly and took a small sip of hot broth. Then a gulping mouthful. He handed it back to her.

"Thanks."

She nodded and pulled the blanket closer around her shoulders. For several kilometers they rode that way, side by side, silent and angry. Finally, Angela shook her head as if she had been arguing with herself, then unwrapped the blanket and offered part of it to Alec.

"Before you freeze," was all she said.

He hesitated a moment, then pulled the warm fabric

across his shoulders. Automatically they slid closer together so that the one blanket could cover them both.

"You told Douglas to come and get me," Alec said to her.

Her face was set in a stubborn frown. "You used me, didn't you? You had no intention of calling for a ship to take us away. Did you think I fell for your lies?"

He shook his head. "I guess I've been outsmarted all along."

"You've outsmarted yourself."

"We'll see."

"Why did you lie to me?" she asked, her tone suddenly more hurt than angry. "Was it just to screw me or to get the radio? Which one?"

"I wasn't lying," he said. Before she could reply, he went on, "I didn't tell you the whole truth, but I wasn't lying when I told you I wanted you to come back to the moon with me."

Angela's frown softened, but her eyes were still wary, searching. "You meant, after you'd taken the uranium."

He nodded.

"You knew that wasn't what I meant when I offered to get you to the radio."

"Yes, I knew."

"Then you were lying."

"And so were you," he countered, "when you offered to help. You knew you were going to call Douglas and trap me."

"I know you'll have to kill him before you get the uranium."

"And you're protecting him."

"I'm trying to protect both of you," she said earnestly, urgently.

"And that's why you lied to me."

She almost smiled. "All right, I lied too. Feel better?"

It *was* funny, Alec realized. "We've both been sneaking around each other."

"But he needs you, Alec. What he's trying to do . . ."

He stiffened. "Douglas? He doesn't need anybody. He's got enough ego to cover the world all by himself."

"And you're blind!" she snapped.

Douglas' base was a shock. They drove up to a well-maintained wire mesh fence that seemed to wind clear across the landscape, over the rolling hills and as far as the eye could see. Where the road penetrated the fence stood a sentry tower, wooden beams weathered by years of sun and rain. Two men lounging at the base of the tower straightened their guns on their shoulders and opened the gate wide enough to step through. Douglas brought the jeep to a full halt and exchanged a few words with them.

They swung the gate wide. Alec saw that there were at least two more men up at the top of the tower. The grim snout of a heavy machine gun poked out from the railing up there.

After another chilly fifteen minutes of driving, with nothing to be seen but open countryside, they came to the first buildings.

"This used to be a base for the United States Air Force," Douglas called back from the driver's seat. "Makes an ideal headquarters for us—ready made."

They drove past row after row of neat wooden buildings, most of them looking as if they'd been freshly painted. Barracks, machine shops, warehouses, mess halls, even a building marked BASE THEATER in barely readable faded lettering. The airfield itself was immense, huge swaths of concrete runways and ramps, hangars and maintenance buildings and office towers built of brick and stone. All in excellent condition. But not an aircraft in sight. *We could land the shuttles right here*, Alec tantalized himself.

And people everywhere. Throngs of people, more than Alec had ever seen before. Walking, working, laughing; many of them waved to Douglas as he drove past. Hardly any of them carried weapons. *Like the history tapes of the old cities.*

They drove past the airfield area, out to a more deserted sector of little hills topped by small clumps of vividly colored trees. No buildings in sight out here, except one concrete blockhouse standing atop a bare grassy hill.

Douglas drove them up to the blockhouse.

"This is where the fissionables are," he said, turning in his too-small bucket seat to face Alec. "Want to see 'em?"

Alec nodded. "Yes."

"Okay . . ." Douglas hauled himself out of the jeep and headed for the blockhouse's metal door. The guard stepped from his side of the jeep and turned to face Alec. His pistol was now in its holster, but he kept his hand on its butt.

Alec climbed out and turned to help Angela, but she had already jumped out on the other side.

Douglas had the door open now, and Alec frowned at the realization that he hadn't watched to see if it had been locked or not. *Doesn't matter*, he told himself. *We can blow it open if we have to.*

Inside, the blockhouse was musty and damp. It was a small room, completely empty and dark except for the light sneaking in through the gun slits in each wall.

"Eh, would you mind?" Douglas gestured toward a metal trapdoor set into the cement floor. "I can't bend as easily as you can."

Alec reached down and grabbed the metal catch at one end of the steel door. He tugged, then heaved. Nothing.

"It slides," Douglas said.

*Thanks for telling me before I rupture myself.* The door slid back smoothly. *Oiled recently.*

They clattered down a long metal stairway into utter darkness, groping along the wall and railing until Douglas said, "Wait a minute . . . the generator switch should be . . . here . . ."

A click, and then from somewhere below them the rumble and whine of a diesel generator set. Lights glowed into life.

Alec could see that the stairs went down another twenty meters and ended in a huge storehouse room. Spread across the floor were heavy dull gray metal cylinders, each bearing the blood-red, three-sided emblem of danger and the printed words: RADIOACTIVE MATERIAL. There were more than fifty cylinders, all spaced at least twenty meters apart.

*Enough to power the processing plants for a century,* Alec thought.

"There's enough fissionable material here to blow up everything between the Great Lakes and the Hudson River," Douglas said.

Alec turned toward his father, who was standing two steps above him. "We need this . . . some of it, at least. We need it to live."

But Douglas shook his head. "No. If I let you take some of this back to the moon, we'd be killing them. You can kill people with kindness, you know. The wrong kind of kindness."

Alec could feel himself going tense, the skin on his face stretching taut. "In another two years we won't have the energy to process the fertilizers and medicines we need. You can't . . ."

"Don't tell me what I can't do!" Douglas boomed, his voice reverberating off the cement walls and metal stairs. "Those people can't survive by themselves. They can't live cooped up in their underground rats' nest. They've got to re-establish contact with Earth. Not just a raid every ten years, but real contact—genetically meaningful contact!"

"So you can rule them!" Alec flashed back.

Douglas' mouth opened, but for a moment no words came out. Then he broke into a roar of laughter: loud, thundering laughter that hadn't the slightest trace of humor in it.

They quartered Alec in a room of his own, in what had once been the Air Base's bachelor officers' quarters. The two-story brick building was an efficient but drab set of rooms. They were spacious, compared to what Alec was accustomed to. His own room was on the second floor, in a corner so that he had two windows. There was a real bed, a desk, and a chest of drawers. Alec smiled at the furniture. He had nothing to put in the drawers, nothing to hang in the closet.

But there was a shower, and it worked! For a slothful long hour Alec luxuriated in the unbelievable pleasure of having actual water sluicing over his naked body. There were two large pieces of cloth hanging next to the shower, and Alec used them to rub himself dry.

Someone tapped at his door. Wrapping one of the cloths around his waist, Alec yelled out, "Come in."

He stepped from the bathroom in time to see Angela entering the main room, carrying a handful of clothes.

"Oh . . ." They said it together.

She simply stood there looking at him. Alec grabbed at the cloth, clutching it at his middle, feeling foolish about it but somehow fearful of letting it slip just the same.

"I was cleaning . . ." he said lamely.

She grinned at him, making his face redden. "So I see." She was wearing a dress, pale blue to complement her eyes and golden hair, with a skirt short enough to show her fine, graceful legs.

"You look very pretty," he said.

"So do you." Grinning.

Flustered, he couldn't reply.

"I brought you some fresh clothes from the supply shop," Angela said. "I hope they fit okay. If they don't I can fix them for you."

"Thanks."

She dropped the clothes on the desk. Looking around the room, she asked, "Is everything okay? Do you need shaving things?"

"No," he answered. "I won't need another depilatory treatment for six months or so."

"Okay."

"Is there someplace to eat around here? Have you had dinner?"

"The mess hall will open in an hour," she said. "If you're hungry, I can fix you something at my place. It's not far froom here . . ."

"Uh, no, that's all right. Guess I'd better get dressed."

"Okay." She started for the door.

"No, wait." *This is idiotic. For Christ's sake, we've made love together.* "Don't go . . . Let's have dinner together."

Nodding, she said simply, "Okay."

Feeling silly, Alec took the clothes into the bathroom and tried them on. Turtleneck shirt, dark blue and thickly ribbed. Gray slacks that were too big around the middle and long enough so that he had to turn up the cuffs. A pair of solid boots, good size. A belt to pull the pants tight.

"How do I look?" he asked as he came out of the bathroom.

She smiled and frowned at the same time. "I wasn't too good about the sizes, was I?"

"Only the pants. The rest fits fine."

So they had dinner in the noisy, crowded, clattering

mess hall, sitting on benches at long wooden tables surrounded by steam and pungent odors and the chattering of other peoples' conversations. They sat side by side, but said practically nothing to each other. The food was hot and solid, nothing fancy, but more of it than Alec had been able to get since leaving the moon.

Outside afterward, it was dark and their frosted breaths hung in the air before them. The buildings were all alight. *Why not?* Alec thought. *He's probably got nuclear generators buried underground somewhere, using the fuel we need.*

They walked under the chilled stars to Angela's place. It was a separate little house, sitting at the head of a row of white wooden houses.

"I have some wine," she said. "The villagers make it."

Inside, the house was a combination of warmth and utilitarianism. The furniture was sparse. The front room was completely empty except for a single old wooden chair with a high straight back and a rug of some sort rolled up in a corner. There was a fireplace that looked as if it hadn't been used in a long time. Angela led Alec back to the kitchen, which had a table and three chairs in it, as well as a small refrigerator, stove and sink, all lined against one wall. Through another doorway, Alec could see the bedroom. Instead of a bed, there was simply a mattress on the floor and a sleeping bag half unrolled atop it.

"You have this place all to yourself?"

"Yes," she said, reaching down to a cabinet under the sink and pulling out a dusty green bottle. "Da . . . er, Douglas has the house at the other end of the row. Will and most of the other leaders live here . . . or really, their families do. Most of the time they're out in the wilds somewhere."

"Will's married?"

She set the bottle on the table next to Alec and took

two glasses from a cabinet. "He was going to marry a girl from one of the villages further south of here. But she was taken by one of the raider gangs. No one's seen her since."

Somehow that seemed to hit Alec like a blow to his midsection.

Angela sat down. "It was years ago . . . he got over it."

"Did he?"

She shrugged. "He functions. He lives. He even sings, sometimes."

Alec shook his head. "It's a lousy world."

"It's the only one we've got. Will you pour, or do you want me to?"

Alec took the bottle and pulled the stopper out of it. Funny, spongy thing. *Cork?* he wondered. Somewhere he had heard about the substance. Very carefully, conscious for the first time in months of Earth's six-fold gravity, he half-filled the two glasses with bright red wine.

It tasted marvelous. Smooth and warm and warming.

"All right," he said, putting his glass down firmly on the table. "It's not the only world we've got. There's an entirely different world, where all this insanity of raiders and killing doesn't exist."

"The lunar settlement," she said.

"Right. Civilization. Where you don't have to carry weapons all the time and worry if you'll make it through the night."

"That's what we've got here," Angela said, looking straight at him. "That's what Douglas has built for us."

"Yes . . . by force, by war, by strangling the people who trusted him."

She quickly shifted the subject. "Tell me about the lunar settlement. What's it like up there?"

With an effort, Alec pushed his anger down. "It's peaceful. It's polite. People can be human beings instead of jungle animals. You don't have this heavy gravity to fight against all the time. You can sail in the aerogymn and dance all the ballets every written."

"Ballets?" Angela looked puzzled.

*Never heard of them,* he realized. "Up on the surface," he went on, "you can see real beauty. I mean, it's beautiful here on Earth, wild and unpredictable and all . . . but on the moon, watching the sunrise takes a whole day. And the stars . . . and Earth itself, hanging there blue and beautiful. You can go for a thousand klicks without seeing another human being, alone, just by yourself, alone with the whole universe hanging up there and watching you . . ."

"It sounds desolate."

"No, it's beautiful. Watching the ice vents outgassing right after the perigee quakes . . . there's nothing like it. There's enough sulfur dioxide in the rocks to tint the vapor pink—it just puffs up and out like a ghost escaping from its grave."

Angela shuddered. "That doesn't sound beautiful to me."

"Wait till you see it."

"I'll never see it," she said. Sadly.

"Yes you will. I'm taking you there, remember?"

"No . . ."

He hunched forward in the chair. "God, you're beautiful. Let's go to bed."

She didn't look surprised. "There's more to it than that."

"What?"

"If Douglas finds out . . ."

Alec's fists clenched. "He means more to you than I do."

She reached out for his hand. "Alec . . . I don't mean anything to you. You can screw me one minute and try to trick me the next."

"You did the same damned thing!"

"Because I knew you were! You didn't fool me, not for an instant."

"Then why'd you go to bed with me?"

Her voice was rising. "Because you saved me and I was scared and you were kind . . . no, you killed those two . . . oh, hell! I don't know. I did it because I wanted to."

"And you don't want to now."

"Yes, I do want to."

It took a moment for Alec to realize what she had said. Then, leaning back in the chair, he wondered, "Then what the hell are we arguing about?"

Angela shook her head. "You don't understand any of it, do you? Not a bit of it."

But she got up from the table and took him by the hand and led him to the bedroom.

The first light of dawn woke Alec. He lay there with Angela's warm softness beside him, her head cradled in his arm, and watched the day slowly brighten through the bedroom window. The sleeping bag was spread lumpily over them.

"Are you going to stay?" Angela asked very quietly.

"Huh? I thought you were sleeping."

She smiled at him. "I've been thinking for the past couple of hours."

"Really?"

"Are you going to stay here . . . at the base, I mean?"

"I don't have a choice. I'm a prisoner."

Pushing away from him slightly, she said, "Oh that. You don't have to worry. Douglas just wanted you to come here without any fuss. He wouldn't stop you from leaving. He does love you, you know."

"The hell he does."

"Don't be a jerk, Alec. Of course he does."

*Then why did he leave us? What kind of love is that?*

"Well?" she asked.

"What?"

"Are you going to stay here?"

"Would you come with me if I left?" he countered.

"No."

"Because *he* needs you more than I do."

She laughed. "Douglas doesn't need me! He doesn't need anybody except one person."

"Who's that?"

"You."

He looked at her. "Don't be funny."

Angela sat up and pulled her knees up under her chin. The cover slid down to her ankles, and Alec shivered; not from the room's coldness, but from the curve of her smoothly fleshed back and hip.

"Look," she said. "What you don't . . ."

"I'm looking," he murmured.

She intercepted his reaching hand. "Not now. You've got to realize something. Douglas is an old man . . ."

"Fifty-five. That's not old."

"It is when you've lived the way he has," Angela said, completely serious. "He needs help. Your help. That's why he brought you here. He was overjoyed that you made it all the way here from Oak Ridge. He bragged about how you got through the summer on your own."

"I'll bet."

"He wants you to join with him, help bring the lunar settlement and his own territory here together. If you two can work together, you can build a real civilization on Earth. But if you fight . . ."

"Listen to me," Alec snapped. "He ran out on us. Not just on my mother and me, but on hundreds of men, women and children. He's stolen the fissionables that we need. Without them we'll die. He won't let us have them."

"Yes he will!" Angela said. "If you'll only agree to help him."

"Help him make himself another Genghis Khan? He can rot first."

"You just don't understand, do you?"

"Wrong! I understand far more than you do. Far more."

She shook her head. "No Alec, you're wrong. You're all wrong about so many things."

Instead of answering, he started to sit up.

"Where are you going?" she asked.

"Back to my own quarters."

"Not yet." She slid her arms around his neck and they eased down onto the mattress again. "You don't have to go now. And stop pouting. What's going on between you and your father has nothing to do with what's going on between you and me."

*Doesn't it? Aren't you doing this to make me stay here, to get me to join forces with them?*

But although he thought it, Alec didn't say anything as they started to make love again.

# Chapter Sixteen

It was easy to slide into the simple routine of life at the base.

The first leaves fell from the trees, the grass turned brown and brittle. The wind came always from the north or west, cold and sharp enough to cut through the heaviest of coats. The sky turned gray as the days shortened. The sun didn't climb far above the horizon and the moon itself seemed to have disappeared from the cloudy night skies. One titanic rainstorm stripped away the last of the leaves, blew off roofs and tore limbs from the now-bare trees. Alec's quarters stayed dry, although the heat and electricity went out for several hours. Angela's house was flooded to a depth of ten centimeters in the cellar.

Then the weather turned dry and fine. Days were cold, invigorating. Nights were colder. More and more, Alec slept with Angela. If Douglas knew about it, he said nothing, even though they dined together frequently in his house with Will Russo and others of Douglas' aides.

It was an easy time. The summer's fighting was over and everyone was preparing for the long winter.

Trucks and wagons came in every day from the outlying villages, heaped with produce from the farm harvesting and gave the farmers tools and guns and ammunition that had been made in the base's shops.

Troops of warriors came in from the hinterlands, reunited with friends and families that they hadn't seen all summer. There were parties, celebrations, even dramatic offerings by self-styled actors and singers in the base's mammoth, bare auditorium.

Alec found their efforts amateurish, but he attended every performance, sitting with Angela next to him. Douglas always sat in the front row and it always seemed to Alec as if the actors and singers were playing especially to him. He appeared to enjoy himself hugely, guffawing at the jokes and applauding every effort lustily.

Will had brought in a cache of whisky, "liberated" from a long-deserted city that his troop had detoured through. He rationed the stuff carefully, except for one long night when he gave a party and they all—including Alec—sang drunkenly until the sun rose.

All except Douglas, who left early in the evening after a few drinks. And by the time they started singing "The Frigging Bird" for the fourth time, Angela slipped away, too.

"I wanted to check on Douglas," she explained the next morning. "He didn't look too well when he left."

Through his thundering hangover, Alec said, "So you had to nursemaid him."

"You were having fun," she answered, smiling.

*And so were you, I'll bet.* But he said nothing. He seethed inside, but he couldn't bring himself to accuse her openly. *What would I do if she admitted it?*

And then he realized that he loved her.

A few nights later they were walking arm in arm from the mess hall to her house. They were heavily bundled in thick coats and woolly hats and gloves. The water in the lake nearby had a thin layer of ice over it already, and the only birds still remaining around the base were hardy brown sparrows who puffed up their feathers and hopped over the dead grass looking for seeds or crumbs.

For the first time in weeks, Alec noticed the moon. It

was only a sliver, sailing eerily among the clouds that scuttled by.

"I wonder if Kobol's back at the settlement."

"He's wintering in Florida, where it's warm," Angela said.

Still staring at the moon, Alec muttered, "What's he up to?"

"No one seems to know."

"He'll be here in the spring," Alec said. "I don't know how he'll do it, but he'll be here in the spring."

"There'll be fighting."

"Yes."

They had reached Angela's house. "And which side will you be on, Alec?"

He thought about it. "I don't know," he answered honestly. "I just don't know."

The first snowfall came early and caught everyone by surprise. Alec, most of all.

He walked out in the howling wind, turning dizzily round and round to watch the strange white flakes bury the world in their clean coldness. They spattered against his face and hands as drifts built up against the buildings.

He trudged to Angela's and dragged her out into the snow. She taught him how to make a snowball and they pelted each other until they laughed themselves into exhaustion.

Then they spent the rest of the day by her fireplace, not thinking of food or anything else except each other.

It was Will Russo who pulled Alec away for a few days.

After more than a week of steadily heavier hints, Will finally asked Alec if he'd like to go out into the woods on a hunting trip. Something in the way he asked implied that he had more on his mind than simply hunting. Alec agreed.

They set off across the frozen lake early one morning, as the sun was just starting to brighten the eastern sky. Alec felt plainly nervous about walking on ice, with all that water under it, but Will was chattering happily and occasionally humming to himself, perfectly at ease. So Alec shifted the heavy pack on his shoulder harness and tried to forget what would happen if the ice broke.

They spent the whole day up in the hills, moving straight ahead, following some inner sense of direction or purpose known only to Will. The snow was thinner up under the fir trees, barely a dusting on the ground.

"Will," Alec asked, pulling up alongside his long-striding companion, "what are we hunting for?"

"Three men," he replied, trying to replace his happy grin with a serious look. He was only partially successful.

"What? Men? With these?" Alec hefted the long-barrelled rifle Will had given him. It fired only one shot at a time.

"Well, maybe we won't have to use guns. They might come peacefully."

"I thought we were going for meat . . . to eat."

Will shook his head. "Nope. Trappers get plenty of game for the table. Oh, we might bag a deer or something on our way back. But only after we deal with the thieves."

"Thieves?"

Still striding along fast enough to make Alec trot once in a while to catch up, Will answered, "They joined one of our scout parties late in the summer. I thought all they wanted was a safe, warm place to spend the cold months. But a couple of weeks ago they took off with a wagon-load of food, guns and ammo."

"A couple of weeks ago? They could be in Asia by now!"

"Nope, they're not. They had to shoot their way past the gate guards, and one of 'em was wounded. Killed two of our guards, by the way. Other guard followed them for a while, and we've had relays of scouts trailing them . . . at a distance. Don't want anybody hurt unnecessarily."

Alec nodded. That made sense. But now, "We're going to take them?"

"Right. They're holed up in a cave, out of food. One of them's still in bad shape from his wounds, I imagine. The other two might listen to reason."

"And if they don't?"

Will rubbed his nose. "That's why we're carrying the rifles."

They camped in the woods overnight and ate from the food they had carried with them. Only a small fire. They slept wrapped in blankets. Alec was shivering when he woke up next dawn.

By midmorning they were halfway up a barren hill. Underneath its coating of snow, where the wind had blown bare patches, it looked as if the ground had been scorched black. No trees grew here and only a few stunted, gnarled bushes stuck their tortured bare limbs out of the snow.

"There's the cave," Will said, pointing with his rifle.

Up near the top of the rocky hill was a black fissure between two large boulders.

A clatter of pebbles behind him made Alec whirl around, rifle cocked and leveled.

The man was old, whiplash thin, with a cold-whitened face that was mostly bones and eyes. His mouth was sunken in, toothless, and his heavy fur hat seemed to be jammed down until it merged with the bulky collar of his rough coat.

"They're still in there. Haven't seen any signs of smoke or a fire for three days now." He said *fie-yuh* for *fire*, an accent Alec hadn't heard before.

"Not much firewood around here, that's for sure," Will said.

"Eh-yup," said the scout.

"Okay. Good." Will wriggled out of his shoulder harness, reached inside the pack and took out two oblate metal objects.

*Grenades*, Alec recognized.

Pushing one grenade in each of his coat pockets, Will said, "You two stay here and cover me. I'm gonna see if they'll talk some sense." He picked up his rifle and started scrambling toward the top of the hill.

Alec kneeled in the snow and clamped his rifle under his arm, pointing it in the general direction of the cave.

"They're bad poison," the scout murmured in his strange accent. "Caught Johnny Fullah last week and shot him through both knees . . . left him crippled to bleed to death in the snow. Lucky I found him."

Alec glanced at the old man, then put the rifle to his shoulder and aimed it dead at the cave opening.

Will was nearly at the edge of the big boulder on the left of the cave.

"Hello the cave!" he shouted.

No reply.

"We know you're in there. You're cold and hungry and your friend needs medical help, if he's not dead already. Come on out and we'll take you back to the base. I'm a medic, I can help your wounded man."

"And then hang us!" a voice shouted back. It sounded high and young and trembly to Alec.

"That's up to the jury. You'll get a trial."

"We ain't comin' out!" It was definitely a young voice, crackling with fear.

Will talked to them for half an hour, patiently, almost pleasantly. He pointed out to them the hopelessness of their situation, urged them to come out peacefully.

Finally the voice said, "Okay . . . okay . . ."

Will grinned back down toward Alec, then rose to his feet. "Good," he said toward the cave. "I knew . . ."

The shot exploded, echoed by the cave walls, and

knocked Will completely off his feet. He tumbled, flailing legs and arms, down the rough hillside. A yellow-haired figure darted from the cave's mouth and dashed off toward the right.

Alec had let his rifle rest on is knee, but without thinking about it he snapped it to his shoulder and fired. The rock chipped in front of the fleeing blond. He skidded to a stop, turned toward Alec. And Alec fired again, slamming him back against the rock. Again, and the figure jerked once more and crumpled to the ground.

Alec swung the rifle back to the cave's mouth. Another shot rang out, and the snow puffed a few centimeters in front of Will's sprawled body.

Alec emptied the rest of his clip at the cave's entrance. The firing stopped. He scrambled up the few meters to Will's side. There was a spreading red stain on his side. His eyes were open, but hazy.

"Don't . . . don't . . ." Will muttered. Alec heard more shots, from behind. He glanced over his shoulder and the scout was aiming a smoking pistol rock-steady at the cave's mouth.

"Give them a chance . . . they're scared . . ." Will said weakly.

"I'll give them a chance," Alec said. He pulled the two grenades from Will's pockets. One of them was slippery with blood. Hooking a finger through their firing rings, Alec grabbed Will's rifle with his free hand and made his way, doubled over, toward the cave's mouth.

There was no more firing. Flattening himself along the boulder beside the cave entrance, Alec yelled:

"You've got five seconds. Come out with your hands up or I'll blow you all to hell."

The same high, crackling voice shrieked, "Wait! . . . Gimme a chance . . . he's out cold . . . I can't drag him . . ."

But Alec was counting, not listening. He reached five,

glanced at Will still sprawled on his back in the snow halfway down the slope, then pulled the pin from one grenade and tossed it into the cave.

"Hey . . . wh . . . no . . . *wait!*"

The explosion sounded strangely muffled. Smoke poured from the cave, and Alec thought he heard a high, keening screech, long and raw and agonized. He yanked the pin and threw in the second grenade. The explosion blotted out all other noises, and by the time the smoke had wafted out of the cave, all was silent inside.

Alec edged into the cave carefully, rifle cocked. It took a half-minute for his eyes to adjust to the darkness. There was enough left of the two bodies to recognize that they had once been human. Barely enough.

He walked out and went to the blond he had shot. The kid—he couldn't have been more than seventeen—still lay where he had fallen. There was no gun or any other weapon near him.

The wind gusted and made Alec look up. The scout was at Will's side, easing him out of his blood-soaked coat.

"Don't look too good," the scout said as Alec joined them. "Think they got a rib. Might puncture th' lung."

"Can we move him?"

"Got to. Can't leave him hee-yuh."

They bound Will's chest as tightly as they dared, Alec tearing strips from his own shirt. Then Alec sent the scout on ahead to get help as he wedged himself under Will's arm, on his good side, and started to help him up.

"What about . . ." Will sagged, nearly pulling Alec to his knees, ". . . those kids."

"Don't worry about them."

It wasn't as bad as Alec had feared. Although they barely made two kilometers before sundown, trudging along with most of Will's weight dragging on Alec's shoulders, just before it got truly dark a trio of scouts met with them. They had a stretcher, and the four of them carried Will to an overnight camp that the old man had set up. They slept by a big, hot fire.

The next morning a wagon came up and took Will and Alec back to the base. Douglas and Angela and half the base's people met them at the first gate.

It was two nights later that Douglas pounded on Angela's door.

She and Alec had eaten supper together in the mess hall, then walked the snow-banked paths to her house. They were sitting in front of the fire, drawing a charcoal sketch on a piece of fabric together. Angela was going to paint it and hang it on one of the walls.

Angela got up to open the door. Douglas strode in and suddenly the bare little room was crowded.

"Well, at least you're dressed," Douglas said.

Alec scrambled to his feet.

But Angela merely replied coolly, "Of course we're dressed. Now close the door or it'll be freezing in here."

Douglas nudged the door shut. "I want you over at Will's place, right away."

"What's happened?" Alec demanded.

"No time for explanations. Come right now."

Douglas turned and yanked the door open. "Well?"

Alec took Angela's hand and the three of them trotted through the icy darkness down three houses to Will's place, while Alec's mind raced: *An infection. Something's happened to Will. Maybe the wound was worse than they thought.*

They burst into Will's house. And there was the big oversized puppydog, sitting on the sofa in the main room of the house, with half a dozen men and women squatting on the floor around him. A merry fire was roaring in the fireplace and they were all laughing and waving glasses.

"Oh-hoh!" Will called as the three of them stepped into the house. "They're here! Give them glasses and let's drink a toast to my companion-in-arms and rescuer."

Someone shoved a glass into Alec's hand. Someone else filled it eight centimeters deep with whiskey. Everyone stood and faced Alec as Will intoned, with great seriousness:

"To Alec, who brought me back alive."

"To Alec," they all said.

The whiskey was beautiful, smooth as free-fall and warmer than sunshine. But then, "What is all this?" Alec asked, slightly dazed. Angela looked puzzled too; but happy.

Will was fully dressed, but the bulk of bandages could still be seen under his shirt.

He said, "My medical colleagues have finally admitted that I'm out of danger and can be up and about . . ."

"In a few days," said one of the older men, trying to look dour. "In a few days."

"Right. In a few days," Will agreed. "So I thought to myself, if I can be up and about in a few days, that means I can go back to Utica and hunt for more whiskey. So why don't we celebrate my miraculous recovery with the bottles we already have on hand?"

"Sound strategic thinking," Douglas boomed. And the party was officially launched.

It went on all night. Toward dawn, a few of the women disappeared, murmuring something about getting breakfast together.

Douglas was sitting on the sofa beside Will. Most of the others had bunched into little knots of conversation in corners of the rooms. Douglas pounded the empty space on the sofa alongside him and said to Alec, "Come here, son. Sit down." It was a command.

They were all drunk enough to drop most of the pretenses that people live with. So Alec, knowing that his grin was as unsteady as his walk, made his way past a quartet of people sitting cross-legged by the dying fire and dropped onto the sofa next to his father.

"Well," Douglas said, in the nearest thing to a quiet conversational tone that he could muster, "you've been with us almost three months now. Still think I'm an ogre?"

Alec could see Will watching him, past Douglas' bulky form, grinning hugely, as if he'd arranged a reconciliation between David and Absalom.

"No," Alec admitted. "I guess you're not a monster. I still don't agree with you, but I think I can see why you did it."

"Good!" Douglas raised both hands in the air, like a victorious gladiator. One of them held an empty glass instead of a sword.

"Now then," he went on, letting his hands drop, "there are a few things to settle. First, I think you'd better marry the girl. She's like my very own daughter, and I'll admit I had mixed feelings . . ."

"Wait a minute," Alec said. "Marry Angela?"

"Of course."

"That's between her and me. You don't have anything to say about it."

"The hell I don't!" he exploded. "She's practically my daughter. You *are* my son. If you think you're going to go fucking around and leave her pregnant, you'd goddam well better think again."

The other conversations stopped. Nobody turned to look at them, though, and they all resumed a polite buzz and made sure they ignored Douglas and his son.

"Now wait . . ."

"No, you wait," Douglas insisted. "You're going to marry her, and then head a delegation to meet with Kobol. There are a few things I want to make clear to him."

"I'm not sure I want to!"

"Not sure? What the hell do you mean, not sure? You can't have your cake and eat it too. You're either with us or against us. There aren't any neutrals around here. Now you just said you're on our side."

"I didn't say that!"

"Then you're against us!" Douglas roared.

Will put a hand on his shoulder. "Hold on, Doug . . . just . . ."

But Douglas shrugged him off and lumbered to his feet. Alec stood up beside him, barely coming up to his shoulder.

"Now you listen to me," Douglas said, his voice low and threatening. "I've let you sit around here and have your fill of food and warmth and shelter for three months. You've sneaked around my back to fool around with my virtual daughter. And what have I asked from you in return? Nothing! Not a goddamned thing. Except loyalty. And you refuse?"

Trembling and white hot inside, Alec answered in a voice so low he could barely hear it himself. "That's right. I refuse."

"Then get out!" Douglas roared, pointing toward the door. "Take whatever you own and get the hell out of here."

"That's just what I'm going to do."

Alec started for the door. Everyone else in the house was staring at him now, all pretense of polite disinterest vanished. Will looked worse than when he'd been shot.

"Just a minute," Douglas snapped as Alec reached the door. "You take whatever you please from this base. But you leave Angela alone. You're not good enough for her, no matter how cleverly you've tricked her."

"I'll take what I want," Alec said.

"Try taking her, and I'll have you hunted down like an animal and killed. I promise you!"

# BOOK THREE

# Chapter Seventeen

Alec stormed out blindly into the frozen night. He passed Angela's house, saw the lights and glimpsed a bustle of women inside. He guessed that they were preparing breakfast, talking together, laughing and gossiping.

He went on past. By the time he had put together his own few belongings and found and saddled a horse, dawn was streaking the eastern sky. But it was a dull, overcast day that arose, with a sky as grimly sullen as Alec's own thoughts. He rode beyond the checkpoints and the guarded fence gates, away from Douglas' base.

He rode most of the day and camped up in the hills, under a stand of firs. Their branches made a poor fire that burned too quickly, then smoldered without heat. By morning he was shaking with bone-deep cold. And hungry.

The only weapon he had brought with him was the automatic rifle he had come in with originally. It was heavy and cumbersome to use on small game, even when choked down to single-shot action. And Alec quickly found that his shooting wasn't good enough to get a rabbit or smaller rodent as it scurried across the frozen, snow-patched ground. His dilemma was painful: squirt a clip of rounds at a rabbit and you might hit the animal, might even have enough of it left to gnaw on; but you'd be out of ammunition in a day or two.

On his third day of wandering it snowed, a heavy

fierce blizzard that howled through the woods and blotted out everything except the very nearest trees. Alec was lucky enough to find a cave and enough hardwood to make a fire that lasted the night. The horse needed it more than he did. There was no forage to speak of, and the animal was weakening quickly.

He spent two days in the cave, locked in by the blizzard. No firewood, no food, nothing but the stench of the horse and the screeching wind. When it ended and the sky shone blue again, the world was completely covered with white. Snow plastered the trees and made their branches sparkle crystalline in the newly risen sun. Drifts heaped up against the mouth of Alec's cave waist high. And the land outside was a rolling, featureless unmarked expanse of white.

Briefly he admitted its beauty. Then his hunger and the fear of dying drove him out into the snow.

The horse died that day. It just collapsed under him in a shuddering groan and floundered in the snow. Alec could feel the warmth of life seeping out of its body. Now he was totally alone. Nothing alive was even in sight. There were no clues, no direction to aim for, no hope.

He stood in the hip-deep snow, wet and cold and trembling between despair and burning fear.

*Sleep, that's what I need. Rest and sleep.*

And the wind sighed, making the trees croon a lullaby. *Sleep . . . yes, sleep.*

But then, from somewhere deep in his memory came a fragment of poetry that he hadn't realized he knew. It spoke itself in his mind, and he jerked erect. He muttered it to himself, then shouted to the trees and wind:

"To sleep! Perchance to dream:—ay, there's the rub;

"For in that sleep of death what dreams may come . . ."

*That sleep of death.* He repeated it to himself. And he

hunched forward and fought his way through the snow.

It was a bitter, exhausting battle, more against himself than the elements. Cold, hungry, weary, he clamped an iron determination over his aching, protesting muscles and pressed onward.

*There are villages all around here,* he kept telling himself. *Look for smoke, or maybe a road.*

He found a road first. He barely recognized it; there was nothing to distinguish it from the rest of the snow-covered landscape except a pair of ruts where sled runners had pressed down. It was easier to walk in the ruts, though. Thankfully, Alec started along the road, heading downhill, away from the base and toward the valley floor where the farmlands stood. And the villages.

It was nearly dark when he staggered into the village. It was either the same one he had taken months earlier or one exactly like it. Then Alec saw the old man who sat at the gate. Underneath his muffling coat and heavy, pulled-down hat he was the same man.

They said nothing to each other. Alec stood by the snow-trimmed gate on unsteady feet, clutching the automatic rifle feebly, puffing with exhaustion. The old man faced him, the same shotgun in his gloved hands, looking uncertain and red-faced in the last dying rays of the sun.

The old man shrugged and beckoned to Alec, then turned and headed into the village. Alec followed him, staggering, down cold deserted lanes where the snow had been pounded flat and solid by the passage of many feet.

The old man led him to a hut. "In there," he said, in a ragged, age-roughened voice.

Alec pushed the door open and stumbled into the room. A flood of warmth from the fireplace was the first thing he sensed. The second was the two men at the table, startled, half out of the chairs, a steaming bowl of something on the table between them.

They were two of Alec's men.

And that was all that Alec noticed. He fell face down and was unconscious before he reached the hut's bare earthen floor.

They spent a couple of days pumping warm food into him and letting him rest on their pallet. Miraculously, Alec realized, he hadn't come down with a fever. A little frostbite and a lot of raw, chaffed skin. But otherwise no damage that rest and food couldn't cure.

The men—Zimmerman and Peters—had decided to stay at the village when Alec's force had broken up. Most of the group had joined Will Russo's squad, once they learned that Alec was Douglas' prisoner. But Zimmerman and Peters remained at the village. Alec slowly realized that they were living together as lovers. He was startled at first, even though homosexuality was fairly widespread in the lunar settlement. But they left him alone, so he said nothing to them. He only wished they had another hut to go to at night.

"And Jameson?" Alec asked them on the third day. "Did he join Russo and Douglas, too?"

Peters shook his head solemnly. He had grown a luxuriant dark beard since Alec had last seen him. "No," he said. "Not him. He didn't stop any of us from doing what we wanted to do, but he said he was heading south to join up with Kobol."

"Russo told you that Kobol had landed?"

"Yes. And he let us make up our minds about what we wanted to do. George and I . . ." he glanced almost shyly at the blond, fair-skinned Zimmerman, ". . . we decided we'd done enough soldiering. We helped the people here to take in their harvest and they invited us to stay. They've been very kind and understanding."

*They probably think everybody from the moon is homo,* Alec thought. Aloud, he asked, "Did any of the men go with Jameson?"

"Four or five."

Alec sank back on the pallet. *There's no one left to join you,* he told himself. *You're completely on your own.*

After a week, the elders of the village came to Alec's hut. They were polite, deferential, even. But they were also firm. They also had no desire to be caught in whatever high politics was going on between The Douglas and his son. So Alec would please leave as soon as he was strong enough. They would give him food and ammunition and even a good horse. But he must leave the village.

Solemnly they led a big, gentle-looking chestnut-brown mare from their communal barn and loaded it with a bedroll, packs of food and ammunition. Peters gave Alec an ancient single-shot rifle, good for small game hunting. Zimmerman gave his own pistol, holster and cartridge belt.

The elders watched without a word as Alec said goodbye to his two former comrades and swung up into the saddle. With a nod to the older men, he kicked the horse and trotted through the gate and out of the village.

*To where?* he wondered. *South to join Kobol?* Instinctively he shook his head, vetoing the idea.

It was midday when he left the village. By the time the sun was low on the brow of the western hills, Alec had found a cave in a little ridge and decided to spend the night there.

*Kobol will be coming here in the spring,* he thought as he unsaddled the horse. *Let him come to me.* But another part of his mind thought ironically, "You've got to weather the winter first."

He pulled enough deadwood from the bare trees outside the cave to make a small fire. He tethered the horse near the cave's entrance. The smoke from the fire wasn't too bad, and he was getting used to it by now. He was almost accustomed to the horse's smell.

Briefly he debated trying Peters' rifle on some small game. But it was already getting dark. He decided to eat from the stores the villagers had given him: a bit of salted meat and some dried grains.

The horse was standing still as a rock. The fire had burned down to a few barely glowing ashes. Alec was stretched out in the bedroll, trying to sleep, trying not to think of Angela. This was the tough time, when there was nothing else to occupy him except thoughts of her. The night outside was dark and still, with only an occasional sigh of wind breaking the wintry silence.

*Would she have come with me? Good thing she didn't; damned near killed myself. Wouldn't want . . .*

A crunching sound. Alec's eyes snapped open, but there was nothing to see in the darkness. The cave was black, its entrance only slightly lighter. The sound had been faint, but—*there it is again!*

Footsteps on snow.

Alec slid his hand down to the pistol inside the bedroll.

*The villagers are coming to get their gifts back. If The Douglas' son just happens to die in some cave, it's not their fault. And why should they lose a valuable horse?*

Listening carefully, Alec thought he heard two horses slowly advancing toward the cave.

"Mr. Morgan?" a young voice called out.

He didn't answer.

"Mr. Morgan?" A silhouette appeared at the cave's mouth. Then another. "We'd like to join with you, if you'll have us."

They were young, not yet out of their teens. And bored with life in the village. They saw in Alec a chance for adventure, an opportunity to see more of the world. Alec tried to dissuade them, told them that all he had to offer them was danger and an early grave. They grinned and insisted that they weren't afraid and they'd follow wherever he led.

So he led them.

First into the nearly abandoned cities, where there were still some supplies. The nearer cities had only a few feral gangs roaming through them, yet were big and complex enough for three stealthy men to find canned food and even some clothes and blankets without running into a fight. But to get more weapons and ammunition they had to ambush a group of a half-dozen savages. Alec planned the ambush carefully, letting the city-dwellers spot him and chase him into an empty building's cellar. A brief clatter of gunfire echoing madly inside the tight confines of the dirty cellar room, and his two followers were able to arm themselves with automatic rifles and more ammunition than they really cared to carry.

They traded some of the ammunition and Peters' rifle for fresh food and an extra horse at a village on the eastern edge of Douglas' territory. They left the village with another recruit, an older man who'd lost his wife and children to sickness and wanted no more memories of them.

And Alec had his plan. *Let Kobol work his way up here by spring. By then I'll have Douglas' defenses completely mapped out. I'll be waiting for him, and I'll resume command of the force he brings.*

But he needed a radio. And he knew where to get one.

Alec waited. With new-found patience he bided his time, waited out the blizzards in caves and forest shelters, recruited more men—youngsters, mostly—from the villages. Craftily, he never attacked a village. He traded with them, lured their sons to his side, hinted that the village elders would be wise to treat him fairly because the days of The Douglas' reign were numbered.

He learned the territory, mapped its folds and hills, its

forests and streams, the roads, the cities, the villages. And Douglas' defenses. A new perimeter of wire fencing was going up, he saw; teams of men digging through the snow to set up the fence out on the outermost edges of his territory. They also built wooden watchtowers every kilometer or so, despite the bitter weather. Douglas was not waiting for spring.

Alec located the firebases on hilltops inside the new perimeter fence. He saw scouting parties and larger armed patrols riding across the countryside, but he kept a few jumps away from them. He wanted no serious fighting. Not yet. Once he thought he recognized Will Russo at the head of a column of men on snowshoes. Alec stayed especially far from them.

The days were getting noticeably longer when he attacked the firebase. He had to lead his men around the long way, through a gap in the still-uncompleted outer fence and watchtower ring. It was still bitterly cold, and the sky seemed to be a constant blank of gray as Alec marched his two dozen men toward the firebase. But toward evening the sun broke under the western clouds, and Alec noticed a tiny blue flower poking its head out of the snow along a hillside.

He smiled to himself. Not at the flower's beauty or the promise of the sunset, but at the correctness of his timing for the attack.

They waited until well after midnight and climbed the hill toward the firebase on foot. It was laid out almost exactly like the firebase Alec had been in. The men stealthily clambered over the snow-packed earthen ramparts and used knives and crossbows on the defenders inside. Alec got to the radio before the base commander could switch it on. He shot the man twice in the chest as he wildly clawed at the console controls.

Only when the commander lay gasping and bleeding to death on the floor of the radio alcove did Alec notice that he was still gripping his unbelted trousers in one hand and his feet were bare.

They took no prisoners. But they carefully disassembled the radio and its generator and packed them onto the firebase's own truck. They used the explosives they found there to blow up the underground dugouts and artillery pieces, leaving no evidence that they'd stolen the radio.

*He'll suspect,* Alec thought of his father. *But we'll stay far enough from his other radio equipment so that he won't be able to monitor our calls.*

The truck slipped and groaned through the night, convoyed by the mounted men. They got safely back outside Douglas' perimeter, only to find that they hadn't been chased at all.

Still, Alec pushed on far into the following day before he tried calling the satellite station. When he finally made contact, the voice that crackled in his earphones seemed totally incredulous.

"We thought you were dead or . . ."

"Or gone over to Douglas' side?"

"Well . . ."

"Never mind," Alec said. "Get word to Kobol that I want to see him or his representative as soon as he can get someone up here. There's much planning to do. I'll keep in touch with you at least every other day and relay instructions on where to find me."

"Yessir. Er . . . I suppose you want to be patched through to the settlement, and speak to your mother?"

Without an eyeblink's hesitation, Alec answered, "No. I can't afford to keep broadcasting that long. It might get picked up. Relay this message to her: Tell her that I'm fine and we'll soon have accomplished our mission."

"That's all?"

"That's everything."

# Chapter Eighteen

Kobol sent Jameson.

He arrived within two weeks of Alec's first radio call.

"How did you get here so quickly?" Alec wondered.

Jameson smiled in his humorless, eagle-fierce way. "By boat. There are a lot of boats down in Florida. And plenty of fuel for them, too. They make the fuel from seawater—electrolyze the hydrogen and then freeze it down to a liquid."

Alec nodded. *There must be more technology in Florida than up here.* Then he remembered. *Of course! The old spaceport. It must still be intact.*

"Came up the Delaware River as far as we could," Jameson went on. "Went past Philadelphia at top speed; it's still slightly radioactive. When we ran out of river we trekked overland."

Jameson and Alec were standing on the brow of a small hill, sheltered by a stand of white-barked beech trees. Their limbs were still bare and snow still covered much of the ground. But the sun was high in a perfectly clear blue sky. Warmth was returning to the land. If you listened closely, you could hear trickles of melted water running beneath the snow. Soon the streams would be flowing noisily again.

"What's Kobol doing down there?" Alec asked.

"He's putting together an army, a real army," Jameson spread his hands outward for emphasis. "Thousands of men . . . he's recruiting them from the locals. They've got four shuttles landing supplies and weapons almost every day now: trucks, lasers, heavy stuff."

"Thousands of men? Four shuttles?"

"Right. The Council's decided that the only way to get the fissionables is to smash Douglas once and for all. So they're giving Kobol everything he wants—there must be more able-bodied lunar men in Florida than there are left in the settlement."

Turning sharply on Jameson, Alec snapped, "Everything *he* wants? I'm in command!"

Jameson shrugged. "You might find that point a bit difficult to get across. The official story was that you'd been killed or captured. The *rumor* was that you'd joined Douglas."

"They're both wrong. I was named commander of this mission and I've never been relieved of command, no matter what Kobol says or thinks."

"He's not going to be pleasant about that," Jameson said.

Alec looked at him, thought a moment, then said, "All right, there's no sense arguing about it here and now. We'll have to settle it between us when he gets here."

Jameson nodded, but still looked unconvinced, even slightly amused.

"I assume Kobol has some plan worked out for getting his thousands of troops here?"

"Indeed he does," Jameson said. "He's been studying terrestrial meteorology and he's come up with the brilliant observation that it's warmer in the southern areas—where he is—than it is up here in the frozen north."

"So?"

"So his plan is to follow the advance of springtime right up the countryside. He's already started to move his men northward, out of Florida and into some lovely swamplands that the natives call Georgia: As the warm weather moves northward, Kobol will move his men along with it, adding new recruits along the way."

"More men?"

"That's right." Jameson nodded. "He says nothing succeeds like excess."

"He stole that. It's a quotation from history."

Jameson looked slightly surprised. "Really? Humph. He's been strutting around like he thought of it himself. Anyway he's been saying that the more men we have, the more raiders and barbarians will want to join us. And the bigger the army we have when we fight Douglas, the easier it'll be to beat him."

Alec scuffed a booted toe on the snowbank along the path they were walking. "It won't be easy to keep an army like that together. Those people aren't going to march halfway across the continent and follow orders. Why should they?"

"Some of them will. Maybe a lot of them. Kobol's promised them all the loot and women they can carry, once they've beaten Douglas."

"Ohhh." Alec finally understood. And thought of Angela.

They spent the day pacing back and forth along the trail that wound across the hill's brow, while the three men who had come with Jameson waited stolidly back at the base of the hill, among Alec's own men.

"So we can expect Kobol's army to reach here just about the time the spring mud's dried and it's easy to move across country," Alec summarized.

"That's his plan."

"The timing's going to be important. He's got to arrive here just when the travelling turns good again. We've been able to survive so far because it's been more trouble for Douglas to hunt us down than we're worth to him. But when the travelling gets easy again, I don't think we can last very long. If Kobol waits a week or so too long, we could be dead when he gets here."

"I know."

Alec said, "So does he."

For a moment Jameson didn't respond, but merely kept his stern bird-of-prey expression as emotionless as he could. "He'll get here in time. He wants to marry your mother and gain full control of the Council through her. He won't let you get killed. Not that way, at least."

Strangely, his words neither surprised Alec nor upset him. *He hasn't told me anything I didn't already suspect.*

"All right," Alec said quietly. "It's vital that Kobol and I meet face to face before his troops get here. I've got a nearly complete picture of Douglas' defenses. In another couple of weeks I'll fill in the few gaps in the information. Even with a big army, he'll need that intelligence."

"I know," Jameson said, a bit stiffly. "He sent me to get the information."

Alec shook his head. "No. I'll talk with Kobol and no one else."

Jameson said nothing, gave no hint of what he felt.

"It's more than relaying information on defenses," Alec explained. "There's the whole question of strategy . . . how we're going to attack Douglas. If you carry back the data I've got about the defenses, Kobol will set up his battle plan before he gets here. That could be disastrous."

"Should I tell him that?"

Alec grinned. "Tell him whatever you like. But I want to see him before his army reaches this far north. I'll leave you to arrange a time and place."

Jameson looked away from Alec, out toward the setting sun and the band of sullen maroon that lined the western horizon. "He won't try to kill you," he said softly, almost to himself. "But he might want to keep you under his eye . . . as a prisoner."

"You mean that a meeting with him might be a trap?"

Jameson said, "It could be."

"Can I depend on you to prevent that from happening?"

Jameson swung around and fixed his hawk-like gaze on Alec. "I'm only one man. He'll have lots of others with him."

"I know," Alec said. "But if it comes to trouble, will you stand with me?"

For almost a minute, Jameson didn't reply. Then he said, "I've served under you and I've served under him. If it comes to trouble—I'll stand with you."

Alec put out his hand to the bigger man. Jameson took it in his grip and smiled. It was like a glacier melting.

"We're both insane, you know," he said.

"I know," Alec answered. "I know."

The meeting was arranged for a mutually convenient time and place.

After several discussions by radio—relayed by the satellite and taking longer than Alec felt comfortable with—they agreed to meet on a boat in the upper Delaware River, at a spot called the Water Gap. The term was a puzzlement to Alec until he saw the place.

The snow was melting fast under the early spring sun and the ground was mushy and slow for travelling. Alec and four picked men made their way on horseback southward, following the maps Jameson had left with them. It took a week of hard travel.

Once they reached the river, they could have found the Water Gap with no further help. The Delaware cut between two high-shouldered mountains, revealing layers of striated rock that had been exposed by millions of years of erosion.

There was a passable road along the shoulders of the mountains, the remains of an old highway. It was broken up and covered with rubble, but the horses stepped over the litter easily and clopped along, making good time. It was a huge relief after the rough going in the mud of the countryside. But Alec and his quartet of men kept wary eyes on the slopes rising above them and across the river. Good places for ambush. The trees and brush hadn't leafed out yet, however, and the ground was bare and difficult to hide in.

At the Gap's narrowest point there was a surprise: the graceful arch of a bridge still standing, spanning the river with steel and concrete that didn't even look particularly begrimed and weathered until they got quite close to it. And anchored at the base of one of the bridge's supporting pillars was a small power boat.

*There can't be more than five or six people aboard a boat that size,* Alec thought to himself as they nosed their horses down a trail that led to the water's edge. *We won't be badly outnumbered—unless Kobol's got other boats hidden further down the river.*

The boat glided close enough to the shore for Alec and two of his men to wade up to its boarding ladder. The other two men, and two of Kobol's crew, stayed on the shore with the horses.

"Good to see you," Kobol said with a toothy smile as Alec climbed aboard. He looked thinner than the last time Alec had seen him: harder and leaner, with more lines in his face. His hand felt leathery when Alec shook it. But his eyes were still hooded, masked.

"Outdoor life seems to agree with you," Kobol said to Alec as the boat started its purring electric engine once more. "You're lost your baby fat; you look good."

Alec grunted a noncommittal reply and noticed that the forward deck and the top of the cabin were covered with solar cells. There were no guns in sight, but something squat and bulky was covered by a tarpaulin at the boat's stern. *A laser?*

They went down into the cabin. It was a tight little compartment with foldup bunks locked against the bulkheads and an oversized table taking up most of the room. Narrow benches lined both sides of the table. Atop it was pinned a photomap of the area of Douglas' base.

"We've pieced this together from satellite photos," Kobol said. "I think you'll find it acccurate."

Alec slid onto one of the benches, studying the map and nodding. The photos were very detailed; he could even see Angela's house. *What were we doing when this picture was taken?* he wondered idly.

Kobol took the bench on the other side of the table and muttered something to one of his men. Sandwiches appeared, and a brownish drink that Kobol called "beer."

"It's quite good," he told Alec. "Slightly alcoholic. One of the first factories the natives got running again in Florida was a brewery. They grow the grain right there and use half the wood in the area to keep the factory supplied with power."

Alec sipped at it. It tasted sour and awful. He must have frowned, because Kobol said with an air of superiority, "You have to develop a taste for it."

"I'd rather not."

"We have milk," a new voice said.

Alec looked up and saw Jameson standing in the compartment's narrow hatchway. Suppressing a smile, Alec nodded and said, "All right, I'll take milk."

They spent several hours poring over the map. Alec fitted in all the details he knew about Douglas' defenses, until the map bristled with inked-in wavy lines representing fences, and circles and squares that pinpointed watchtowers and firebases.

Kobol looked impressed. "We'll have to concentrate everything in one massive onslaught—straight up this major road." He swept his hand along the map.

"That's just what Douglas would expect," Alec countered, shaking his head. "He'll stop you here . . . ," he pointed to a spot where the road snaked between hills, ". . . or here, where the streams and lakes will force you into a narrow line of march."

Kobol tugged at his mustache. "He doesn't have the strength to stop us. We'll have nearly five thousand men by the time we get here."

"The defense always has at least a two-to-one edge," Alec quoted at him. "With someone as clever as Douglas, you'll need every man you can get. Remember, he's been preparing these defenses for years. Why throw the men right into his guns?"

"And what would your military genius suggest?" Somehow, when Kobol became angry or upset, his voice went from its normal irritable nasal tone into a positively adenoidal whine.

Alec glanced up at him. "You have an advantage in numbers. Use it! Attack over a broad front, spread Douglas' troops thin trying to defend such a large area. Bypass the firebases and strongpoints . . ."

"And have them chop us to shreds?" Kobol flared.

"They can't. I've seen what they've got there. No more than ten rounds apiece for most of the heavy guns. They'll shell you until they're out of ammunition, then they'll either have to come out and engage us in small patrol kinds of actions, or sit on their hilltops and wait until we come after them."

Kobol said nothing, but his head was rocking back and forth in an unspoken negative.

"The firebases can discourage small attacks, or attacks that are localized enough—where the attackers are so concentrated that a few high-explosive shells can tear them apart. But a broad, thin screen of attackers, moving quickly and staying as far away from the firebases as possible, will make the firebases almost useless."

"Makes sense," muttered one of Kobol's men, sitting on the bench beside him.

"If he's right about the amount of ammunition they have for their big guns."

"I'm right," Alec snapped. "If it'll make you feel any better, we can grab a couple of the closest firebases the night before the attack. But the others, deeper inside Douglas' territory, we should bypass."

Kobol shook his head more vigorously. "I don't like leaving pockets of enemy troops in our rear. They'll be fully armed and able to . . ."

Alec slammed a fist on the table. "Dammit, what's our objective? Capturing hilltops or Douglas' headquarters? *Here's* what we're after!" He jabbed a finger at the base. "If we inch along one hill at a time, he can spend all summer delaying us and gathering strength from the farther countryside. By autumn we'll be surrounded and starving. We've got to strike hard and fast. Here." He touched the base area again.

"And those men in the firebases and strongpoints will just sit there and let us walk in?"

"That's right!" Alec insisted. "There are only ten or so men in each spot. No more than twenty apiece. But they're heavily armed. If we try to attack them, they can hold us up until Douglas brings his reserves onto the scene. But if we bypass them, what can a dozen or two men do to a whole column of troops? They'll be surprised, confused, cut off from help. If they come down from their hills to attack, they'll be cut to pieces."

"They've still got that artillery."

"After the first half hour of fighting, the artillery will be out of ammo."

"They could still knock off a lot of trucks and men."

"Not if we move fast and stay spread out."

"I don't know . . ." Kobol hesitated.

More quietly, Alec said, "I *do* know. We're going to

do it this way. We can win quickly and with low casualties." The back of his mind was whispering, *And I can get to Angela before anyone else does.*

Kobol was staring at him, eyes glittering. "It's not your decision to make."

"Yes it is."

His hands spread flat on the map, as if to ensure ownership, Kobol said, "You can't possibly assume that you're still . . ."

"I am in command," Alec said evenly. "No one has relieved me of command. You'll take orders from me, Martin."

Kobol tried to laugh, but it froze in his throat. His mouth twitched. He glanced at the men sitting on either side of him.

Alec said nothing. For a long wordless minute they sat facing each other; Alec with his two youngsters and Kobol with his men flanking him.

"I think Alec's plan will work," Jameson said. He was still leaning against the hatchway. The gun at his hip loomed enormous. He was slightly turned, facing Kobol, gunhand free and resting easily at his side.

"The men I've assembled don't know you," Kobol said to Alec. "They won't take orders from you."

"They know me," Jameson said flatly. "They'll follow where I lead them."

Kobol glared up at Jameson and let his breath out in a hiss of frustrated rage. "So that's the way it's going to be."

"That's the way it is," Jameson answered, as calm as a hawk circling its prey.

"All right," Alec said. "To prevent any misunderstandings, Martin, I think you'd better stay with me until the army gets here. Ron, you take this boat back and assume command of the troops."

A smile flickered across Jameson's face. "You're giving

them a lot more dignity than they deserve. They're not troops, they're just a big gang. Hardly any discipline. They'll come up here for the spoils, and they'll fight—your way, Alec. They'd never stand up in a toe-to-toe battle."

"Whatever you want to call them, then," Alec said. "Get back to them and move them up here. As soon as the ground's dry enough to move fast, we attack."

"And when you get back to the settlement," Kobol seethed, "I'll have you executed. I'll make your mother sign your death warrant!"

Alec smiled at him. "That's assuming that *you* make it back to the settlement, Martin."

# Chapter Nineteen

The rain was steady, heavy, and driven by a numbingly cold wind. The ground beneath the horse's hooves was unending mud that made obscene sucking noises with every laborious step. The horse was big, but it couldn't go much further without rest, Alec knew.

But he pressed on, urging the horse forward with his boots. He was heavily muffled inside a leather coat and hood, but the wetness had seeped into him until he felt that icewater was trickling through his veins.

Squinting into the rain and mist, Alec saw that the little stream he had reached had turned into a churning white-foamed channel that carried tree branches and other debris madly onward.

*He won't be able to ford that*, he knew.

"Ho-ho!" a familiar voice called. "There you are!"

Turning slightly in the slippery saddle, Alec saw Will Russo's bulky form pacing slowly out of the mists, leading a tired-looking horse step by sloshing step through the mud.

"How'd you cross the stream?" Alec blurted.

"Oh, further upstream. It's not so bad up there."

Alec got off his horse and walked toward the advancing man. "Is your wound all healed?" he asked.

Will nodded and a thatch of red hair, glistening with dampness, flopped down from under his hood. "Been fine for months now. Got back to Utica and, by golly, the rest of the whiskey was still there. You?"

"I'm okay."

Will grinned at him. "Look, let's get out of this weather. There's a little cave a bit further upstream."

They led the horses through the mud and rain for a few minutes and found the cave. It was more of a purposely dug shelter than a natural cleft in the hillside. The inner walls were smooth and even, Alec noticed.

"I was glad to get the message your scout gave our scout," Will said once they had pulled the horses inside the narrow shelter. "I was worried about you, you know."

Alec was unbuttoning his coat. "Nothing in here for a fire . . ." he muttered.

"That's okay." Will rummaged through the pockets of his voluminous coat. "Brought a little . . . aha! Here it is." He produced a small dark brown bottle. "Saved you some of the whiskey."

They both took long pulls from the bottle. Alec could feel the liquor burning out the dampness inside him.

"Well," Will said, as pleasantly as if they were lounging together on the moon, "what did you want to talk about? Not the weather, I presume."

Alec laughed. "No, not that." Then, more seriously, "You know what's going to happen when the ground hardens, don't you?"

Will tried to erase the smile from his face, but he was only partially successful. "Yep. Kobol's bringing a whole raft of raiders and swamprunners up here to attack us. It's been tried before."

"You don't have to look so damned cheerful about it!" Alec snapped.

"Should I run and hide? Look, we've been through this kind of thing before. Why, the first winter Douglas and I . . ."

"You've never seen an army this big," Alec interrupted. "And they'll be better armed than any gang that's been put together since the sky burned."

"H'mm. Well. Is that what you came to tell me?"

"Yes. I want you to get out. Take Angela with you. I don't want either of you hurt."

"Leave Douglas? She'd never do that. Neither would I."

"You've got to!" Alec insisted. "There's no way for you to help him. He's the reason for the fighting, he's the one they're going to be after. If we can get him without risking your lives . . ."

But Will was shaking his head. "You don't understand, Alec. I can't leave Douglas. I'd sooner chop off my arm. We're friends, closer than brothers, really."

Alec said nothing.

"It's really Angela you're worried about, isn't it?"

"Yes."

"She's worried about you, too. She was damned sore when you left without even telling her you were going. I think she would have gone with you, I really do."

Alec shook his head.

"Well, that's all in the past. She sure as hell won't go anywhere now. She'd never leave Douglas, not with all this trouble brewing up . . ." A thought seemed to strike him. "Unless . . ."

"Unless what?"

Will grinned and answered, "Well, maybe if you were there at the base, helping us to fight off these riff-raff of Kobol's, then if things got really bad you could get her out and get to someplace safe."

Alec stared at him. *He's not putting me on,* he decided, watching the big man's innocent face. *He really believes what he just said.*

"Will," Alec said softly, "don't you realize that I can't fight on Douglas' side?"

"Oh, I don't know. There are a lot of things you don't realize, you know. He tried damned hard for a lot of years to get them to listen to reason back at the settlement. He didn't just decide to go off and make a kingdom for himself here on Earth. He was pushed. By Kobol and the others."

"The others?"

"Other members of the Council. Douglas was pushed out of power by those he trusted most. By those he loved most, too."

"Meaning my mother."

Completely serious now, Will nodded. "Alec, you probably won't believe me, and you may wind up hating me for even saying it, but . . . well, dammit, your mother helped to push Douglas into doing what he did. She knew he had no choice. She gave him nothing to return to, and they both knew it when he left on the mission to Earth. She didn't want him back."

The coldness clamped itself over Alec's body again. "You're right," he said, deadly soft. "I don't believe you."

The big redhead made a helpless gesture with his hands. "It's the truth."

"Maybe. Perhaps it's what he told you. But I'll never believe it. Never."

"That's . . . too bad."

"There's something you ought to know," Alec said. "I'm not just joining up with Kobol's forces. I'm leading them. I'm in command."

"I was afraid of that."

"Why?"

"Because we're going to have to try to kill each other. And we're friends," Will said.

"That's why I want you to get away. And take her with you."

"No, I can't do that. He's my friend too. And your father."

"I'm coming after him. Don't stand in the way. Don't try to protect him."

Sadly, in a voice so low that Alec barely heard it, Will said, "Don't make me choose between you and him, Alec. You'll lose."

"We've already made our choices," Alec said. "They were made ten years ago."

# Chapter Twenty

Even though they assembled as quickly as possible, it still took more than a week for Kobol's army to straggle all its various units together in a valley on the edge of Douglas' territory.

Alec had never seen so many human beings before. He stood on the crest of the highest hill in the area, under a maple tree that was just breaking out in young fresh leaves and watched the awesome sprawl of trucks, jeeps, horses, guns and men.

Ron Jameson was standing beside him. "That ought to be enough men to conquer the whole world," he said.

"I don't like having them all bunched together like this," Alec said. "If Douglas' people spot them, and if he's got any nuclear weapons or airplanes . . ."

"We've intercepted all his patrols," Jameson said calmly. "And I doubt that there are any nukes or planes left in the world."

"It would only take one."

With a slight shrug, Jameson countered, "We can be ready to move in two days. I think we can keep Douglas' patrols from finding us for that long."

"Two days?"

Nodding, "Check. The men have moved hard and fast to get here. They need time to catch their breath, get their weapons ready, and absorb your battle orders."

*That leaves me two days to deal with Kobol,* Alec thought.

"If we sit still for more than two days," Jameson added drily, "the different packs in this glorious conglomeration will start fighting each other. There's not an overabundance of trust or friendship down in that valley."

Alec nodded. "All right. Let's get to work."

It was fully night, after the evening meal, before Alec was able to get to Kobol. The older man was being held under virtual arrest in one of the caves that honeycombed the valley's hillsides.

His "room" was a small cavern whose sloping walls and roof were laced with stalactites of a thousand different colors. The only entrance was a narrow passage, barely wide enough for a man to squeeze through sideways. Alec had posted an armed guard at the outer end of the passage.

Kobol was sitting on an ancient, creaking bunk, his legs folded under him and his head bent down as he intently wrote in a rapid script on a paper he held in his lap. Alec saw that the bunk was covered with sheets of paper, all filled with his writing.

"Good evening," Alec said.

Kobol hardly looked up. A slightly raised eyebrow was his only greeting. Then he returned to his writing.

Alec said, "There's something I haven't told you."

"Oh?" Still not looking up.

"I know where the fissionables are stored."

The pen stopped moving across the page.

"I want you to head a special force to seize them before Douglas has a chance to destroy them."

That straightened Kobol's back. He pushed the paper off his lap and unfolded his long legs. Somehow it reminded Alec of a snake uncoiling. "You think he might sabotage them?"

"It's a possibility. He might even have them booby trapped, or set to go off in a nuclear explosion that will take everything with it."

Kobol frowned thoughtfully and ran a finger through his mustache.

Pulling the only chair in the room next to the bunk, Alec straddled it and went on, "You know more about the fissionables than any of us. It's a risky job, but a necessary one. Are you willing to do it?"

Almost smiling, Kobol said, "If I do, I'll only be in charge of a small suicide squad, while you're leading the grand army. If I succeed, it's under your command. If I fail, you get rid of an enemy."

"If you fail," Alec said, "we get rid of each other. And everyone else."

"And the settlement dies for lack of fissionables."

"Yes."

"When I get back to the settlement I'll still accuse you of treason."

Alec let a smile form itself. "Won't that be a bit hard to prove if you have the fissionables?"

"I'll prove it."

"Go ahead and try."

Kobol swayed back a little, then seemed to tense, as if poised to strike. "If I accept this job and get the fissionables, do you promise me safe conduct back to the settlement?"

"You mean, will I have you shot after we win the battle?"

"That's one way to phrase it."

"You'll be safe. We can settle our differences back at the settlement."

"My safety for the fissionables," Kobol mused. "It's a deal."

Alec nodded. Neither man offered his hand to the other. Alec rose from the chair and started toward the passageway entrance. Halfway there, he paused and turned back to Kobol.

"I haven't asked you for a similar guarantee—that you won't try to kill me before we get back to the settlement."

Kobol started to reply, but Alec went on, "I don't need your promise. I couldn't trust it, anyway. Just keep this in mind. If you try to kill me, I'll kill you. Even if you're successful, there are a dozen or more men who'll chop you into bite-sized pieces afterward. That's a promise."

He left Kobol sitting on the bunk, looking angry.

On the morning of the third day the attack began.

It had been a hectic two days, getting the men and equipment ready, keeping Douglas' increasingly heavier patrols from penetrating to the valley, briefing Kobol and putting together his special unit of trucks, keeping in touch with the satellite for constant updates on the weather forecast.

It rained the night before the attack. The troops moved out of the valley and spread to their positions, arcing across nearly half of Douglas' defensive perimeter. They moved swiftly despite the rain, most of them on horseback, but the shock wave all on trucks and jeeps. Each unit was completely mobile, no foot soldiers. The armored trucks mounted lasers, the jeeps bore machine guns and rocket launchers. The cavalry carried everything from automatic rifles to crossbows.

*The rain's kept Douglas' patrols down and screened our deployment*, Alex told himself. Then he added, *I hope.* He stood on the laser mount platform of an armored truck. The sun was just starting to edge above the eastern hills, turning the still-clouded sky pink and mauve. The rain had stopped half an hour earlier, as predicted by the satellite observers; the ground was wet but not especially muddy.

Alec wore a battle helmet, and could hear the crosstalk of a hundred different unit commanders by switching frequencies on the dial on one of the earphones. They had chosen the frequencies carefully to be out of the range of Douglas' radio receivers. Each sector commander checked in, and finally Alec asked Jameson, "Ron, how's it look on your end?"

Jameson's voice was crisp and calm in his earphones. "Everything all set here. All unit and sector commanders ready and eager to go."

Alec glanced at his wristwatch. Five-fifty. The attack was planned to start at six, when Douglas' men should be starting their breakfasts, looking to their cookfires rather than watching for an attack.

As he waited for the watch hands to crawl along, Alec's mind filled with images of all the things he had been through: the storms, the cold, the mud. And the nights with Angela, the warmth of the fire, the heat of their passion. And the towering gray old man who had driven him away.

With a shake of his head, he focused his thoughts on the reality before him. The morning was clearing rapidly, the clouds breaking up and scuttling away on a fresh, clean breeze. The sun was bright and already starting to feel warm on his shoulders and neck.

"Minus ten seconds," he muttered to himself.

Turning the dial on his earphone to the general frequency, Alec heard the chime tone that confirmed that the frequency was tuned in and open.

"All sector and unit commanders . . . commence attack. *Now.*"

The truck he was standing on lurched forward, then gained speed smoothly as it climbed toward the top of the hill on which it had been waiting. Behind it, three other trucks and a pair of jeeps trundled along. The jeeps passed Alec's truck, speeding toward the crest of the hill.

They reached the top and started downslope. Putting the binoculars to his eyes, Alec could see the thin strand of fence wire winding across the rolling countryside, several klicks ahead. Two watchtowers were in view, and a hill crowned with a firebase stood off near the horizon.

*They've seen us now,* he knew, watching the figures atop one of the towers moving rapidly and gesticulating. *Are they surprised? Or have they been waiting for us? Are they as scared as I am?* And Alec realized that his heart was racing, he could feel it pounding in his throat, hear it in his ears, amplified by the 'phones clamped to the sides of his head.

They sped toward the fence and off to his right Alec could see a squad of cavalry troops riding hard to keep pace with them. The jeeps were up ahead, flickers of fire danced at the tops of the watchtowers, but Alec could hear nothing except the rush of the wind as his truck tore forward.

The lead jeep fired a missile at the watchtower and Alec followed its smoky exhaust as it passed within a few meters of the tower's top, then arced into the empty ground inside the fence and exploded.

"We're in range of the fence," shouted the gunner, sitting in the plastic jumpseat that jutted out to one side of the massive laser mount.

Alec turned to him. "Burn it down."

The laser's special power generator hummed into life and then its vibration was drowned out by the high-pitched whine of the laser itself. The beam was invisible, but where it touched the fence the wire mesh flashed into incandescence and charred and curled like the wick of a candle.

The jeeps swerved toward the opening and the laser

gunner swung his attention to the watchtowers. The nearest one was still firing until the energy beam touched it with its burning finger. The tower top burst into flame.

And then they were through the fence, racing across the bumpy countryside. The wind tore at Alec's face. The jeeps were both intact and pulling even further ahead of them, swinging left to put as much distance as possible between themselves and the firebase's artillery. Glancing toward the rear, Alec saw the cavalry squad pouring through the gap in the fence without hesitation. Both watchtowers were burned and silent.

He saw a flash from the hilltop and an instant later the ground erupted far off to his right. The dull heavy roar of the explosion reached him as the black cloud hurled visible chunks of earth high into the air.

*Get past the firebases and engage Douglas' mobile reserve.* That was his mission. *Leave the firebases isolated and concentrate your forces on the reserves. Smash them before they can organize a counterattack.*

Two more artillery shells hit in front of them. The shock and noise hit simultaneously and the driver veered the truck hard to the left as debris pelted down on them. Alec could see a pair of smoking craters where the shells hit; they looked raw and painful in the gentle earth.

More shellbursts, but falling further behind now. Then one struck close enough to knock one of the jeeps over. It rolled crazily, scattering broken pieces of men and machinery across the grass, and finally came to rest on its side. As the truck swept past it, the jeep burst into flames. *No time to stop for the wounded. Not now.*

A gently sloping ridge rose ahead of them. Alec knew the countryside by heart. If there was going to be trouble anywhere, it would be at this ridge line. Douglas had been turning it into a natural defense line, adding man-made earthen embankments where the ridge itself flattened out, so that the ridge line completely encircled his base, twenty klicks out from the innermost fences. Between the ridge and the fences was nothing but open flat country.

They charged up the ridge, Alec hanging grimly to the rail of the laser mount, expecting land mines, more artillery fire, ground troops dug into trenches up at the top.

Nothing. The ridge was bare of defenders. The flat meadowlands stretched out ahead, and Alec could see other units of trucks, jeeps and cavalry dashing across the grassland already.

*Too easy*, he told himself. *Douglas couldn't possibly be taken so easily.*

But they plunged on, bouncing at breakneck speed down the ridge's rear slope and slewing out onto the flatland. Occasional explosions reminded them that the firebases were still active, but the artillery fire was desultory and did nothing to slow them. If anything, the hundreds of drivers urged extra speed from their electric motors whenever a shell burst near them.

Tense with a mixture of exhilaration and fear, Alec clicked his radio dial for Jameson's frequency. "Ron, where are you now?" he spoke into his helmet mike.

A heartbeat's delay, then, "We've just crested an artificial ramp of earth, about twenty klicks from the edge of the main base area. Not much opposition. Lost a truck that fell into a shell crater and a squad of cavalry that took a direct hit. Everybody else is moving at top speed. No sign of real resistance yet."

"All right. Keep moving and stay alert." He dialed the general frequency. "All unit commanders, report any delays or ground resistance other than artillery fire."

No response at all. The radio buzzed to itself.

Alec said, "All sector commanders, sound off in order."

"Sector one. No delays, no resistance." Jameson's voice.

"Sector two. No problems."

"Sector three. Goin' like hell, nobody in our way."

"Sector four . . ."

Alec's attention was pulled away by a tug on his sleeve. The gunner was leaning far forward in his seat, gesturing toward the rear of the speeding truck.

A trio of squat, heavy-looking gray shapes was topping the ridge behind them. With the sector commanders still reporting, Alec turned and raised his binoculars.

They were ugly-looking tracked vehicles, painted dark green and brown. Long cylinders poked from turrets. *Tanks!* Alec recalled seeing them on history tapes. The cylinders were cannon. *They might have lasers, too.*

"Hey, this is sector three. We've just picked up some sort of trucks or somethin' followin' us."

"All units," Alec shouted, "report on the numbers and positions of enemy tanks. They're rolling forts, heavily armored and carrying cannon."

As if in answer, one of the three tanks in Alec's rear belched flame and a shell exploded close enough to jar the speeding truck.

*That's Douglas' plan. He's had the tanks all along, probably spotted them at the firebases last week. Now he's got us caught between the tanks and his reserves.*

"Listen to me!" he yelled to the unit commanders. "Engage the tanks at your longest possible range with the lasers. Use your jeeps and cavalry to get behind them and destroy them at close range. Try to immobilize them. Go for their treads."

The radio sizzled with confused reports of fighting and losses. Alec clicked it off as another shell-burst lifted the truck entirely off its wheels momentarily and slammed him against the railing. Debris pelted him and stung. He tasted blood in his mouth.

Crouching down near the driver's cab, he shouted, "Zig-zag, dammit! Keep them guessing." He straightened and shouted to the gunner, "The treads, aim at their treads! Their armor's too thick to get through."

Then he realized that the gunner was hanging limply in his seat harness, head lolling, mouth agape and eyes sightlessly staring.

Alec reached over and unfastened the harness catch. The gunner slid out of his seat, rolled over the edge of the mount platform and bounced onto the ground. Another shell rocked the truck as Alec climbed into the seat, suddenly feeling as exposed as a patient stretched on a surgical table.

He swung the laser's sighting mirrors around and tried to hold them on the nearest tank. Flicking the fire controls onto the shortest possible pulse, he rattled off a train of microsecond bursts. The ground near the tank smoked and sputtered, but the tank itself appeared unhurt. The truck lurched violently as he tried again.

*Where the hell is everybody else?*

Alec fired three more times as shellfire racked the truck. He heard debris clanging against the truck's sides, then caught a glance of another truck as they zipped past it. It was gutted, wheels splayed, front end smashed in.

One of the tanks seemed to be turning in a tight circle. *Got its left tread!* Alec rejoiced. A half dozen mounted men were pulling up alongside it, unlimbering the rocket launchers and grenades they carried.

He turned his attention to the second tank and saw, beyond it, that the third was crawling with men clambering over it, like ants swarming on an invading scorpion.

*If we can knock off the tanks before Douglas' reserves get here . . .* Alec dialed the frequency for the other truck in his unit. "Get on the left side of that tank that's still fighting. I'll swing to his right. Spray him!"

They swung to the tank's flanks. The turret turned toward Alec's side and he fanned the laser beam to maximum width and sprayed the entire turret area. *Blind the bastards*, he raged to himself, hoping that the infrared energy would at least damage the periscopes poking from the turret. Then the tank bloomed into a roar of flame. The other truck's laser had found the engine ducts. The tank shuddered, then burst open like an overripe melon. Its fuel and ammunition exploding inside it, the tank's top turret hatch blew high into the air. With smoke and steam hissing from every joint and port in the heavy armor, the tank died like a dragon consumed by its own internal juices, hissing and rumbling and slowly disappearing in smoke.

It seemed like minutes, but it actually took nearly two hours before the tank counterattack was cleaned up. Alec's units helped each other where they could, but most of them had to fight their own battles, individual jousts of two or three tanks pitted against a handful of trucks and jeeps. The cavalry made the real difference. The horsemen scattered at the sight of the tanks, then while the tanks were engaging the trucks and jeeps, reformed in the rear and attacked with grenades and rocket missiles. Men leaped from horseback onto the tanks and stuffed grenades into the engine ducts or cracked the periscopes and rangefinders that poked vulnerably out from the armor. Blinded or immobile, the tanks were more deathtraps than weapons.

Douglas' reserves came up to join the battle long before the last of the tanks were destroyed, but they were either on horseback or riding lightly armored trucks. And they were spread thin. The breadth of Alec's attack had foiled Douglas' planned defense before the battle began, though neither side recognized this while the fighting raged.

As the battle eddied away from his sector, Alec ordered his truck back up to the top of the ridge that had masked the tanks' advance. From the high ground he could see much of the swirling, dust-clouded fight; and he had time to check his commanders by radio and direct their actions. *The tanks were a good idea,* he realized. *If we had come in a massive single thrust, they would have converged on us and clobbered us.* But with a broad, fluid advance there were no heavy concentrations of troops to squeeze in on, no massed targets for the tanks' guns.

Now, as he watched the field peppered with burning pyres and saw his laser trucks slicing through Douglas' lightly armored reserves, Alec calmly spoke orders into his helmet mike. Douglas' men were beginning to retreat; in some places, they seemed to be panicking and blindly racing away, especially where the laser trucks were burning everything they could reach.

It wasn't pretty. Alec knew his own casualties were mounting. The stench of death reached him, even high up on the ridge: burned flesh and the bitter fumes of explosives and burning oil. The noise was incessant, even through his heavy earphones: explosions punctuating the constant chatter of automatic weapons; roars and groans that might have been the voices of men, but so distorted and tortured that they were unrecognizable.

He climbed out of the gunner's seat and stood on the laser mount platform. His knees were shaky and his vision blurring.

*This is what you came for,* he told himself as he watched several thousand men trying to kill each other. *This is what your entire life has been aimed at.*

He grasped the binoculars that still hung on his chest and started to put them up to his eyes. But he hesitated. *What if I see Will's body out there?*

Jameson's flat unemotional voice in his earphones snapped him back to reality. "They're breaking on this end. All the fight's out of them."

"All right," Alec heard himself say. "Don't bother with the stragglers. Let them go. Make a dash for the base itself and try to take it before they can set up a last-ditch defense. I'll join you from this end of the line."

"Check. What about Kobol and his special unit?"

"He'll follow my squad."

"Right. I presume you'll give the necessary orders in your usual crisp, military fashion."

Jameson had sensed Alec's depression. Despite himself, Alec grinned. "Yes, yes. Move out in five minutes, no more."

"We're moving."

Alec quickly checked with the other sector commanders. The battle was disintegrating into a series of separate little skirmishes. Douglas' troops were struggling for their lives now, trying to escape or simply survive. Alec ordered all commanders to ignore retreating enemy troops and offer a surrender to pockets of men still fighting. Half of each unit he ordered to race for Douglas' headquarters.

As his own truck started bumpily down the ridge to take the lead of one column that was forming up, Alec relayed his orders to Kobol, who had been waiting back at their takeoff point.

"Now?" Kobol sounded shocked. "You're heading for the base now?"

"That's right," Alec said as the truck lurched past a clattering collection of other trucks and jeeps. "We've broken Douglas' main force. It's nothing more than a mop-up operation now." He silently added, *unless Douglas has more surprises up his sleeve.*

Kobol mumbled something vaguely sounding like

congratulations and promised he'd be on his way immediately.

"Steer clear of the firebases," Alec warned. "They're still enemy-held. Those guys might be in a mood to spend the rest of their ammunition on you."

Before Kobol could respond, Alec clicked the radio off, grinning to himself.

*It can't be this easy*, Alec warned himself. But he answered, *What else could he have? He's used more men than I ever saw at the base. He can't have much more.*

As they sped over the battlefield, whizzing past burned-out tanks and trucks, past twisted bodies and moaning, maimed men, past gaping shell holes and grass made slippery with blood, Alec began to realize that it hadn't been so easy after all. Quick, but not easy.

He directed his column to a road, one of the packed-earth trails that he and Will Russo had ridden. It turned around the shoulders of the last few hillocks, darted under a copse of newly leafed maples and beech trees, and then the first buildings came into view.

The column of trucks and jeeps fanned out across the hummocky grass as they approached. The lasers burned down the fence quickly. The watchtowers here seemed to be empty, unguarded and unguarding. Alec scanned the base area with his binoculars as they raced past the still-smoking remains of the innermost fence. A few people were dashing about in the streets, racing for the shelter of buildings.

Jameson reported, "We're less than a kilometer from the western end of the base. No resistance. Hardly any sign of life."

"Slow down," Alec commanded. "Proceed with cautions, but keep advancing." He pulled a hand-drawn map of the base from his jacket and told Jameson which buildings his troops should seize. "Get the defenders out of the buildings and into the open. Herd them onto the runways of the old airfield."

"Check," Jameson said.

Alec gave similar orders to all his unit commanders, then headed his own truck straight for the row of houses where Angela and Will and Douglas had lived. As the truck rolled alone through the streets between three- and four-story buildings, Alec realized what a target he made for snipers, standing alone on the back of the truck alongside the gleaming metal bulk of the laser.

*So shoot*, he silently told his enemies. *You'll never get a better chance than now.*

But there was no firing anywhere. Not even a sign of life in this part of the base. The houses looked cold and empty as the truck pulled up along the dead-end street that they lined. *They've gone*, Alec told himself, and realized that he was a fool for thinking they might still be here.

He made the driver stop in front of Angela's house. Swinging down off the truck, pistol flapping at his hip, heavy helmet on his head, Alec remembered the night he had left. Somehow he had never pictured his return as being quite like this: the conqueror striding into the desolate enemy camp.

The house was empty. The fireplace cold. It looked dusty, abandoned, as though no one had lived there for weeks. Perhaps months.

Grimly, Alec marched down the street toward Douglas' house. He knew it was foolish, but still . . .

He glanced over his shoulder at the driver, sitting alone in the buttoned-up armored cab of the truck. The man had lowered the front armor panel so that he'd have more than just a slit to allow fresh air inside. He wore his helmet and his hands were on the steering wheel. *Ready to leave at an instant's notice*, Alec saw. *Constructive cowardice. The man who wants to save his ass is the man who's got a chance to live through the day.*

Fifteen paces from Douglas' house, Alec froze.

A mechanical whirring sound, faint but real, stopped him. Like the sound of a gun mount tracking. He edged off the walkway and stepped close to the shrubbery that was just beginning to turn green, next to the house. One hand on his pistol, Alec carefully looked over the empty-seeming street.

Nothing.

Then the sound came again, from behind him. He whirled and crouched as he drew the gun from its holster. Still nothing in view. But there was *something*. Something was different, something that hadn't been here before.

A glint in the corner of his eyes. A metal pole, strapped hastily against the house with an antenna jury-rigged at the top of it. New, still bright in the late afternoon sunlight that lanced through the smoke-grayed sky. A cable led down from the antenna to a second-floor window.

The antenna turned, making a mechanical whirring sound as the little electric motor moved it.

Alec tightened his grip on the pistol and commanded himself to stop trembling. He waved to the truck driver to get his attention, then tapped his helmet earphones. It took a few moments before the driver understood and asked, "Yeah?"

Whispering, Alec ordered, "Get Jameson and tell him to bring a squad of men here. On the double."

"Right."

Slowly, as quietly as he could, Alec moved along the side of the house and around to the back door. It was unlocked. He pushed it inward gently, almost smiling at Douglas' insistence on good maintenance: the hinges did not squeak.

Once inside, he could hear a muffled voice from upstairs. It sounded like Douglas. *Alone? Why would he be here, and not out in the open with his men?*

Alec took the steps three at a time, but very slowly, crouching low and keeping the gun ready for any surprises. With all the stealth he could manage, he got to the top of the stairs and moved to the door of the bedroom where Douglas' voice was coming from.

Then he flung the door open and leaped into the room.

The door banged against the wall as Alec landed on the balls of his feet, crouched, balanced, gun rock-steady in his hand.

Half the room was filled with radio gear, gray and black boxes jumbled together, dials glowing. A wild tangle of wires linked the seeming chaos to a thick cable that wormed its way out through the window that was jammed shut over it.

Douglas sat in the bed, an old-fashioned microphone in one huge fist. His left leg was poking out straight from the hip, encased in a white plastic cast. His trousers had been cut away at the hip. His face looked thinner than before, his hair and beard grayer. His clothes and the bedsheets were rumpled and sweaty-looking. A carbine lay on the bed beside him, with several boxes of ammunition stacked on the table next to the bed.

For an instant Alec stood there unmoving.

Then Douglas said, "Well, it's about time you got here. What kept you?"

# Chapter Twenty-One

Alec blinked at his father. "What happened to your leg?"

Glowering, Douglas said, "Thrown from a goddamned horse, would you believe it? Four days ago. Have to sit out the whole goddamned battle here and try to run things by radio." He tossed the microphone down on the bed. It bounced and clattered to the floor.

"You could save a lot of lives by telling . . ."

"I've already ordered my people to stop fighting," Douglas grumbled. "That's what I was doing while you were trying to sneak up the stairs." He waved a hand at Alec. "You can put that popgun away, I'm not going to try to shoot you. This thing isn't even loaded."

Alec went to the bed and took the carbine. He leaned it against the doorjamb, then holstered his gun.

"You fought a smart fight," Douglas said grudgingly. "I didn't expect you to be spread out."

Pulling up the room's only chair, Alec heard himself responding, "I didn't expect you to have tanks."

"Think I showed you everything?" Douglas laughed.

"Where is she?"

"Angela? I packed her off to one of the villages a week ago. Told her to stay there until the fighting's over. She'll be back."

"And Will?"

Douglas shook his head. "Last I heard, his horse had

been shot out from under him. Don't worry about him, though; he leads a charmed life."

Suddenly there was nothing to talk about. Everything to be said, but nothing to talk about.

Douglas broke the silence. "So you've won."

"Yes, I've won."

"What are your plans?"

Alec glanced out the window, then returned his gaze to his father's haggard face. "I came for the fissionables. I'll take them back to the settlement."

"You know where they're stored?"

"You showed me, remember?"

"Oh . . . yes, that's right."

"Kobol's got a trained crew to take care of them."

"Kobol. H'mm."

Alec blurted, "They'll want to execute you. You're a traitor."

"I've known that all along," Douglas said easily. "If it weren't for this damned leg, though, I wouldn't have been so easy to catch."

"He's going to marry mother."

"Kobol? Good! Serves him right. She'll have him sliced and neatly served on a platter inside of a year. They deserve each other."

Alec felt his insides tightening.

"No, don't go stupid, son," Douglas said. "Kobol's been after her for years. And she's been letting him chase her. Even before I left. In fact, it's one of the reasons why I did leave. They were being damned obvious, even then."

"You expect me to believe that?"

Grinning wickedly, Douglas said, "I don't give a damn what you believe. I've accomplished what I set out to do. My work's just about finished now. Yours is just starting."

"What? What do you mean?"

Before Douglas could answer, a trio of trucks pulled up in front of the house and the voices of two dozen men filled the air. Doors slammed open, boots clumped on stairs.

Jameson stepped into the bedroom. "You okay?" he asked Alec.

Nodding, Alec got up from the chair. "This is Douglas Morgan," he said. "Keep this house guarded. No one goes in or out unless I personally grant permission. I'll set up my headquarters in the first house on this street, where my truck is parked."

"Right," Jameson said.

Douglas spoke up. "I presume the condemned man will get a meal sometime this evening?"

Alec couldn't look him in the face anymore. To Jameson he said, "See to it."

Then he left his father sitting on the bed, surrounded by the armed strangers.

Alec ate his dinner alone in Angela's house, the first hot meal he'd had in many days. He was almost finished when Kobol burst into the tiny bungalow.

"We've got it!" he crowed, pushing past the protesting guard who had been stationed outside the front door.

Alec looked up. Kobol was jubilant. "Got what?" Alec asked.

"The fissionables! Enough to last the settlement fifty years, at least."

"And then what?"

Kobol stopped. He stood uncertainly before the rough wooden table at which Alec sat. His smile of triumph began to crumble.

"What do you mean?"

And suddenly Alec began to understand part of what Douglas had been telling him. "What then? What happens to the settlement after fifty years?"

Kobol shook his head, a short snap to either side, like a horse shaking off a gadfly. "They'll find more, of course. Fifty years is a long time; we won't be around to worry about it."

"No," Alec said. "I suppose not."

"I'm ordering a pair of shuttles down to start loading the fissionables at first light tomorrow."

"All right."

"And I want Douglas packed aboard too. They'll be waiting for him back at the settlement."

Alec pushed his unfinished plate away from him and stood up. "No."

"Eh? What do you mean?"

"I mean *no.* You're not taking Douglas back to the settlement. We'll handle him right here. I'll take care of it."

"No you won't." Kobol's tone hardened. "You've been riding pretty high, but it's time you realized that I'm a Council member and I have the final say in . . ."

Alec pulled his gun from its holster. "Martin, you can take the fissionables and yourself back to the settlement tomorrow. I'll follow you there shortly. But Douglas stays here. He chose to live on Earth, he might as well be buried on Earth. If you want to be buried here too, then just say one more word." Alec's voice was as soft as the fur of a leopard. "One more word. Go ahead."

Kobol's mouth opened, but no sound came from it. He snapped it shut with an audible clicking of teeth.

"Good," Alec said. "Now get out of here and go about your work. Leave Douglas to me. And keep your hands off my mother until I return to the settlement. You can be killed there as well as here. Remember that."

His face red and seething, Kobol turned and stamped out of the house.

Alec holstered the gun and sat down to finish his meal. But he was no longer hungry. Suddenly he felt old, grayer than his father, weary and miserable and completely alone.

The guard opened the front door a crack. "Sir?"

"What is it?"

"We have a prisoner here . . . someone you said you wanted to see."

"Will Russo?"

"That's who he says he is, sir."

"Send him in!" Alec rose again and came around the table.

Will was caked with grime, and his clothing was torn in several places. But when he stepped into the house and saw Alec, his big sheepish grin spread across his face.

"You weren't fooling about a big army, were you?"

Alec had his hand out and Will grabbed it.

"Are you all right?" Alec asked. "Have you eaten? Are you hurt?"

"I'm starving, but otherwise okay . . . your boys had us pinned down for six hours; never saw so many guns and lasers in my life."

Alec sat him at the table and told the guard to bring food. He watched as Will wolfed down everything in sight and washed it all down with a liter of fresh cow's milk.

"Which village did Angela go to?" Alec asked as Will ate.

"Dunno," Will said, his mouth bulging. "But she'll be here. She'll want to see Douglas, tend to him."

*Tend to him,* Alec thought jealously.

"You took a lot of casualties?" he changed the subject.

Will nodded. "It was pretty heavy out there. You had us outgunned and outsmarted."

"I'm glad you weren't hurt."

Will grinned. "So 'm I!" Abruptly, he grew somber. "But a lot of good men died today. A lot of good men."

"Yes," Alec agreed. "But at least it's over now."

"Over? Oh no. By golly, it's really just beginning."

"Begin . . . what do you mean?"

"Ask Douglas about it," Will replied. "I'm surprised he hasn't told you about it already."

"Told me what?"

But all Will would say was, "Ask Douglas."

"Dammit!" Alec snapped. "You know he's under arrest for treason. Kobol wants to bring him back to the settlement and make a public exhibit out of him."

"You won't let them?"

"No, I won't. But I can't let him live, either."

Will shrugged.

"Technically, you're as guilty as he is," Alec added. "But it's Douglas they want to punish. You won't have to . . ."

"No," Will said. And there was iron in it.

Alec stared at him.

"I'm Douglas' man. What happens to him happens to me. I'm as guilty as he is. We planned this thing together. Kill him and you've got to kill me, too. Or else."

"Or else what?"

"Or else I'll hunt you down and kill you."

"Hell's fire, Will! You're talking like a medieval barbarian."

"Maybe that's what I am. Maybe that's what we all are. I love you like my own son, Alec. But if you kill that man I won't be able to rest until I've revenged him."

"Jesus Christ."

"Exactly," said Will Russo.

It was late when Alec walked down the lonely street to Douglas' house. Late and dark. The spring night had turned cold; the stars glittered with winter hardness. The street was deserted except for the two guards lounging near the truck parked at the cul-de-sac end of the street.

All of Douglas' people in the base had been disarmed and penned into a few of the big barracks buildings. No women at all had been found in the base. Tomorrow, Alec knew, the women would start returning from the outlying villages. So would the crews of the firebases.

The guards straightened up when they recognized Alec. He saw that they had a small grill plugged into the truck's generator, and were warming themselves with it.

"Chilly night," Alec said to them.

"Sure is."

He nodded to them and went inside Douglas' house. Two more men were drowsing in the living room. They snapped to their feet when Alec let the door bang shut.

"Everything quiet in here?" he asked.

"Yessir." They both looked embarrassed, even a touch fearful.

Without another word, Alec tiptoed up the steps and pushed at the door to Douglas' room. The old man was sitting on the bed in almost exactly the same position that Alec had left him earlier. He was wearing glasses now, however, and reading a battered, well-thumbed book. Alec squinted at the cover, but it was too worn to make out the title.

"Come on in," Douglas said, barely looking up from the book. "I've been waiting for you."

Alec stepped into the room and took the chair. Something was making him feel edgy, nervous. As he sat down, he realized that Douglas' voice was no longer the booming, demanding, self-assured roar it had once been. He was quieter, his voice subdued. *From defeat?* Alec found that hard to believe.

Douglas waggled the book. "Found this in a city library, years ago. Hemingway. *The Fifth Column and the First Forty-Nine.* Forty-nine short stories, that is. Magnificent."

Alec shrugged.

"So." Douglas put the book down on the table beside his bed. The radio equipment had been cleared away; nothing was left except the torn end of the cable still hanging from the room's one window. "You've come to see if I'm comfortable and enjoyed my meal?"

"No."

"Come to read my death sentence?" Douglas actually looked amused.

"Not that either," Alec said. "I've come to find out what you meant when you said your work's nearly finished, but mine is just beginning. Will said something very much like it a couple of hours ago . . ."

"You've seen Will?" Douglas asked eagerly. "He's all right?"

"He's fine. Hungry as a bear . . ."

"And thirsty, I'll bet."

Alec felt a grin bend his lips. "Yes, I imagine so."

"But you've finally started to tumble to the fact that there's more to life than beating your old man, eh?"

Alec hunched forward in his chair. "I want to know what all these mysterious hints are about."

"It's not too complicated," Douglas said. "Everything's worked out pretty much as I had planned it. I admit that I expected to beat you today, rather than the other way around. But the plan can work either way."

"What plan?" Alec demanded, suddenly irritated.

Douglas smiled at him. A genuinely benign, paternal smile. "The plan to reunite humankind. The plan to rebuild civilization."

"That!"

"Yes, that. It happens to be the reason for everything I've done over the past ten years and more. But now it's going to be up to you to put the plan into action."

Alec shook his head.

"Listen to me!" Douglas snapped, with some of his old fire. Jabbing a thick finger at him, he said, "It's finally been accomplished. Don't you understand that? Look around you, what do you see? And I don't mean just this room. What's happened out there today?"

"We beat you."

"Who beat me?"

"We did—the army that Kobol put together and I led."

"And who's in that army?"

Puzzled, Alec answered, "Who's in it? People from all over: as far south as Florida, as close as some of the villages just over the hills from here."

"And who else?" Douglas' eyes were gleaming.

Alec thought a moment. "Us," he finally realized. "Men from the settlement."

Douglas leaned back on his pillows, satisfied. "Excellent. You got the right answer with only a few prods. You might make a real leader yet. An army made up of bands of men who've been fighting each other for the past fifty years—raiders and farmers, city barbarians and fishermen from the warm country—plus you lunar people with your high technology. For the first time since the sky burned, an organization of Earth and moon people, working together."

Alec blinked at him. "What's so marvelous about that?"

"I'll tell you." Douglas was obviously enjoying this, and his voice had regained some of its former strength. "When the sky burned, civilization on Earth ended. But on the moon we were all right—for the time being. Then the leaders in the settlement got the notion that there was nothing they could do to help what was left of Earth's people."

"They were right," Alec said. "They were barely able to survive themselves, those first years."

"They were right, *at that time*," Douglas corrected. "But that doesn't make the decision right for all time.

From that first decision, it was a short step for the next generation to tell itself that the lunar settlement could survive on its own, and all they wanted from Earth was an occasional supply of the things that couldn't be produced on the moon."

"The fissionables."

"And medicines, plants, other things. So while the lunar people were looking down their noses at the so-called barbarians of Earth, it was the settlement people who were really acting like barbarians: raiding Earth for what they wanted but could not or would not produce for themselves. *That's* barbarism!"

"Now wait . . ."

But Douglas plowed on, "The truth is, the settlement can't survive on its own and never could. Genetically it's a dead end. Already the cancer rate and birth defects are skyrocketing."

Shaking his head, Alec said, "We've been through all this before."

"Indeed we have. But now we have the opportunity to set things straight. "You're in command of a joint Earth-moon army. You're sitting on the fissionables that the settlement wants. You can *force* them to start working with the people here on Earth, to start rebuilding civilization in earnest. What I've done is to set the stage. Now you can make the dream actually happen."

Alec felt the strength sag out of him. His jaw fell open. When he realized he was gaping, he straightened up in the chair and said, "Me? You want me . . ." He ran out of words.

"Yes, you," Douglas said gently. "I've been waiting for you for ten years, son."

"But you tried to kill me!"

"No I didn't. I tried to see what you were made of. I set up conditions that would test you, so we could *both* find out what you were made of. You came through in good shape. You survived. What's more, you learned. You understand now exactly what I'm saying, and you agree with every word of it, I can see."

"No . . ."

"Yes!" Douglas was beaming now. "*You're* the leader of this entire ramshackle alliance. *You're* the one man with the power to force those hothouse lovelies in the settlement to rejoin their brothers here on Earth. Alone, separated from the knowledge and technology of the moon, Earth's civilization will never be rekindled. Nobody knows that better than I do! I've spent ten years bringing a minuscule number of people back from absolute barbarism as far as a feudal society."

His fists clenched. "But the lunar settlement—alone, separated from Earth, cut off from the lifeblood of the human race, the genetic pool—the settlement will die. There's no other word for it. They'll all be dead within another two generations. Three, at most."

Alec heard Kobol's voice in his mind, his response to Alec's question about what would happen when the fissionables ran out: "*Fifty years is a long time, we won't be around to worry about it.*"

"You're worrying about my children," Alec said to his father.

"Your grandchildren."

"But why did you set up this battle? Why couldn't we have done this peacefully?"

The grin on Douglas' bearded face turned sardonic. "Would you have believed me? I tried to tell you. And do you think those barbarians out there would have kindly consented to work together in sweet brotherhood for the furtherance of an ideal they can't even imagine? They have no conception of what civilization means, you know. Not even the best of them. Oh, they'll follow a leader that they trust—someone who brings them victories and loot. But all they really understand is survival, and survival means fighting." He paused, but only for an instant. "What brought all those fine fighting men here? A yearning for culture or a chance for loot?"

"Loot, of course," Alec answered.

"Damned right. And you'd better keep them happy, too, until you can halfway civilize them. Get them at least up to the standard of loyalty of the old Mongol hordes. You can build a civilization with warriors like that, even though they themselves are barbarians."

But a new thought was buzzing into Alec's awareness. "You . . . what am I supposed to do with you?"

Douglas snorted. "Kill me, of course! I'm superfluous now. I'm a problem for you. My men will stay loyal to me as long as I'm alive, and the people in the settlement won't trust me and won't trust you if you let me live."

"But your men won't follow me if I have you executed." *It's insane! You don't sit in a bedroom and talk to your father about killing him!*

"They'll follow Will, and Will is fully aware of the plan. That's why it was important for both of you to survive the battle."

"It's crazy," Alec muttered.

"No," Douglas corrected. "It's politics. A little rougher than the polite debating orgies you've seen in the settlement, but basically the same thing. To make yourself leader of the whole coalition, you've got to get rid of me."

"I came to Earth to kill you."

"Good!" Douglas boomed. "Then we're agreed on it."

Alec jumped up from the chair, knocking it over backwards behind him. "No! I can't do it. I can't!"

"Don't be an idiot," Douglas snapped. "You've got to."

But Alec bolted from the room and ran down the stairs and outside into the night.

# Chapter Twenty-Two

Alec didn't sleep that night. Not that he could have, even if he tried. Because the motley collection of troops that made up his army had already started to loot the base.

The first thing that they found was that there were no women. Then they realized that Alec had ordered Jameson to lock up all the weapons, ammunition, and vehicles. These and the prisoners—Douglas' men—were closely guarded by lunar troops. So they turned to the warehouses, out along the old airfield, and started to tear them apart. They found enough food and wine to bolster their spirits, and enough flammables to start several of the buildings ablaze.

Jameson was waiting for Alec when he returned to the bungalow after visiting his father. Striding down the short street, Alec had seen the glow of the warehouse fires.

"Might be a good idea to let them have their fun tonight," Jameson said.

"They've enough fun already," Alec countered. "Get fifty men and four laser trucks. Find Will Russo and get him to join us, with a dozen of his most reliable men."

Jameson let an instant's skepticism flash across his face.

Alec said, "If we let them dissolve into rabble they'll be killing each other by sunrise."

"There is that," Jameson admitted thoughtfully.

In less than an hour, they met at the motor pool, an ancient garage where voices boomed hollowly off the metal walls and silent trucks. Alec didn't discuss the situation, he laid down a battle plan.

"They're rampaging through the warehouses, burning whatever they can't carry. We'll converge on the warehouse area from three different directions," he traced lines with his finger on the map spread across the oil-smeared table before him, "and get them under control."

Jameson was still doubtful.

"If they decide to fight us . . ."

"They won't if we work things properly," Alec said.

Will Russo nodded his agreement.

Three columns of heavily armed troops converged on the burning warehouses and the drunken, raging men. In the guttering light of the fires that crackled through warehouse windows and roofs, the looters slowly realized that they were being hemmed into one open area where the streets in this sector of the base came together.

Alec stood on the back of a laser truck with a powerphone in his hand.

"Listen to me," he commanded, his voice magnified to the dimensions of godhood. "Listen to me, because the men who don't will be dead before the sun rises."

They stood in a befuddled, drunken, sullen mass draped with blankets and sacks of flour and wine bottles and new boots and less identifiable booty. They listened, while the fires groaned at their backs.

"That's all the fun we're going to have tonight," Alec said. "From here on, there will be no more looting. You are part of an army, a fine, victorious army, and you have a right to be proud of your victory. But you are also going to follow my orders and maintain discipline. Anyone who can't follow orders can leave. Now. Go back where you came from, or go anywhere you please. But you can't stay with me unless you follow my orders.

"Those of you who stay will become the richest men

of Earth! Not from looting, but from a fair share of all the riches that this land can provide.

"If you want to take your chances as raiders and looters, go right ahead. Leave this base tonight, now, and you'll be allowed to leave in peace. But those of you who stay will never have to worry about a meal or a bed. You'll live longer and better than any raider ever has. And we—all of us, together—will rule this entire land. Now who wants to leave?"

There were more than a thousand men standing there. The crowd surged, shuffled back and forth. But no one made a move to leave.

"If you're still here by sunrise, you will be members of my army. You will not loot and steal because you won't have to. You'll get what you want, and more of it than you ever dreamed was possible."

"What about the women?" somebody shouted.

"When you're a raider, a looter, the women run from you and hide," Alec answered. "When you're a member of the army that rules the Earth, the women will chase after you!"

They laughed. Alec could feel the tension easing out of them.

"All right then," Alec boomed at them. "When the sun comes up, those of you who are still here will be members of the army that will rule the world. You'll have to follow orders. If you want to leave, slink away while it's still dark. When tomorrow dawns, the world will see something it hasn't seen since the sky burned: a new force that will conquer everything that stands in its way!"

They cheered. They actually cheered. Alec thought to himself, *Will they always be this easy to control?* He realized he was riding atop a wild animal. Grimly, he told himself, *It will always be a battle to stay on top.*

He spent the rest of the night touring the base, riding

atop the battle-dented truck and checking on every street and building in the base complex. Quiet prevailed. The men were tired from battle, drunk with the wine they had found and the exhilaration of being alive when so many others had died. Now they were exhausted. A taste of discipline was only the excuse most of them needed to fold up into the oblivion of sleep.

With the sunrise came Angela.

She came in a horse-drawn wagon, protected by six village youths armed with old rifles and shotguns. The posted guards stopped her at the edge of the base. She asked to see Douglas. The guards radioed for Jameson, who in turn informed Alec.

He had her driven to his quarters, the bungalow they had shared months earlier.

Alec was waiting for her inside the house when the wagon creaked to a stop. She jumped down and walked straight to the front door; without hesitating, she entered. She looked tense, worried, thinner, tauter, just as beautiful as ever.

"Where's Douglas? Why can't I see him?"

Alec had to fight to control his voice. "You'll see him. He's all right . . ."

"No he's not. You don't understand." She seemed genuinely frightened, her eyes wide with fear.

"It's all right," Alec said, crossing the tiny room to reach her. "No one's going to hurt him. Don't be afraid."

They stood in front of the dead ashes of the fireplace. Angela was actually trembling as he took her in his arms.

"Alec, please, you've got to let me see him. I don't know what he's told you . . ." Abruptly she pushed away from him. "Damn! I don't even know if I can believe what you're telling me. You *want* him dead, don't you?"

"No . . . that's over now."

"But it would help if he conveniently died, wouldn't it?"

"That's what he said last night."

"You still don't understand what he's doing, all the plans he's made."

"Yes I do . . ." But suddenly Alec knew that there was still more for him to learn.

"Alec, take me to him," Angela urged. "Please, right now, before it's too late."

He hesitated only a moment. "All right. Come on, he's still in his own bedroom. We didn't move him because of his leg . . ."

"What about his leg?"

"He broke it in an accident a few days ago . . . fell off his horse . . ."

"No!" she screamed. "He's been in that room for the past month! He's been sick . . . deathly sick!" She dashed for the door.

Alec raced after her. They tore down the street, past the startled villagers, running toward Douglas' house. With the perfect clarity of adrenalin-aided vision, Alec saw the guards loafing sleepily in front of Douglas' front door. Heard the shots. Saw the guards jerk to attention and burst into the house.

"No!" Angela was screaming. "No . . . don't . . . he can't . . ."

More shots. Then no sounds except Alec's own gasping breath and the pulse hammering in his ears. He outdistanced Angela and ran to the house, pushed through the open door and skidded to a halt.

Douglas was sprawled at the foot of the steps, his legs resting on the bottommost stairs. There was a machine pistol in his hand, its wire stock bent grotesquely under his heavy hand. His chest and gut were covered with blood. The room smelled of gunsmoke. The two outside guards were standing frozen, guns still hot in their hands. Upstairs, the third guard was kneeling against the stair railing, babbling:

"He came at me, he came at me. Shooting. He was shooting."

None of the guards was scratched. The cast was gone from Douglas' leg.

His eyes were open, his chest heaving in rapid painful gasps.

Angela clattered into the house and broke into a racking sob. Pushing past Alec, she sank to her knees next to Douglas.

"Nooo," she crooned. "Noooo . . ."

"It's all right," Douglas said, his voice a throaty groan. "Better this way . . ."

"He was shooting," said one of the guards next to Alec. "You can see the bullet holes all over the walls. He was trying to get out."

The bullet holes were all up near the ceiling, well above head level. Ignoring the guard, Alec stood beside Angela, next to his father. "Why?" he asked. "I would have saved you. I wouldn't let them take you."

Douglas managed to grin at his son. "How do you . . . ," a gasp of pain, ". . . think I found out about the cancer rate in the settlement?"

Alec sank to the floor.

"Only had . . . a few months left," Douglas panted. "Sorry to scare your boys . . . tried not to hurt them . . ."

He closed his eyes.

Angela collapsed over the dead body. *Tears won't help him.* Then Alec realized that the tears were always for the living, not the dead. *All right then. Cry for both of us.* He couldn't cry. Not now. Perhaps not ever. But surely not now. There was too much to be done. Too much unfinished work that hung in the balance.

He straightened up and turned to the guards. None of them had moved a millimeter. They were staring at Alec, their own lives showing in their eyes.

"It's all right," he told them. "You saved us all a lot of trouble."

They didn't relax, but that didn't matter.

"You," he pointed to the one nearest the door. "Get Will Russo and Ron Jameson here. There's work to do."

Then he glanced down at Angela's broken, sobbing form. To the other guards he said, "Get outside and don't let anyone in here until I tell you to."

They hurried out of the room. The guard who had been upstairs had to step, shakily, over Douglas' body. Then he ran to the door and left.

Alec knelt down beside Angela again and took her tear-streaked face in his hands. "It's time," he said, as gently as he knew how.

She looked at him searchingly. "Time for what?"

"To begin."



6-74